# The Cartels Daughter

## by D. D. Carmine

This is a work of fiction. The authors have invented the characters. Any resemblance to actual persons, living or dead, is purely coincidental.

Compilation and Introduction copyright © 2010 by Triple Crown Publications
PO Box 247378
Columbus, Ohio 43224
www.TripleCrownPublications.com

Library of Congress Control Number: 2010929113
ISBN 13: 978-0-9825888-5-7
Author: Marcus DeGeorge
Cover Design: Valerie Thompson, Leap Graphics
Editor-in-Chief: Vickie Stringer
Editor: Cynthia Parker
Editorial Assistants: Deidre Dailey

First Trade Paperback Edition Printing June 2010

10 9 8 7 6 5 4 3 2 1

Printed in the United States of America

# Dedication

*I dedicate this book and all that comes with it to three special women in my life. You three women make me want more, make me try harder, and push me to pursue my dreams as long as I live. I will never give up.*

*To you, Krystal, this dedication is more than just words on paper. You accepted me from day one and never gave up on me no matter the circumstances. Every step I took, you took with me. When I laughed, you laughed with me. When I cried, you cried with me. So when I succeed, YOU succeed with me. I cherish the bond we have and thank God every day for you. You make me whole baby sis. I love you always.*

*To you, Satia, my love for you cannot be expressed in words. You mean more to me than you could ever know. You make me try harder for you and your sister because I want to give you everything you ever want.*

*To you, Dream, this is just the beginning. I will make sure you and your sister will have a comfortable future. I love you very much, and always will.*

*Krys, I told you to check me out. So...what do you think? I'll always find a way, I promise you that. Failure is not an option Short Body.*

*I want to be what everybody in my past didn't want me to be. Successful.*

# Acknowledgments

First and foremost I want to thank God for all things good and bad. I'm saying thank you for all that was given to me and taken away. I am truly grateful for all my blessings and truly appreciate the greatest gift of all, LIFE.

Loving God allows me to love myself, and that, in return, allows me to love others. To me this is a beautiful cycle, one that I will continue in until my days are no more.

I would also like to thank you, Ms. Vickie Stringer, for having the vision and drive to accomplish what is now the largest urban publishing company in the world. You built a company that is giving individuals like me the opportunity to express themselves.

Thank you for solidifying the fact that I can do anything I put my mind to.

I also want to thank you, Ms. Christina Carter, for your enthusiasm in my writing and for lifting my spirits when I needed it most.

Thank you to the entire Triple Crown Staff and everyone who helped bring my dream to reality.

Thanks to all the people who read my manuscript in its infant stages. You all told me that I had something worthwhile, but I was still skeptical. You were all right.

I want to say thank you to my brother Tony for being with me every step of the way. Through all my ups and down you were with me to make sure that I made decisions that were right for me. You've always given me the support I needed, no questions asked. Thank you for having my back. Love you Big Bro.

I want to thank my Auntie Sharon for lighting the fire inside me, and thank you to Ms. Albena, for your support and encouragement. Thank you to Frank for being who you are. I'm trying to be a better example of a big brother (work with me).

I want to thank my brother from another mother, Mario Keene AKA (Rio), for having my back and giving me your undying love and support.

I also want to thank my man Nate, AKA (Redman/Max), for putting up with me and my issues. (You still owe me some moonlight).

I also want to thank all my peoples for traveling with me through the good and the bad times.

Marco, (What up King), "Oates" (you know who you are), Quick (What up Solid), my big brother Sweat (What up Solid), Chacho, J.D. (You predicted it), Jedi (I made you famous), Lefty, "Big Heazy 424," My man Vic, my two P-Cola hitmen, Mondo and Dre. What up O.G. (Fat Cat), Chi 4 Life, My man T.Y. stay cool homie, Adam, What up Jay, get at me son, you don't have to wait until Puerto Rican Friday no more. Doc, good looking on all your help and advice. What up Jay "The Plumber," Hey Trav, get at me Cradshaw. Mikhial, I'm still waitin on "OCK." What up Fire, get at your main man. Stay true Dred. What up Joe Washington AKA (The Fog), stay real baby. What's the business Tonio AKA (Gambino), Big Cuz got you baby!

And to all my Uncles, Aunties, Cousins, Nieces and Nephews, thanks for the love.

Last but not least I want to say thank you to my Mom and Dad. See, I saved you two for last because you were the most important. You see what I did? I used my mind and creativity to say something, to express myself. All the same things I have been trying to do with you over the years. There was no handbook on parenthood for you to use, so you did your best. That I do understand. But know that sometimes the child can teach the parent, if you just listen.

I used everything I was taught as a child and a young man and articulated my thoughts to create something that will outlive all of us. All the good memories and the bad ones were completely worth it. But understand me now...the past and the future DO NOT matter. All that matters is now, this moment. It's up to us to use it wisely.

To you, your silence has only made me stronger and more aggressive toward succeeding and not giving up, not ACCEPTING failure. All I ever wanted was your support, not your selfishness. But make no mistake, without you...I wouldn't be ME. You taught me how to survive but didn't teach me how to succeed. Don't get me wrong, I thank you for that, but I want to do more than just survive.

Here's something for you to think about, the ones hardest to love are the ones that need it most.

# Prologue

**Shielded by the cover** of night and a mist of seawater that hovered in the air like fog, Soltan and company came up to the stern of the large Colombian freighter in fast-boat dinghies. Arriving in pairs: Soltan and B.B., Crow and Sammy, Prince and Rome, they all knew going in that there was a chance everyone wouldn't make it back alive. But to these six men, the proposed payday was well worth the risk. They climbed up to the deck of the boat using grappling hooks attached to knotted lengths of industrial-strength climbing rope. There was no turning back now.

Each man was outfitted in a black wetsuit and armed with 45 Socom HK Mark 23's equipped with Trijicon night sights, laser aiming modules and Knight's Armament suppressors. All of which were carried in Wilcox tactical thigh holsters.

Once topside, they fanned out in their pre-arranged pairs. The 400 foot long and 150 foot wide cargo ship was at least 30 years old. The rough international waters of the Caribbean had not been kind, as it showed signs of rust, rot and decay. No matter the looks or its condition, the ship still maintained its purpose, buoyancy.

Prince and Rome crept starboard toward the control booth looking for an entrance below deck to begin their search for the drugs and money stored on the ship. Knowing the cargo ship would be well guarded and patrolled by armed men, this band of pirates took no chances at detection, making all movement deliberate and deadly.

Soltan and B.B. came across three armed Colombians with their backs turned, quietly speaking in Spanish. Soltan looked at B.B. as they crouched in the shadows of the large boxes on deck and put a finger to his mouth. He made circular motions with his hand, signaling B.B. to flank them. Understanding, B.B. stepped away from Soltan, drawing his half moon-shaped blade, clutching its polished engraved handle in an attack position. The blade was one of a pair crafted alike, with no others like them in the world. The other blade was in the hand of the only other person who knew what the engraved symbols on the handle meant. Soltan was the one who had given B.B. the blade, letting him know that until they met on the other side their goal was to milk this life for all its worth.

As Soltan watched B.B. step away from him, he stuck his left hand into the small pocket on the leg of his wetsuit, pulling out a small ball bearing. He tossed that ball over the heads of the three Colombians, with it landing not far behind a stack of cargo boxes. Soltan knew that B.B. was in the immediate area. The bearing had the effect Soltan wanted, making the Colombians look in the direction where it landed. With a nod, the oldest looking of the three motioned for one of them to go check it out. The younger soldier took off eagerly but cautiously, carrying his machine gun in the ready position. The soldier circled a stack of crates, checking to make sure no one was hiding there. As he made his way around them the soldier didn't see B.B. come from behind with the quickness and stealth of a wild predator, wrapping him up tight like a boa constrictor. Grabbing the Colombian by surprise with one hand covering his mouth and the other dragging his blade across the throat, B.B. cut until he heard a crunch and the gurgle of blood in the young man's throat, leaving the body limp and lifeless. Holding the man tight, B .B. rode him to the ground and then pulled him out of sight.

As Soltan watched the Colombian soldier disappear, he noticed two shadows coming from the other side of the deck. He wasn't concerned with who they were, he was concerned with how much noise they were going to make, as they headed straight for the remaining two Colombians who were still deep in conversation.

The shadows came in so fast the two soldiers never knew what hit them. Crow and Sammy collided with them like wrecking balls to skyscrapers. Making short work of the Colombians, snapping their necks with what seemed like little effort, they looked up to see Soltan walking toward them spotting a grin with a hint of teeth.

Below deck, Prince and Rome were also making short work of every Colombian encountered. They had managed to remain undetected, leaving nothing but dead bodies in their wake. When they had the main door to the berthing area open and were satisfied there weren't any more Colombians to dispatch, Rome spoke out, "Yo, this is it, we could find what we came for and have it all to ourselves Prince, we don't need Soltan. We could leave him on this tub with the rest of these dead motherfuckers and start our own journey to the states like we talked about."

"I don't know Rome, Soltan's been good to me. Plus

we wouldn't have made it this far if it wasn't for him. Think about it, he didn't have to let us in on this. I really don't like the idea of crossing Soltan, man," Prince replied.

"Man, fuck Soltan, the only reason he still alive cause everybody think he some kind of voodoo priest or some shit. That nigga just as grimy as us. Think about it, what makes you think he really gonna split the wealth with us anyway. We just two low life mercenaries he using to help take out these fuckin Colombians. I wouldn't be surprised if his whole plan was to leave us dead on this ship with the rest of these chumps. We ain't part of his regular crew. Think man, Think!" Rome spat out, "Man, Soltan dies tonight and if you don't like it you can die with him."

Rome raised his gun to Prince's head, looking him in the eyes.

~ ~ ~

"You seen Rome and Prince?" Soltan asked Crow and Sammy.

"Last I seen as we fanned out was them going under," Sammy said as he nodded at the stairs which led below deck.

B.B. came from the shadows behind the crate, wiping his blade clean across the thigh of his wetsuit saying, "Let's finish the job and be gone, no time for conversation."

"Alright, make sure that the boat is clear and find those two so we can get what we came for and be done," said Soltan to the men standing before him.

Before they all walked off, Crow and Sammy drug the two dead Colombians into the shadows, hiding the bodies behind some crates while Soltan and B.B. covered them.

Below decks, Soltan and B.B. began their search of

the cargo hold, checking every place a person could be hiding or waiting to ambush them. Going the opposite way, Crow and Sammy joined the search as well.

During the search of the lower deck of the ship B.B. came to a doorway that led to the berthing area, hearing what he thought were voices. He approached slowly, not because he thought it was more Colombians, but because he recognized Rome talking to someone who had to be Prince. What really drew his attention was the conversation he was hearing. "Man, fuck Soltan the only reason he still alive cause everybody think he some kind of voodoo priest or some shit, that nigga just as grimy as us, think about it..."

By this time Soltan had walked up on B.B. with a curious look on his face, realizing that B.B. was listening to something. While standing there he couldn't help the evil grin that spread across his face as he listened.

"...what makes you think he really gone split the wealth with us anyway, we just two low life mercenaries he using to help take out these fuckin Colombians. I wouldn't be surprised if his whole plan was to leave us dead on this ship wit the rest of these chumps. We ain't part of his regular crew. Think man, think! Man, Soltan dies tonight and if you don't like it you can die with him."

Exchanging a look, Soltan and B.B. both raised their weapons and walked into the room where Rome was pointing his gun in the face of Prince. Seeing Soltan and B.B. seemed to snap both Prince and Rome back into reality.

"You were right to think I wouldn't share the fruits of our labor, Rome."

While Soltan talked, B.B. circled Prince and Rome, who seemed to be frozen in place, and disarmed both of them. As soon as B.B. had taken both their weapons and stepped clear, Soltan put a bullet into the left knee of

Rome, while B.B. kept his gun trained on Prince.

"Aagh!" yelled Rome, as the bullet tore through flesh and bone with a crunch. Falling to the floor, Rome tried to gather his senses as he grabbed at his leg, trying to fight the pain. But the pain of the first bullet was dulled by the second bullet that was fired into the right side of Rome's chest, away from his heart, knocking him flat on his back. It looked as though Rome had passed out but he was still conscious, the pain now having him in a non-moving state of shock. Soltan watched with that evil grin that was almost a snarl as Rome lay there on his back bleeding heavily.

Turning to Prince he said, "What do you have to say for yourself?"

"Soltan man, I ain't want to have nothing to do with that shit he was talking, man. You see he was going to kill me if you didn't find us when you did," Prince said, shaking with fear.

Without saying anything more, Soltan holstered his gun and pulled out his ivory-handled blade. His attention now back on Rome, he bent down on one knee and tucked the curved end of the blade between Rome's legs, and with a heavy jerk of his arm he began dragging the blade upward toward his stomach. The blade was cutting like a warm knife through butter. Seeing this, Prince began to turn his head away so that he wouldn't have to see the grotesque display, but B.B. grabbed him from behind, placing the barrel of his gun against Prince's head, and pointed his face back in Rome's direction, forcing him to watch.

"Watch him die or die with him," B.B. said to Prince.

Not knowing where it came from, Prince felt the edge of something sharp against his throat now. As Prince watched in more astonishment than fear, Soltan dug his blade deep within Rome's bowels and continued on his

*Triple Crown Publications presents . . .*

upward journey towards the man's chest. Rome had faded in and out of consciousness a few times, but the look on Soltan's face filled Prince with more fear than he had ever known. Soltan looked as if he was performing a work of art, and not cutting open a human being. Hearing footsteps, Soltan turned to look at Crow and Sammy as they walked into the room.

"Soltan, we found the money, can you hurry this along so we can get off this damn boat. I'm getting fuckin' seasick," said Sammy.

"Gimme that bag, Crow," Soltan spoke, ignoring Sammy's statement.

Crow reached inside his wetsuit to pull out a large freezer bag of green bottle-fly larvae, known to chew through 40 pounds of soft tissue in one day. Soltan took the bag and laid it on the ground next to Rome's bleeding body. Grabbing at the edge of loose skin, Soltan pulled at it, ripping and tearing apart the tissue that held it in place. Using his blade, Soltan cut away muscles and tendon to further expose Rome's rib cage.

Reaching inside his wet suit he pulled out a pair of stainless steel rib cutters and began separating ribs one at a time. Once Soltan had snipped a straight line through the sternum, he reached in with both hands and pulled the two cages of bone apart. Prince was the only who visibly flinched when the cracking and splintering started. It was a completely unnatural sound for any man to hear. Not being able to take it anymore, Prince began throwing up over to the side as B.B. held him, while Crow and Sammy looked on unconcerned. With enough of Rome's insides exposed, Soltan picked up his blade and proceeded to free the heart from its cavity. Cutting the aorta, the superior and inferior vena cava and the surrounding pulmonary artery and veins, Soltan lifted Rome's heart in the air.

At that moment Sammy finally spoke up. "Soltan you are a sick muthafucka, you know that?"

"Fuck you" responded Soltan, as he put Rome's heart down and picked up the bag of larvae. The little flesh eaters were clearly visible through the large plastic bag as they squirmed around aimlessly. Opening the bag, Soltan poured the maggots into the chest cavity, letting them find their own way. Retrieving Rome's heart, Soltan stood up and walked around Rome, squeezing the heart, dripping blood around the body. Once the circle was complete Soltan carved a cross on Rome's forehead with his bloody blade.

Turning to his audience, "You guys ready to get paid? Come on, let's go," as he motioned for them to follow him.

Taking a quick look over at B.B., where he held Prince, he ran his index finger across his throat in a slashing motion. There was no reason for him to leave Prince alive. Prince probably would never have the guts to go against him, but he was tight with Rome. And for that alone he had to go. That's the price you pay for befriending the son of a Haitian President who wouldn't listen to reason.

As they walked out, two pops, more like muffled firecrackers, broke the silence of the night air. When everyone turned around, B.B. was standing over the body of Prince, looking down at him with a neutral expression on his face. The three men didn't even bat an eye at the sight. When they turned to walk away, Soltan spoke over his shoulder to B.B. "Don't waste too much time on him, we need to get moving."

B.B. heard the comment, but was already in a zone as he knelt down with his blade in hand and starting cutting.

As they walked back to the stern of the ship they

each carried two large army duffel bags bulging with money. B.B. came up behind them at a full sprint from across the deck, and stopped in front of Soltan breathing heavily. Sammy was lowering himself back into the dinghy when B.B. spoke in a hushed tone.

"Everything is set. Are you ready for a new life?"

Soltan looked at B.B. as he pulled two nails from his pocket, handing one to B.B. Still clutching Rome's heart, Soltan walked over to a nearby crate and hammered the nail through it with the butt of the gun, posting it on the wooden box. B.B. followed, doing the exact same to Prince's. Turning now to face his friend, Soltan stated bluntly, "I am new life," placing his hand on B.B.'s shoulder.

# *O*ne

**New Year's Eve showed no signs** of the traditional night before the New Year. The night was cool and breezy but had no bite to its chill factor. City streets remained busy and most local businesses were still open. It was 9:00 pm when Soltan pulled onto the grass of the place he and his crew dubbed "The Junk Yard." Putting his car in park, he sat still for a minute, wondering what else the city of Charleston had to offer. He enjoyed the city very much, especially the woman, but deep in his soul he believed it was time to move on. There were many cities in the United States, and he was sure he would find one just as enjoyable or possibly more so, that he had yet to see. America was the land of opportunity, and he wanted to experience any and all it had to offer.

Getting out of his black Impala SS, he walked up to the porch door of the house that sat in the middle of the block. The house could pass for abandoned at a quick glance, with boarded-up windows and its deteriorating structure. Being one of many run-down homes in this high crime area of North Charleston, it fit in perfectly. At the door, he was greeted by Crow, who had his arm around a woman he'd never seen before. She was attractive enough, but not his type.

"We've been waiting for you to get here so we can get started," Crow said to him as he stuck his tongue in the woman's ear.

With nothing on but a halter top and boy shorts that showed off the smoothness of her chocolate thighs and shapely legs, the woman spoke up, extending her hand to Soltan. "Hi, my name is Tasha."

"Nice to meet you, Tasha," he answered, shaking her hand.

Noticing other woman in the house, he walked past Crow and Tasha into what looked to be a stripper's night out. Everywhere he looked there was a half-naked woman standing around, eyeing him and smiling. Entering the living room he saw B.B. coming from the hallway that led to the bedrooms. "Sammy, dim the lights," B.B. called over to him.

Sammy, being the player of the bunch, was sitting on the far wall across the room with two beautiful women on each side. He cooked the cocaine into what is known as crack, and they distributed it to the lower level work-ers. But the skills he used on the two women next to him were not skills he learned in the kitchen. He had a gift when it came to women - whatever he said women ate it up, the two sitting with him being no exception.

The one on Sammy's left was a peach complexion Clydesdale, having some of the thickest thighs and calves ever seen on a woman. The other female was a petite brown cutie-pie, who could pass for an actress if it weren't for the six inch heels and tons of makeup she was wearing.

As Soltan took a better look around, he noticed

everyone was there. Some guys were sitting at a table in the corner playing cards, almost oblivious to the women surrounding them.

Sammy was there, a number cruncher, the math wizard of the operation keeping track of the profit and loss margins, ratios, and inventory. He loved numbers so much in school in Haiti he sometimes would correct the teacher in class. Crow had convinced Soltan that Sammy would be an asset to the whole operation, keeping all the money flowing in the right direction. Having grown up together there was never any problem with camaraderie because they all wanted the same things in life - money, power and respect.

B.B. walked to the couch and lit a blunt he had rolled in his favorite backwoods tobacco leaf. B.B. was a somewhat different story. While they all grew up in military homes, B.B. took on not just the traits of a soldier, but those of dark magic as well, known in his region as voodoo. His main influence and teacher was none other than Soltan, his brother, comrade and mentor. The lights started to dim and the air flooded with the distinct smell and smoke of reefer. Soltan watched a woman approach him.

Standing no taller than five-six and weighing about a hundred thirty pounds, with the smoothest brown skin he had ever seen, she definitely had his attention. She eased up to him and handed him a gold bottle of champagne that still had ice sliding down the sides of it. Her advance was more than sexy, it was predatory. She looked like a goddess in the flesh. Taking the proffered bottle in one hand, he used his other to grasp her wrist, pulling her closer to him. Her face was almost angelic, with her eyes betraying her seductiveness and her mouth showing the promise heaven intended. Her nose was short and button-like, and her lips had a natural pout to them. Licking them, she stepped away from him and began to speak. "My name..."

"Not yet, turn around for me, let me look at you from behind," he said, putting the neck of the bottle up to her mouth before she could finish.

She grinned and took a drink, but she didn't turn around like he asked. She just shook her head no. Soltan was caught up in desire and confusion – he wanted to look at the shape of her ass, and he wasn't used to women telling him no. The confidence of this woman made his penis jump in anticipation. Usually when he got the jolt and tingling sensation he knew that the woman he was looking at would be a sexual workout.

Soltan bent down and kissed her on the neck and then whispered in her ear, "You're wit' me for the rest of the night, ma."

Looking into her face, he saw her smile at him as she responded. "You're gonna have to work harder than that to get my interest."

Soltan said, "I'd work all night just to get your interest for a minute."

She smiled at that and rested her head on his chest, and wrapped her arms around his waist. Soltan couldn't help but notice that she smelled wonderful.

Looking around now, Soltan noticed the other women had all taken their clothes off. Now naked, the women Sammy had with him were on their knees, taking turns with their heads bobbing up and down on Sammy's cock as he sat on the couch. B.B. had one of the women bent over with her hands on the wall, hitting her doggy style as he smoked his blunt. One guy had a video camera and was filming everything, going on amusing himself with his own commentary as he caught couples in the spotlight attached to the camera. Standing naked in the center of the room, the guy with the camera soon had his own leech on her knees, holding him at the waist as she tried to suck the life from his main vein. He didn't make it easy on her, moving around and sticking the camera in private spots and from different angles, but she did her best trying to keep up.

One woman, sick of taking turns, turned her attention to the upturned ass of the other girl who was sucking on Sammy like her life depended on it. She dug her face in between the woman's ass cheeks and made the woman throw her head back in ecstasy as she climaxed. The guy with the camera looked like he was getting all this on tape, but he was having a little trouble concentrating on anything, because the head doctor he had shifted into overdrive. To Soltan's disgust the room had turned into an all-out orgy. Nobody really seemed to be interested in anything going on around them because they were too busy doing their own thing.

Soltan looked down at the woman under his arm. She had noticed what was going on too. She said, "What kind of key party shit is this? You into that stuff?" Seeing her expression and hearing her words, he pulled her into a bedroom, and then closed and locked the door. Sitting on the bed, he pulled her to him so that she was standing between his legs. With his hands on her hips, he slid them down slowly and begun to caress her ass. She pulled his hands away and stepped back.

"You guys don't waste any time, do you? I like guys who go after what they want, but I also like to know who I'm dealing with," she said.

"Ok, my name is Derrick, what's yours?"

"I'm Lauren Gonzalez, nice to meet you," she said, smiling.

"I didn't know this party was going to be a free-for-all. I came to have a good time but not like that," Lauren said, motioning her head toward the living room.

Soltan watched her as she talked, knowing that he wanted what she had to offer. It was New Year's Eve so he was ready to bring in the coming year with a bang, literally.

"So that's not your type of party out there?" Soltan asked, trying to figure out a way to get her naked. But he had work to do first.

"No. I'm not into audiences, or strange people that I don't know. But you intrigue me, you have an air of confidence about you that I like."

"I'm happy to hear that, 'cause you definitely have something that I like," he said, eyeing her body lustfully. But if you're not into orgies, then why are you here, especially dressed the way you are?"

Soltan was referring to the fact that she and the girl he met at the door, Tasha, had on identical outfits, and Tasha was in the living room making her own sex tape.

"I came to do a little dancing to make a little extra money. I got bills to pay and I was told that I could make enough here tonight to pay them. I came here with my girl Tasha, she says she's been here before and that you guys would pay good just to see a little ass, so here I am. I didn't know it was going to turn out this way, for real."

Soltan looked long and hard at her, admiring that she would go to such an extent just to survive. A woman like her could turn out to be useful if she was used right.

"You're down to take your clothes off, but you're not into group sex. What about sex with a guy you just met?" he probed, smiling.

"What, a one night stand? I'm not above fulfilling my needs from time to time," she teased him, rubbing his neck and the top of his head, leaning into him so that her breasts were close to his face.

"It might not be a one night stand, you never know. Relationships have started out in stranger ways," he said, now getting hard feeling her softness pressing against him.

"I'm no whore, Mr. Derrick."

Inhaling the sweet scent of her, Soltan leaned back on the bed, pulling her down on top of him, looking into her face. "I never said you were, but what I will say is you don't look like the type of girl to be involved in this type of action."

She looked down at him as if in some kind of trance, not being able to control her own body while it reacted on its own accord. It wanted this man, a complete stranger. It knew him, craved him.

"To be honest, when I saw you come through the door you caught me off guard." She said, now rubbing her secret place into the bulge she felt. "You don't look like the rest of them in there. To me, you look more reserved. I don't know why, but I am drawn to you," she continued.

Looking up at her, Soltan became quite curious as to what potential this woman had and what he would love to do to her right here and now. Rolling her over onto her back, he looked down into her eager face.

"I've got something special in mind for you. Come on, let's go," he said, then pressed his penis hard between her legs before standing up. Extending his arm, she took hold of his hand as he helped her off the bed.

"Go where? What are we doing?" Lauren asked.

"We're leaving."

"I can't leave my girl, we came here together," she said, a little unsure.

"Tasha?" He asked quizzically. "Your girl is in good hands, trust me," Soltan shot back before reaching for the door knob, unlocking it. "But here's my thoughts on it. You came here to make money, but you don't want no orgy, right? I don't blame you. So why don't we get out of here, and I'll give you the money you would have made if you had stayed back there all night. Then we can hang without any of those distractions."

Walking out into the hallway with Lauren in tow, they reached the living room and noticed the party was still in full swing. The only thing different was some of the original partners had switched up. Now there were people on the floor having sex, with continuous moans and grunts coming from every direction. Lauren said, "Yeah, I'm definitely gettin' up out of here."

This had really turned into some kind of porno, with bodies overlapping and the distinct smell of sex everywhere. Reaching the front door, Soltan looked back. Catching the eyes of B.B. on him, he gave him a nod and walked out, locking the door on his way out. Walking to his ninety-six Impala, Soltan pressed the button on the remote of his key chain and the doors unlocked as the front and rear lights flashed twice. Getting in the car, Soltan pulled out his cell phone to call B.B. who picked up on the second ring. "Yo."

"Happy New Year."

"Happy New Year, my brother, and take it easy on l'il one, she's probably the most innocent out of the bunch," said B.B., referring to Lauren.

"I don't know about that, she don't look innocent to me," Soltan said looking her over, then said, "Keep on fucking. New Life," before ending the call.

"New Life," B.B. Repeated, then got back to the girl whose leg he was holding in the air.

Backing out of the yard, Soltan began to think about what hotel he was going to take Lauren to for the night. He didn't have time to deal with her right now, so he wanted to stash her away until he did.

# Two

**As they drove along,** Lauren thought about what she was doing. She was extremely attracted to this guy, but didn't know him at all. *He looks decent enough, but so did Dahmer and Manson,* she thought. She didn't like leaving her friend either. *She'll be alright, shit, she didn't look to concerned with anything else going on around her, especially as that dude was putting that pipe on her ass when we left. Damn! What about my money? Tasha said we was gonna get paid good tonight and I ain't made a single fuckin dollar. Shit, this dude look like he got some money, too. He said I would get paid – I hope I don't have to do nothing too freaky to get it.*

Looking over at him as he drove, she continued to think. *I don't know why, but I'm feeling this dude. It's funny though, 'cause I feel safe with him but don't even know him. I know one thing though, he sure smells good and from what I felt earlier he is definitely packing some meat down there. I wonder if he knows how to use it. Probably not, but I sure hope so.* With that last thought she reached over and put her hand on his thigh and began rubbing back and forth, trying to see what kind of reaction she would get.

Soltan turned to look at her and asked, "What's up?"

She returned his gaze and stated, "I don't know where we going, but I can't wait to get there."

Soltan just smiled and couldn't help but to think, *I like this one, she's aggressive.*

Pulling under the awning of the Embassy Suite Hotel in downtown Charleston, he parked right in front of the door. When the valet walked up and opened his door Soltan put a twenty dollar bill in his hand telling him, "I won't be long, so don't hide it."

Walking over to her door, he opened it and helped Lauren out of the car, holding her hand as he pulled her to the front desk. Soltan noticed a couple of people staring at them as they walked, but didn't mind, he enjoyed it, feeling kind of excited on the inside. As they approached the desk, the clerk asked, "Good evening sir, what can I do for you tonight?"

"I'm looking for a suite with a king-size bed, preferably on a vacant floor," Soltan said.

"I'm not sure if we have a vacant floor sir, but I will try to get you one as secluded as possible," the desk clerk said, smiling as he punched keys on the computer in front of him.

Soltan noticed the young clerk was stealing glances at Lauren, but he knew he probably couldn't help it, 'cause the damn girl didn't have any clothes on.

"Ah, here you go, I've got one suite left, Suite 621 and it's in the easternmost corner, where I'm sure you should have the type of privacy you're looking for," the clerk said, smiling again as he caught the look Lauren gave him.

"The rate is two hundred and seventy two dollars for the night," he continued, now looking at Soltan.

"That's fine, I'll take it," Soltan said as he reached in his pocket, pulling out a stack of bills. The clerk processed the information printed out a receipt as Soltan handed him the money.

"Here's four hundred, make sure I'm not disturbed, you understand?" Soltan asked firmly.

"Yes sir I do, I'll just need your signature here," the clerk said, pointing to an electronic signature pad.

As Soltan signed, the clerk glanced at Lauren with raised eyebrows, wondering if she was going to be worth it. Lauren returned his look with a scowl of her own, not liking what he was saying non-verbally. When Soltan finished, the clerk handed him two key cards, saying, "Have a nice evening sir, and enjoy your stay at the Embassy Suites. If you need anything don't hesitate to call."

Taking the cards, he grabbed hold of Lauren's arm at the wrist and walked to the elevator, smiling at the clerk's words. At the elevator, Soltan pressed the up button and waited for the doors to open. "What's so funny?" Lauren asked.

"You seem to draw a lot of attention, you have such a magnetic personality," he laughed, knowing her looks got more than her share of stares and pick-up lines.

"Whatever, I didn't like the way that guy was looking at me. I don't think it's funny."

"You sure, I could call him when we get upstairs and tell him to come up and join us. I'm sure he wouldn't turn down the opportunity," Soltan teased, looking her up and down.

"You got jokes huh? Wait till we get upstairs and we'll see who's funny," she teased back, running a finger down her cleavage.

The elevator door opened with a ding, and they stepped in. Pushing the six on the number panel, Soltan waited until the doors closed before he turned around to look at her again. "What?" she asked.

Soltan said nothing, he just watched as she showed her frustration. Minutes later they were standing at the door of the suite. Soltan slid one of the cards into the slot provided on the wall. When the red light turned green, the lock clicked and he turned the knob and walked in with Lauren still on his heels. Soltan walked though the room as the door closed behind her, checking out the bathroom and then the window. He turned around to see she had climbed onto the bed, motioning for him to come to her.

Soltan walked over to the bed, sat down in front of her and spoke, "Look, I have to go, I'm not going to stay here with you. I brought you here so I wouldn't have to hunt you down tomorrow. I didn't bring you here to have sex with you, so relax. I have somewhere I have to be tonight. I'm not trying to waste your time or mine. I'll be back, if you're here, good, if you're not, then enjoy the room."

"What makes you think you could get some of this anyway, Mr. Sexy?"

Soltan laughed. He reached in his pocket, retrieving his stack of bills again, and counted out two thousand dollars as Lauren sat stunned. "Here's the money you were probably going to make tonight if you had actually stripped, plus some more," he said, handing her the money.

"You're just going to leave me here? What time tomorrow? What am I supposed to do?" she asked, now with an attitude, holding the money like it wasn't two thousand dollars.

"You'll know what time when you see me."

With that, he stood up, leaned over and kissed her on the forehead, then placed the keycards on the dresser and asked, "Do you think you can handle this?"

"Huh," She pouted in response.

"Just think of it this way. You just made two nights' worth of money, and you ain't had to do shit for it. That's a pretty good deal."

Soltan turned around and walked out the door, not saying anything else. He was leaving to make some money pickups and to drop off some product. New Year's Eve is a good night for selling coke, and he wanted to make sure his people had plenty of stock available. It's a good thing Lauren didn't ask what he was doing. He wasn't going to tell her about his business yet. He reached the elevator and decided he would stop at Deb's last. Definitely.

~ ~ ~

Lauren sat on the bed starting at the door for a long time. She shook her head and blinked as though waking up out of a trance. Then she remembered the money he gave her. More than enough to cover her bills for three months. And in one night's work! Shit, it wasn't even work.

Lauren counted the bills, and her grin got wider with each one. It's wasn't all about the money – but money sure does help.

# Three

**Getting in his car after his** last drop-off, Soltan decided he wanted to get a bottle of champagne before he went to Deb's. There was a 24 hour pharmacy on the way to her house he could stop at, he reasoned. Picking up his cell, he called her.

"Hello," Deb answered.

"Wassup?"

"Hey baby love," she cooed, "You coming to spend the night with me? It's New Year's Eve."

"I'm on my way. You need anything before I get there?"

"Just you baby, you're all I need."

"Alright, I'll see you in a few," Soltan said and ended the call.

Deb was the closest thing Soltan had to a girlfriend. She was someone he knew he could trust, but she wanted more that he wanted to give. Deb wanted a full-fledged relationship; something he wasn't ready for. He liked her, no doubt, and would almost do anything for her, but commitment was where he had to draw the line. She lived with her mother and aunt, both of whom were drug addicts. He had offered numerous times to get her own place but she wanted to remain where she was. She said she was comfortable with her mom, plus she didn't have to go far to make her money. Deb was a dealer, quite a good one in Soltan's eyes, but she didn't have to be. Soltan was more than willing to take care of her, but she constantly refused, wanting to be an independent woman. Soltan couldn't help but respect her and her wishes, so he made sure he was with her when he was able.

Pulling into Walgreen's parking lot, Soltan figured the store was fairly empty, if the parking lot was any indication. He parked next to a car he believed was his partner Donte's. Donte was a guy he had gotten close to when he first arrived in Charleston. But Donte was in state prison right now serving out a twenty four month parole violation for failing a drug test. Soltan's suspicion of the vehicle was confirmed when he saw Lori, Donte's girlfriend, come out the store. Rolling down his window he spoke, catching Lori by surprise.

"What's up Easter Bunny?"

Stunned at the words, Lori stopped dead in her tracks until she found the origin. "Derrick, you scared me, what are you doing here?"

"I should be asking you the same thing," he eyed her suspiciously, "You stepping out on my guy?"

"Please, I couldn't mess with nobody in this city without somebody knowing and Donte finding out, so why bother? He ain't got but another six months left anyway," Lori said, waving her hand in the air dismissively.

"How's the baby?" Soltan asked.

"Actually, she's the reason I'm here. She has a cold so I had to buy some cough syrup."

"You straight now?" he asked.

"Yeah, I'm cool. I got everything she needs. But what

are you doing? Shouldn't you be with one of your groupies getting some TLC? It's almost twelve, you know," she said looking at her watch.

"Ease up, ease up, I'm cool. I just came to pick up a bottle of champagne and then I'm going in for the night," Soltan said, dodging the groupies remark.

"You need some money?" He asked her.

"Naw, I'm straight, but Donte did tell me when he called earlier to let you know he needs to talk to you."

"When is the next time you expect him to call?"

"Probably tomorrow or the next day."

"Alright, when he calls you back, patch me in on three-way," Soltan said.

"Yeah I got you. Let me go so I can get back to my baby, I left her with my sister. I'll holla at you later." She said, stepping to her vehicle before getting in.

When she was gone, Soltan went into the store and bought a bottle of 1995 Salon, Blanc de Blanc's. Being familiar with the particular brand made no difference because it was pretty much the only normal bottle of champagne left.

Back in his car, Soltan received a message on his international pager. Calling to check the message, he waited until the second ring before an automated voice spoke, "Welcome to Skynett mailbox services, to check your mailbox please type in your four digit access code, followed by your pin number."

"**** ****-**"

"You have one new message, you have no saved messages."

Pressing one, Soltan listened to his only message.

"Call me," was all the accented male voice said.

Soltan didn't need to hear anymore, he knew exactly who left the message.

Region.

# Four

**Pulling into Deb's complex,** Soltan noticed that it was a fairly quiet night for New Year's Eve. He pulled around the back of Deb's building and parked in his usual spot. Parking back there kept his car out of sight.

Walking toward the building, he heard music coming from multiple apartments, and wondered how many people were having parties tonight. Walking past Deb's window, he knocked on the glass to alert her to come open the door. At the front door he heard what sounded like a party going on here as well. Knocking on the door he could hear someone say, "Who is it?"

Before he could speak, the door opened and he found himself looking at Donna, Deb's auntie.

"What's up, yellow Haitian?" she spoke out excitedly, then turned to give him room to come through the door.

Walking in, Soltan could see there was a New Year's celebration going on alright. Deb's mother had a couple of her friends over, and they were getting their drink on. He could see liquor bottles on the table in front of the couch.

"How is everything going tonight?" Soltan asked, looking around.

Acting like she never heard the question, Donna said, "Yellow Haitian, Deb's in her room." Clearly inebriated.

He gave a quick nod, turned and walked toward the hallway, noticing Deb's mom sitting on the love seat by the door. She was clearly intoxicated as well and never bothered to look up at him as her eyes fluttered open and closed. She was flanked by two men who looked just as drunk.

Walking in and closing the door, Soltan climbed into the bed on top of Deb. Pressing all his weight onto her, he began to kiss her face repeatedly. Under the comforter, Deb spread her legs to give him a cradle to lie in, then reached up and grabbed him behind the neck with both hands.

"I missed you," he said, staring down into her eyes.

Soltan adored Deb She was so innocent looking and did everything he asked of her. She put you in the mind of a young Mya, with a body to match. They could have easily been twins. He did everything he could to shower her with the affection he thought she deserved. There was almost nothing he wouldn't do for her, but he kept that to himself. He didn't want her taking advantage of him.

Rising up off the bed Soltan began taking off his clothes. Once he had them folded, he placed them in a chair by the window. Then he bent down to look under the bed, checking that his nine millimeter was in the same spot he left it a few days ago. Picking it up, he checked the clip. Satisfied, he replaced it under the bed.

With Deb looking on with a smile, Soltan asked, "How long has the celebration been going on up front?"

"Shit, they been at it since this afternoon. They will all be passed out before too long."

Climbing back onto the bed, Soltan lifted the comforter and slid next to Deb's warm naked body. Pulling her closer he could see that she was grinning from ear to ear. She reached out and grabbed hold of his penis and began to lightly massage it to his delight. He submitted to the feel of her warm body and soft skin, letting it soothe him and turn him on simultaneously. Taking a deep breath of her, he smelled fresh strawberries and that took him over the top. She pushed him over until he was on his back and then climbed on top of him, kissing is neck.

Deb was short, around five-foot-one and at a hundred pounds she was very petite. Now mounted on top of Soltan she began grinding her wetness across his stomach and penis.

Palming her ass, he pressed her harder against himself as he felt her juices coat his stomach and shaft. Scooting down just enough that her pleasure spot stayed in contact with his penis, she grabbed his right nipple between her teeth, gently biting and licking it. After a few playful licks she began to suck it, reaching over with her left hand to massage the other one.

Soltan loved the way she used her tongue and the feel of her hot mouth was all he could think about at the moment.

Reaching down between her legs, he began stroking her clit with his fingers. Every few seconds he would insert his middle finger inside her wet cave as far as it would go. The moans that escaped her throat made his penis swell more and more. It had gotten to the point that it was throbbing in time to his heart beat.

She could feel him jumping, just like she wanted, enjoying the rhythm of his pulse on her stomach and between her thighs. Now that she knew he was ready for her, she wanted to fill her mouth with the length of him before she gave in to the desire at her core. Kissing a trail down the middle of his chest, down to his nether region, she grabbed him with both hands, swirling her tongue around the head of his shaft. Slowly, methodically, she snaked her tongue all the way down his shaft then back up again. When she got back to the tip, she eased her mouth around the head, letting her lips envelope it while drawing it into her mouth slowly. Flattening her tongue underneath his shaft, blanketing it, she deep-throated him. With his swollen member touching the back of her throat, she used her cheeks to create a vacuum while her lips made a puckering sound at the base of his shaft.

All he could do was lay there, grabbing at anything he could hold onto. He knew Deb had experience but every time she did this to him it felt like the first time. As she began to ease back off his penis, she began stroking it as her head bobbed up and down.

He noticed that she had found a nice rhythm because he could feel that tingling sensation working its way to the finish line. Grabbing her head gently, he slowed her down until she came to a stop. Then reaching down to her shoulders he grabbed her arms, easily pulling her back up his body.

She complied, crawling back up and centering herself right over the head of his now heavily lubricated sword. Reaching down between her own legs, she guided the head to her own swollen and slick genitalia. She eased down onto him with ease as her love tunnel opened itself up to receive him. Once all the way down, she began rotating her hips so that she was grinding her clit along his shaft.

Grabbing her by the hips, he helped increase the pleasure by pushing her back and forth. Then he lifted his ass off the bed giving her as much of himself as she could take. As he thrust upward, she arched backward, throwing her head back as moans of ecstasy escaped her lips. Bracing herself by grabbing his legs, she began to bounce back onto him in rhythm to his thrust.

As he pumped harder and faster, he noticed that Deb's breathing was becoming shorter and more shallow. Reaching up, he grabbed her breasts, squeezing and massaging them as he continued driving into her hot, soaking wet crevice.

With a scream, she came, flopping forward onto his chest, squeezing her thighs tight against him. She wrapped her arms around his head even tighter, burying his face between her breasts.

He could feel the power of her climax as her inner muscles contracted around him. He teased her with short strokes and swiveled his hips, helping her milk the explosion for as long as possible. When her breathing got back to normal, he slid himself out of her and then switched places with her, letting her spread out flat on her stomach.

Behind her and between her legs, he grabbed her thighs, spreading them apart. Snaking his arms underneath them, he stretched himself out flat on the bed so that his face was now level with her wetness, her plumpness poking out at him from this position. He took a quick second to enjoy the sight of the glistening pinkness before diving in. The moment Soltan took one of her juicy lips into his mouth, a half a scream came from front of the bed. Without looking up, he heard the sound being muffled as she screamed into a pillow.

Lapping at the juices, darting his tongue back and forth, in and out of her pink hole, he felt his own body tense to her reactions. Pulling one of his arms free, he stuck a finger inside her as he continued to lick as if trying to swallow every drop of her sweet nectar. Caught up in Deb's moans and twisting motions he fingered and licked at her core, he ran his tongue around her anus.

Feeling him work his magic, Deb continued screaming into her pillow not being able to help the fact that she had now come four times and felt another orgasm on the way. He never licked her ass, so what he was doing now felt so good she didn't want him to stop. But she did want him back inside her and hoped he would penetrate her again soon.

Spreading her ass cheeks apart with both hands, he buried his face in the middle of them. He couldn't help but savor how good she smelled and tasted.

Leaning back on his knees, he quickly grabbed her by the hips, raising her so that she was now on her hands and knees. He couldn't take it anymore, he had to get back inside her, his body flooding with lust. Lining himself up with her, he guided himself back into her from behind, and began a slow rhythm in and out, savoring the warmth and slickness. She thrust herself back at him and they began to pick up the pace together. Before long, he was slamming into her so hard that their bodies made a slapping sound every time they made contact.

She knew when he finished she was going to be sore, but the way he was fucking her was worth it. He listened to her cries of passion and the louder she got, the harder he thrust. They were both dripping with sweat now as he felt himself getting close. Snatching himself out of her, he squeezed his penis as he began to come on her back.

She quickly turned around, grabbing his rod with her hands, immediately inserting the head into her mouth, stroking his shaft as she sucked and swallowed, trying to ingest every drop of him.

Feeling her lips on him as he came made him jerk back and forth with the pain and pleasure of her assistance. Grabbing her head with both hands, he tried to hold her still, to stop her from moving as he steadied himself in her mouth. But she kept sucking and pulling despite his efforts to control her movements, and didn't stop until she felt his last jerk and throb.

Pulling out of her mouth, Soltan turned over on his back, then pulled her onto his chest and dozed off into a blissful sleep.

# Five

***Waking up, Soltan felt around*** for Deb, but she was-n't in the bed. Looking at the digital clock on her dress-er, he noticed that it was thirty-two minutes after nine. When he rolled over to the edge of the bed, Deb entered the room, wearing just an oversized t-shirt. She sat on the bed and then leaned over and kissed him on the cheek, her eyes bright like stars. "Happy New Year, baby."

"Where's the money?" He asked.

"Damn, back to business already? Hold on then." She walked over to her dresser, opening up her bra and panty drawer. Reaching in, she came out with two stacks of bills, wrapped in rubber bands.

"This is twenty thousand, I'll have the other five by Monday."

Being that it was Saturday, Soltan decided that was pretty good. She hustled harder than some of the other people he had working for him, pulling seventy-five to a hundred grand a month. She only had the last package for four days and she was already trying to get more.

"When are you going to make another drop?" she asked.

"I'll see you again before the day is out, I got some other things to do, so it'll be later. How much you got left?"

"I got enough. I was just making sure we touched base. The last package went pretty fast, so I didn't want to run into a situation and run out," she said as she sat down on next to him, crossing her legs Indian style.

He stood up. "That's settled then. Girl, you make money fast." She smiled at the compliment. "But Deb, I gotta get a shower now and then head out. More work to do."

She pouted a little at that. "You want me to join you in there?"

Soltan smiled, and then picked her up and carried her into the bathroom.

~ ~ ~

After drying off and getting dressed, Soltan walked out the front door of Deb's apartment headed to his car. He checked his messages while he waited for it to warm up. Noticing he had quite a few, he listened to them as he put his day together mentally. The last message was from B.B., telling him to call when he got the message. Finished with all the local messages, he checked his Skynett voice mailbox to find another message that plainly stated, "We need to talk."

Pulling out of his parking space, Soltan drove to the entrance of the complex. Before turning onto the street he called B.B.

"Yo."

"Yeah, what you got going on?"

"Where you at? I been calling you all night."

"I'm on my way to OZ, meet me there," Soltan said, dodging the question.

"OZ" was the code name for the storage unit he and B.B. used to store their equipment.

"You got a message from Region?" asked Soltan.

"I got two already, why, what's going on?" asked B.B.

"I don't know, but I got two also, I'll see you in a minute."

"Yo."

Soltan thought, *What could Region want now? Probably just another job for us, that's all.* But he knew for Region to be calling two days in a row it must be urgent.

Driving to the storage unit he thought about what Region had said when he was younger: "Always play for keeps and never expose your hand."

Thinking about this, Soltan wondered if he had made any mistakes recently. Had he exposed his hand so much that the truth was now out in the open? Had he not covered his tracks with the Colombian situation? It was too early to speculate on anything so he just drove.

# Six

**Rome's father wanted answers** and he wanted them yesterday. Being President of Haiti, Jean-Pierre Casi wanted to know what his son was doing on a Colombian freighter in Buenaventura. His son was mutilated so badly that he was almost ashamed to identify him as his own. Did the killer know Rome was the President's son? Estranged, but still his son, Rome had grown to like the freedoms that crime and deceit had to offer. He did not by any means want to follow in the footsteps of his father. But now there would be no footsteps to take, his boy was dead and now he would exhaust any and all resources to find his killer. On top of it all, he had the Colombians dodging all inquires about the incident, because of the possibilities of a cartel breaking out. At this time all the Colombians could promise was that a thorough investigation would take place. But as it was, Casi wasn't sure that a political approach would be the best way to handle the situation. He didn't want to get any deeper in the cocaine wars than he already was.

~ ~ ~

Arriving at the storage facility, Soltan noticed B.B. was already there and walking toward him as he pulled into the parking lot. Parking his car, he got out, greeting B.B. with a hug.

"How was your night?"

"Eventful. I didn't know that a woman would profess her undying love for you after choking her half to death as she came," B.B. stated, confused.

"Sounds like you enjoyed yourself then," he shot back.

As they talked, they walked past a row of storage buildings until they got to theirs. Turning down the aisle, they both came to a stop at a six by eight by fourteen foot storage compartment. Taking out a key and unlocking the unit, B.B. asked, "So what do you think Region wants?"

"I don't know, but we're going to find out real soon, that's my guess."

Soltan walked into the unit, flipping the light switch to reveal an assortment of electrical equipment, laptops, printers, scanners, portable GPS and cell phones with satellite capabilities. All of it was equipment they used to stay under the radar and off the record, making their own identification, activating their own phones and pagers and so on. This type of equipment was illegal in the U.S., but Canada sold it daily. Although being manufactured in the states, Soltan had to import what he needed though secret contacts across the border. He made it a point to conduct his transgressions discretely in order to stay away from the FCC and their regulations.

Standing guard at the entrance, B.B. kept watch, looking up and down the aisle of the storage compound, making sure they were alone. When Soltan got the OK, he walked over to a laptop stationed on a table, turned it on, pulled a program disk from his pocket and inserted it into the drive. Walking over to a large box in the corner, he picked up a satellite dish and stand, then placed it at the entrance of the compartment connecting the cord to the laptop. Inserting the cord into the USB port on the computer, he punched a few keys and the screen came alive with what looked like radio waves floating across it. He picked up a satellite phone box, taking out the contents and put the phone together. Once the battery pack was on it, he walked back to the laptop and connected the phone to the computer using another USB connector. When he had a strong enough signal, Soltan cloned the phone, disconnected the cord and dialed Region's number.

On the fifth ring, Region picked up. "Yes."

"You left me a message."

"Things are not going according to plan. There have been many questions and accusations on both sides. Our friends have not been satisfied with the results they are getting. Inquiries are being made. While people search for the truth, it is your job to insure that our secrets remain so."

"What do you want me to do?"

"I will send instructions soon. Until then continue business as normal," answered Region.

With that statement the phone went dead, and Soltan knew exactly what was coming. They would be killing anybody and everybody they had to in order for Region's plan to work.

Handing the phone over to B.B. he looked at him and shrugged his shoulders.

"What's the word?" asked B.B.

Soltan didn't speak right away, but waited until he had carried the satellite dish back inside and shut down the laptop. "The boat is still an issue, the old man is a little more upset then we thought he would be, losing a piece of shit like Rome."

"So who's next?"

"Well find out soon enough, but for right now we continue as planned," Soltan said as he walked out of the storage unit and pulled the door down, placing a brand new lock on it.

Walking back to their vehicles, Soltan thought about this whole plan, wondering if it really was going to work. Even though he had his motives, he didn't want things to get so much out of hand that there would be more suffering than before he started.

Standing at their cars Soltan told B.B., "Meet me at the zoo later, I want to feed the animals before it gets too late."

"Cool, I'll get everyone together so it won't take all night," B.B said before sliding behind the wheel of his rental Maxima.

Getting in his own car, Soltan continued his train of thought. What they were doing wasn't just risky, it was a death sentence. He dearly wanted to help his own, but he was in bed with some very dangerous people. He was so deep inside the womb of treason that there was no turning back. He almost felt bad for dragging everyone else into this charade, but they were their own men. All they truly wanted was freedom, and equality, but his own motive went a lot deeper. To him, it didn't matter how many lives were sacrificed, in the end it would be worth it. He would have his wish, even if he had to go to the gates of hell to get it.

~ ~ ~

Soltan pulled into the driveway and watched the valet approach him. Tipping him a twenty, he realized he still had the twenty thousand that Deb gave him this morning stuffed in his pockets. He spoke to the valet, "My car needs to be washed and detailed, there's a car wash two blocks away next to the quick mart on the left. Make sure the windows get cleaned without scratching the tint."

"Yes, sir," answered the valet.

Getting to the elevator he pushed the up arrow and waited patiently for the doors to open. When a bell chimed and they did open, he had to step inside to let a couple with a small child exit before he entered. Pushing the number six button, the doors closed and Soltan began to wonder if Lauren had stayed or taken the money and left as soon as he walked out the door last night.

On the sixth floor, he was walking down the hall when a thought hit him. Pulling out his cell, he called information and requested the number to the hotel. Still walking while the connection was being made, he stopped a couple doors away from the room Lauren was in. Five rings later the hotel operator picked up.

"Thank you for calling the Embassy Suites Hotel, my name is Tammy, how may I be of assistance?" That was the energetic voice of the young woman he passed at the front desk in the lobby.

"Room six twenty-one please."

"One moment sir." Then soft jazz came through the line for about three seconds, followed by a click. Four more rings and Lauren picked up.

"Hello?"

By this time Soltan was standing right outside the door with his ear pressed against it, checking to see if she was still alone in the room. It really didn't matter to him because he had the nine from Deb's house in his right hand now. He just wanted to know what to expect if something was to go wrong.

"Did you sleep well?"

"No, I would have slept better in my own bed," she

teased. "Are you coming to get me now or do you want me to pay for another day on this room?"

Hearing this brought a smile to Soltan's face, because he knew she didn't have any plans of letting him get away. She would do whatever he asked until she had no more use for him or his money. He thought, *Great minds think alike* and said, "Yeah, I'll be there in about an hour to pick you up, meet me downstairs at the front door."

"Ok."

Ending the call, he listened a few more minutes for any activity going on in the room. After being satisfied she was alone, he knocked on the door.

"Who is it?' Her voice faint from the other side.

"Me."

Cracking the door with the security latch in place, she saw him standing there and smiled as she released the safety measure to let him in. Once they were face to face she taunted him. "Trying to find out if you can trust me, huh?"

"I don't know you princess, but I plan to change all that real soon," he said, walking into the room and sliding his gun back into the holster hidden on the inside of his waist band. If she was surprised at all about seeing the gun she didn't show or say anything about it.

As he entered the room he noticed she still looked as fine as she did the night before. But now wasn't the time for carnal pleasures, it was time to get down to business. Soltan knew she was eye candy from the beginning, but he wondered about her mentality. Where she at mentally, besides sacrificing herself for money?

Handing her the jogging suit he picked up at the store on his way over, he said, "Here, I got this for you until you can get some real clothes on."

Still smiling, she took the package, stepped to him and kissed him on the cheek. "What was that for?" She said as he smiled down at her.

"Just my way to get you. You could have left whenever you wanted, you have cab fare. Or you could have called your man to come get you," he said, paying close attention to her response as he probed.

"I don't have a man, and why would I leave? I want to see what's going to happen next. I came this far with you, I didn't see any reason to bail out now. Like you said, I made as much money as two nights of working, but didn't have to do shit but eat bad hotel food and watch BET. Not a bad deal."

Lauren said that, but it wasn't totally true. Lauren knew exactly why she didn't leave - she had an undeniable attraction to this guy and she was curious. She had never been whisked away to a plush hotel before where the man didn't at least make a pass at her. By Soltan not even making an attempt to bed her made him all the more alluring. She thought about him through the night, trying to figure him out, but the trait that stood out the most was that he was calculated. Understanding that he did everything for a reason made her eager to stick around. Recognizing these traits were simple because she grew up around people like him, and where they went people followed.

"You don't know me. I could have some wicked intentions toward you," Soltan said.

Looking at her, Soltan originally thought her main goal was money, using her body as a tool to get it. But as he looked closer he saw strength in her eyes. The kind of strength you can only get from having the knowledge of being able to take care of yourself. Having the knowledge of things that normal people are afraid of.

"You're right, but the only wicked intentions I see in your eyes are sexual. I could be wrong and you could be the Big Bad Wolf, but I don't think you want to hurt me.

I think you want to fuck me," she gave him a seductive look and pose that pushed her hip out.

"That's what you think?"

"Am I wrong?"

"Not entirely."

"Really though, I feel comfortable around you. You make me feel safe and secure, what can be bad about that? I still can't figure it out, for someone to meet a complete stranger and then take them to a nice hotel like this and not try to get some ass, then leave two thousand dollars behind, unh, unh," she said in an attempt to get him to reveal his intentions. "You got a lot of game mister, very clever. It's clear you got money, so you using it to lure me in, smart, I like that. But what you didn't know is you didn't need money to get me. But as I thought about the situation as a whole, it was a test wasn't it, tell me I'm wrong, you just put me through a test of some sort, right?" She paused, looking at him, waiting for him to tell her she was crazy.

"You got something up your sleeve, and it ain't just about fuckin', right?" She stopped, again staring into his eyes.

When he made no attempt at saying anything she added, "One last question though, how did you know I wouldn't set you up? You let me see you have money, how could you trust me? I seen your gun, so obviously you were ready for something, but I could have been ready for you too. I know that's why you called, you wanted to see if I had someone waiting on you in here, but how do you know that I won't try and get you later on?" She tested him now.

When she finished talking, he broke things down for her, all the while thinking that he was right - she has been around.

"You're smart as well as attractive, I like those qualities in a woman. So my assumptions are right. But now that I've listened to you, I will answer some of your questions. I'll start with this, yes I have plans for you, some definitely sexual if you game. As far as you setting me up, I don't see that in you. Yeah I might have shown you a few thousand, but I think it's just money to you. Just something to pay the bills. Sure, it pays your bills, everybody wants to do that, but for you it's not the end-all be-all, am I right?"

"Maybe."

"Yeah, I think I'm right, you're looking for a reason or a purpose and money ain't it," he smiled at her now. "And just for the record, if you had tried to set me up I would have killed you when I walked through the door," he said, looking her straight in the eyes.

Watching her reaction, he could see her whole demeanor changed along with her posture as her eyes widened. He could tell he had touched a nerve, and that he was on the right track.

"I'm not afraid of you."

*Bingo,* he thought, "That's good," he said aloud.

"I've been around real dangerous people before, you don't strike me as a man who would harm a fly," she said, knowing when she said it that it was a lie. She could see the coldness in him for sure.

When he didn't speak and just held her eyes she knew the truth, and he knew she understood.

"Now how about you get dressed so we can get this day started," he said, breaking the silence.

Startled, Lauren didn't know what to think. Was this guy worth dealing with? Had she misjudged him? No, that she hadn't done, she knew enough about him at this point to know he was everything she had thought; cold, calculating and deliberate. Looking at him a few seconds, she made her choice and started to dress in the new jogging suit.

"Just like that, huh? You tell me that you would kill me and then say let's get moving like we were discussing the weather," she said.

"Just like that." He responded, smiling at her sarcasm.

He watched her cover the luscious skin of hers with the cheap jogging suit, knowing he was going to enjoy sex with her. "Where do you live?" he asked, trying to take his mind off her body.

"Greendale. They're townhouses. With my roommates, one of them you already met last night, Tasha. Why do you want to know that?"

"Because you're moving out today," he answered.

"Are you serious?" she asked, truly surprised.

"Yes. Do you have a car?"

Lauren gave him a strange look as she pulled the sweatshirt over her head.

"No, I don't have a car, I guess you're going to get me one of those too," she said sarcastically.

"I knew you were a smart girl the first time I laid eyes on you, but I didn't know you were a genius," he smiled, with a mock look of surprise.

She let out a small giggle then put her hands on her hips, staring at this man, this man that she wanted more of.

"Did you eat breakfast this morning?"

"Yeah, I had room service, I figured since I was in this nice hotel I might as well enjoy the perks."

"Good, one less stop to make. Let's go, we have a lot to do today."

"Yes, daddy," she teased.

*What am I getting into?* She thought to herself. *Something fuckin' amazing.*

# Seven

**Back at the junkyard,** B.B. walked in the door to see Crow getting head on the couch in the living room. The woman between his legs, her head bobbing up and down, looked familiar to him as he approached. Crow looked over and says, "What's up B.B., you want some? She'll do you when she finishes. She says it's her favorite pastime." Placing his hands on top of her head, she moaned in compliance but never slowed down to look up, not missing a beat.

B.B., looked at Crow asking, "Isn't that one of them freaks from last night?"

"Yeah, so what?"

"Man, get that bitch outta here, we got work to do."

Walking over to Crow, B.B. reached down and grabbed the woman by the arm, pulling her to her feet.

"Party's over Super-Head, it's time to go."

Getting to her feet, Tasha wiped her mouth and gave B.B. a hateful stare like she was seriously upset he had stopped her feeding. Reaching back down by the side of the couch, she picked up her purse and stomped towards the front door.

Watching Tasha storm out of the house, Crow tucked his dick in his boxers and pulled his pants up, and tightened his belt. By this time B.B. had walked down the hallway into the room on the left. Coming back into the living room he looked at Crow, asking, 'Where's the rest?"

Zipping up his fly, Crow answered, "They're at the zoo. They are trying to get the next box ready."

The zoo was an apartment on the other side of town they used to cut, bag and store cocaine. It was only occupied when they were working on putting more product on the street.

"Then why are you still here?" B.B. asked sarcastically.

"I was busy until a minute ago, plus I got to make a few more pick-ups."

"You haven't made your pick-ups yet?" B.B. Asked, anger creeping into his voice. "Are you fuckin' stupid? If Soltan finds out there's still money out there he ain't gonna be happy," he continued.

Another thought hit B.B. "Shit, if Soltan found out, I'm pretty sure you wouldn't be a happy camper either," implying that Crow knew what the consequences would be.

As Crow walked out the door, B.B. thought Crow's dick was going to get him in trouble one day. B.B. was Soltan's right hand, the lieutenant of this outfit. He himself wasn't immune to Soltan's wrath, but the others were the ones who mostly feared Soltan, not him. They were brothers till the end and nothing or no one could change that.

Alone now, he took the satellite phone that Soltan gave him and placed it in a shoebox in the closet of one of the bedrooms. Walking back into the living room he noticed the video camera, and picked it up as he was leaving the house.

~ ~ ~

Arriving at the zoo, B.B. walked in the door and found the guys getting the next shipment ready to go back to Haiti. They were sending money in huge marble vases with false bottoms, the kind that landscapers would put in front yards with bushes in them or small trees. Very expensive sculpted marble ones. Once filled with cash, they would weigh about six hundred pounds or more. Looking around he noticed another stack of money in the corner of the living room. This stack of money was without a doubt going to one of the many offshore accounts set up by Soltan so they could have some place to stash their earnings. B.B. understood they made plenty of money, but he also knew that seventy percent was sent back to Region through an Import/Export company owned by Soltan. B.B. never knew the actual destination of the vases, but assumed Region was receiving his money directly. As B.B. thought more about things, he realized he had never talked to Region face to face, or even laid eyes on him.

*Soltan's seen him,* he thought. *We wouldn't be going all this for someone he's never seen before.*

B.B. trusted Soltan beyond understanding, but he had a feeling something was off, and he couldn't shake it. He and Soltan had been together since they were little boys, always having each other's backs. He would have to talk to Soltan about this feeling, just to make sure nothing was amiss.

# Eight

**Soltan was struggling with** a dilemma. He was trying to figure out where he wanted Lauren to stay. It had to be somewhere he could go and feel relaxed, but also close to the interstate. Being able to get to and from a location efficiently was imperative because of the amount of money he planned to store there. The interstate made getting pulled over and searched less of a problem, while it also served as a good escape route.

As she rode shotgun, Lauren thought: *If nothing else, this guy is a serious dude. He didn't beat around the bush and he's not the abusive type. All I know for sure is that I feel good around him - and he smells fantastic.* Looking out the window she noticed they were on Remount Road, a main car sale strip, and wondered what kind of car he was thinking about getting her. She wasn't used to the men she encountered being generous. *Hell,* she thought, *the only place things like this happened were on TV.* Looking over at Soltan she asked, "Are you serious about this, you really going to buy me a car? And a new crib?"

He looked at her for a second and then cracked a smile.

"If you haven't noticed yet, I'm not into games. I do what I want, when I want. I don't need anyone's permission or approval. I try to make things as easy on myself as possible. Unfortunately, I have some good news and some bad news. Everything that's going to happen to you from this point on has a price."

Lauren looked at Soltan as a feeling of cautiousness, along with excitement, passed through her.

"So what's the price?" she asked.

"What kind of car do you want?" Soltan asked, side-stepping the question.

Realizing he was not ready to expose his card yet, Lauren answered, "Since I can't get an answer out of you right now, I'll leave that alone until you're ready. But to answer your question, I don't like cars, I like SUV's."

Soltan smiled at the thought, because that was even better. "Nice", he said, looking over at her. "I'm happy you said that."

Pulling into a GMC dealership, they parked, got out and walked toward the main building. Soltan noticed Lauren looking around the parking lot at different vehicles.

"Anything catch your eye?"

"How about one of those Denalis over there?" she said.

Soltan looked in the direction of the Denalis as they walked into the dealership office.

Immediately upon their entry a salesman came to them saying, "Welcome to Combs GMC, my name is Eric. Is there anything I can show you today?"

"We are looking to buy a Denali," said Soltan.

"Do you already know which one or would you like to browse a bit?" asked the salesman.

"Not at the moment, but I'm sure that if you take this young lady and show her your selection I have no doubt that she will find something to her liking," Soltan answered.

The young, clean-cut salesman turned his attention to Lauren as if seeing her for the first time, now wanting to treat her as if she were someone special.

"Miss, if you would just come this way I'm sure we will have something to accommodate you."

Before she could walk away, Soltan reached down, grabbing her wrist and whispering to her. "Tell him exactly what you want, don't worry about the price, but make sure of two things; get the sport package, and make sure it's brand new, not pre-owned. You got me?"

Lauren looked up at Soltan, smiling, "Whatever you want, you crazy bastard." Then stood up on her tiptoes and lightly planted a kiss on his lips.

In an hour's time Lauren had picked out a Navy Blue Denali with the works. Using his platinum American Express card Soltan paid for the truck, signing his name on the paperwork. Lauren was excited but was trying to stay cool in front of him, knowing she was going to reward him the first chance she got. She had already forgotten that he said there was a price to his generosity.

When all the paperwork was in order, the salesman handed the keys to Soltan and they shook hands. Soltan and Lauren walked out of the dealership office at the same time the truck was being parked in front by one of the GMC employees. Standing there in front of the truck, Lauren grabbed Soltan's hand, looked at him and pulled him down gently to kiss him again on the lips. Smiling, he looked at her and returned a kiss to her forehead and held the keys out in front of her, saying, "Congratulations, you're the proud new owner of a GMC Denali. When the title comes I'll sign it over to you."

Grabbing the keys, Lauren asked, "So what are we doing now? Oh, damn, I am so excited."

"Damn, no thank you, nothing?" Soltan said, shaking his head back and forth in mock disbelief. At this point Lauren grabbed him around the waist and pulled him close so their bodies were pressed against each other.

With her arm wrapped around him, she looked up, saying, "That's what the kiss was for. Thank you sincerely." Standing on her toes she kissed him again, this time with much more passion and lust.

When the kiss was over Soltan looked at her, saying, "You ready now?"

"I been ready," she answered rubbing herself against his erection.

"Not that, I'm talking about are you ready to leave? We still have things to do."

Lauren nodded.

"Then let's go, follow me."

As she released him she walked around the front of the truck. At this point Soltan reached out and patted her on the ass and then walked to his Impala. Leaving the dealership with Lauren trailing behind him, Soltan pulled his phone from his pocket and connected the cigarette lighter adapter to it and dialed B.B.'s number. Two rings later the line came to life.

"Yo."

"Is everything ready?"

"Almost, we're still waiting on a last drop-off."

"Alright, make sure you're done by five so you can beat the rush. I'll be through around six."

"Yo," B.B. said before ending the call.

As Soltan drove, he thought about making sure he had some more insurance just in case he needed it one day. This was the main reason he was doing what he was for Lauren. The call he made to Region was still on his mind; things didn't always go as planned, so he had to be careful. He would have to show up at the Export company sometime today to make sure everything was in order. He could let B.B. take care of it, but he always wanted to be sure himself that everything was right. Not that he didn't trust B.B., but he know one mistake could cost them all too much, so he didn't take any chances.

~ ~ ~

Soltan and Lauren looked at several apartments in numerous locations and finally found one they both liked. A condo-style loft close to the highway convinced them both to end their search.

Having two bedrooms and a master bathroom with a Jacuzzi, he and Lauren finally made the agreement. Signing a year lease, paying for the deposit and year's rent up front, Soltan sent Lauren back to the Embassy to get another room, then realized it was five thirty-seven. He didn't think he would have enough time to pay the utilities for the apartment so he called his secretary, Susan. It took four rings before the phone was answered.

"Good Afternoon, thank you for calling Diamond Import and Export, this is Lisa, how may I help you?"

"Hey Lisa, is Susan around?"

"Oh, hi Mr. Jones, she's in her office, hold one sec while I transfer you," cooed the receptionist.

Soltan could hear the flirty tone in her voice but he didn't mind. He knew that Lisa wanted to sleep with him, but it would never happen. Business was business, as long as she didn't go too far he wouldn't address the issue.

"This is Susan."

"Susan, I need you to do something for me."

"Shoot."

"I need you to get the utilities turned on at this

address," and then he gave her the information. "Did the vases arrive yet?" he continued.

"Yes they did. They arrived around four thirty, and I must say they are beautiful," she gushed.

"Good, don't worry about shipping them yet, I want to see them before they leave. I will be in tomorrow morning."

"Yes sir. Would you like me to put the utilities under the company account or you personal one?" she asked while the sound of papers being shuffled came through the phone.

"Put it under my personal account, but make sure it is direct withdrawal and put the receipts in my box."

"No problem, anything else?"

"No, that's it. I'll see you tomorrow, take care."

"Ok, bye."

Soltan thought about Susan for a quick moment. She was a white woman, in her early fifties who took damn good care of herself. She was fit and in shape, like someone in their early thirties. She had light brown hair that was cut into a short bob, and did everything he asked without hesitation. He was happy to hire her, knowing right away she was trustworthy and discreet. Susan ran Diamond I/E with minimal supervision and he paid her well for it.

Knowing the vases were there and ready to be shipped on time, Soltan knew he wouldn't have to go to the company today, so he decided to go first thing in the morning. But as for right now, all he wanted to do was go home, take a shower and change clothes.

# Nine

**Soltan lived thirty minutes outside** of Charleston in a three bedroom house in a predominately white neighborhood. The house had cost him three hundred and twenty-five thousand, all of which was paid by Diamond I/E. No one but B.B. knew where he lived and that made it easier to relax. The neighborhood was very quiet and his neighbors minded their business. He would see strange looks from time to time because he kept God awful hours, but they never imposed on him. Pulling into his driveway he noticed his lawn needed to be cut. He would call the kid down the street tomorrow. For fifty dollars a mow, the youngster never let the grass get this high before.

Opening his front door and walking in, he noticed that it was too cool for him. Once inside, he locked the door and walked into the hallway, adjusting the thermostat to seventy-eight degrees. Walking back into the living room, Soltan picked up a remote off the glass table in front of the couch and then turned on the TV. to BET with its music videos. He stood there for a minute, enjoying the images. Satisfied, he muted the sound and turned on his stereo system, pressing buttons on the CD changer until the sultry voice of Sade' came through the speakers. Dropping the remote on the couch, he slid off his shoes and socks and then headed to the bathroom. Turning on the shower, he closed the curtain, watching the steam rise to the ceiling before he headed to his bedroom to take off his clothes. Taking his phone out of his pocket, he placed it on its charger sitting on the night stand. Then placing his money and wallet on his dresser, he entered his closet, putting his gun and blade on a shelf. Grabbing a towel and some fresh boxers he went back into the bathroom to shower.

Finished with his shower, Soltan dried off, got dressed and then went into the kitchen. Wanting something quick and easy, he fixed himself a turkey breast sandwich with pickles, tomatoes and mustard and then poured himself a glass of orange juice. Before he could eat, he had to give thanks, so he left his food on the table in the living room and walked into the den.

Facing the fireplace, Soltan grabbed the box of wooden matches sitting on the mantle, taking one out and striking it on the box. In front of him was what some would call a shrine. The skull of his father, which sat on a folded Haitian flag, sparkled brilliantly. Gleaming white and polished, the skull was flanked by scented candles on both sides, made personally by Soltan. Lighting the candles, Soltan extinguished the match, then knelt down, placing both knees on a circular rug. He then looked up at the oil painting of his father in his military uniform. His father's short and long sword were crossed on a plaque mounted on the left side of the painting. To the right was the topcoat of his father's uniform, folded in such a way as to only show the medals pinned to it, while being framed behind glass.

Soltan closed his eyes and began his meditation session. Sealing off his mind, he blocked out the outside world, letting his mind take him to the spirit world. He reached out to a force so cold and dark that he could actually feel the chill take over his body. He searched for the keeper of souls, the ruler of the crossroads, the one who had given him the strength and power that he now possessed. In this special place in the spirit world they could meet and talk. Having been torn apart by the loss of his parents this is the place where he sought guidance and comfort, and Baron Samedi had given him that from the first day he summoned him. Letting the Baron know of his plans to exact revenge on his enemies, the Baron had given him the tools and knowledge he needed. He also taught him how to gain the power of others' souls. His first ritual had him addicted, the power he felt through the soul extraction Samedi taught him created a craving that would live within him forever. It was like a drug, that when taken made him hungry for more. His lust for it had become insatiable. He kept himself in control by bedding numerous women, which was a bonding of souls itself, giving him only a portion of the power he wanted, but it was only a temporary fix. In Soltan's mind, women were nothing but a tool, an alternative drug. He used women's bodies to keep the urge to kill from overwhelming and consuming him. This he knew would eventually not be enough to hold him within sanity's limits. But there was no turning back now, so whenever he got the chance he called upon the Baron to relinquish the remnants of the power gained and receive more knowledge.

Opening his eyes, Soltan rose, rubbed his father's skull and then planted a kiss on it. He gave a slight bow before going back into the living room. Now that his mind was clear he could eat and relax.

# Ten

**As Lauren drove to her** roommate's house, she had a hard time believing her luck. She was driving a new truck that Derrick said was hers, but not only that, she had a new condo of her own with a decent view of the city right off the highway, that she would be moving into soon. She didn't know what she would do about the furnishings but she was sure she didn't have to worry. Derrick was extremely straight forward, except for the fact that she didn't know what the price was for all she had received. That made her feel a little uneasy, not knowing what she was going to have to do, but the way she was feeling right now, she didn't have a problem with whatever curve ball he threw her way. It was just something about him that made her feel secure and sure of herself. They hadn't known each other for forty-eight hours and he was already showering her with gifts.

Pulling into the driveway of the house she shared with her two roommates, she saw one of them looking out the window. Getting out of the truck, the front door opened to reveal Tasha and Stacey walking out in unison asking, "Whose truck is that?"

"It's a friend's truck," said Lauren.

"Where you been all night and why did you leave me at the party?" Tasha asked, angry.

Tasha was the first person Lauren had met when she came to South Carolina. They met at a T.J. Maxx clothing store where Lauren was looking for some clothes and Tasha furthered her career as a booster.

Hitting it off immediately, they became friends and Tasha invited her to her house where she soon became her roommate. "You went with that light-skinned dude, I bet that's where you were," said Tasha.

As they looked at each other they knew Stacey didn't know about what went on at the party. She was a lot like Lauren - she really wasn't a wild one, or a partygoer. All she did was go to work at the local Pizza Hut and come home. Tasha had asked Lauren to go with her so she could feel safe. It wasn't until later that Tasha had told her she could make some money stripping. Lauren was skeptical at first but desperately needed the money so she agreed to go. Seeing her friend Tasha having sex with those dudes kind of amazed her, but she always knew Tasha was easy, capable of doing almost anything for a dollar. So as she stood there being questioned, it took all of her resolve not to ask about Tasha's extracurricular activities of the night before in front of Stacey.

"I'm grown Tasha, meaning I don't have to answer to you or anyone else. Who I was with last night is my business."

As Tasha and Lauren went back and forth, Stacey walked around them to inspect the truck. "This truck looks brand new, Lauren. What's up? Is it a rental or something?" asked Stacey.

"I said it's a friends, now stop asking me questions," Lauren said as she passed Tasha, walking into the house. Walking through the hallway to her room, she noticed Tasha was hot on her trail. Going into her room she tried to close the door but Tasha was right there.

Going into Lauren's room, Tasha closed the door behind her and said, "You think you slick bitch, you left with that dude last night and fucked him, but you trying to play the innocent role."

Tasha stared at her as if she was trying to see through her, then continued. "I see through you ho, you ain't no better than me, I seen that look you gave me outside."

"The look I gave you outside was a look of disgust, I can't believe the things you did last night. You said we were going to be stripping, not fucking, Tasha!"

"Listen at you, you so innocent," Tasha taunted. "I'm going to make money anyway I can. My pussy should be sold bitch, it's just that good. If them suckas want to pay for it, then I'm gonna sell it to them. And they pay well too, I might add," Tasha said as she stuck a fingernail between her teeth making a sucking sound as if she had accomplished something. "I made four hundred dollars bitch, you feel stupid now, don't you?" Tasha continued.

"You know what," Lauren said with a half grin, "you should be on somebodies ho-stroll cause you damn sho got the skills. Now if you will excuse me I would like to get myself together."

Tasha rolled her eyes, turned on her heel and walked out of the room, slamming the door behind her. Talking to herself as she entered the living room, "I got to find out what is going on with this bitch, and where the hell she get that damn truck from. I bet it's that nigga she left wit last night."

"So what she say?" Stacey asked when Tasha sat back on the couch next to her.

"She said it's a rental."

"That's what I thought," Stacey said as she turned her

attention back to the television, not giving Lauren another thought.

Back in her room, Lauren knew she was going to have to be real careful with how she moved around Tasha now. Her jealousy could cause her more problems than she needed, so she had to play this just right. Getting herself some clothes together and grabbing her purse, she didn't know if she wanted to shower now or wait till she got to the hotel. Deciding to wait, she picked up her overnight bag and headed for the front door. Walking past Tasha and Stacey she saw Tasha shoot her a look of abhorrence for not being involved with whatever was happening to her. The door closing behind her she heard Tasha scream the word "HO!", but paid no attention as she walked to the truck.

Getting in, she forgot that Derrick had given her a cell phone with all the attachments she needed. He had also said he had pre-programmed his number in it, but she couldn't remember if he said thirty-four or forty-four. Starting the truck and backing out of the driveway, she tried the first set of numbers. Nothing seemed to happen. Now headed back to the hotel, she looked in the bag with all of the attachments, pulled out the cigarette lighter adapter, plugged it into the phone and then the cigarette lighter. With the low battery chime gone and a strong signal now, she tried the next set of numbers, forty-four and the phone started ringing.

"Yeah."

"I'm on my way to the hotel, I had to go home to get some clothes and my purse."

"Alright, call me back with the room number and I'll see you later," said Soltan.

"Ok, I'll be waiting."

~ ~ ~

Sitting on his couch watching TV., Soltan wanted to

wait until dark before he went back out. He knew that packages had to be dropped off, but he would have to oversee that later. Right now he just wanted to continue relaxing and possibly take a nap before he got going again. Knowing that Lauren would be waiting for him at the hotel gave him a little incentive, because he knew she was going to be everything he thought she could be. In more ways than one.

# Eleven

**Sitting in his office** Jean Pierre Casi was now deep in thought. Reflecting on his country's history, remembering that his people had won their independence through a slave uprising. Haiti had officially declared its independence after a long fought and bloody war in 1804. Thinking about the strength of Jean Jacques Dessalines, the independence leader who led Haiti to victory, Casi hoped he possessed the same strength as he went up against overwhelming odds. The ability to meet adversity head on, and willingness to face death for the cause were possible and necessary. And so far he was maintaining his stance, not wavering, even though he blamed himself for the death of his son.

Jean Jacques Dessalines was murdered in 1806. Casi knew that his time was also coming, but his son's death would not be in vain. Haiti had come a long way since its independence from France. Holding its first free Presidential election on December 16, 1900, the people voted in Jean-Bertrand Aristide with 67% of the majority. At this time western elites were intolerant to resistance of any kind. So by Aristide being perceived as a barrier against the complete implementation of the neo-liberal agenda, he was ousted on September 30, 1991 by a coup d'état.

Casi knew that anything was possible, but as the President, he hadn't feared this particular fate until now. Before his death, General Francois Marsay had insured not only his safety, but had been his friend, showing loyalty, respect and admiration to Casi and his views. Being a fine general to his Army, the general ran his well-trained military with unyielding precision.

During one of their many conferences, the General had conveyed his disdain for foreigners leaching off his country's resources. At the same time, Canadian mining companies KWG Resources and St. Genevieve Resources were waiting to exploit an anticipated five billion pounds of copper in a Haitian deposit. These companies in partnership with Haitian businessmen would have had unfettered access to a further 522,000 tons of gold ore. General Marsay knew that the several million dollars in profits belonged to his countrymen and that they shouldn't be exploited or divided by anyone. So with a strong sense of pride and commitment Casi had managed to thwart other countries attempts to tap their wealth.

Now, Casi faced a new problem, one that demanded his special attention. Jose Gonzalez had taken over the Colombian based Gutierrez cartel. Known as El Plaga, Jose Gonzalez was trying to use Haiti and its ports as a satellite warehouse and substation. El Plaga offered Casi a portion of the cocaine profits if he cooperated. But to the dismay of the one called "The Plague", Casi refused. And they have been enemies since. Which began the cocaine war. As much as Casi tried to keep his people from being involved in the drug trade, someone on the inside had unlimited access to the product. And this created the competition with the Colombians which in return put Haiti against Colombia on a much more deadly level. The Gutierrez cartel has been the world's most powerful and feared drug organization for the past ten years. But now under the command of El Plaga it was revered. Most country's governments were not immune to his persuasion tactics.

To deny El Plaga was to have your entire family tortured and killed. This was the process until someone accepted his offer. So now with the tragic murder of General Marsay, Casi bore the burden alone. With no doubt that El Plaga was responsible for Marsay's death, it was now his own family that was being sacrificed. He silently wished his son hadn't been a casualty in this war. This was between him and El Plaga. If he could, he would lead his country's Army into Colombia and kill El Plaga himself. But that was just a pipe dream, Casi was no soldier, he was a politician. There was no way he could make something such as that happen. It would be ultimate suicide. Having his Presidential guard protect him was one thing, commanding a whole Army was alien. With the arrival of the Colombian ship to take port, the only way for this to happen was for someone in his cabinet to give the OK But who? As far as he was concerned, everyone was as loyal to him as General Marsay had been. Not to mention that his son was on the ship. Was he lured on, and if not, why was he on it? These questions needed answers and at this time he had none. How long would he be able to hold off El Plaga? How much more time did he have before he joined his son? To these questions he had no answer, so he sat quietly in his office trying to devise a way out of his mess. Trying to save his family, his legacy. Trying to find a cure for the plague.

~ ~ ~

Never knowing his father personally, Emilio Gonzalez knew who he was. Knowing, but never really understanding the circumstances, he grew up with pictures, letters and the love of his mother. Emilio also received money from the time he turned eighteen. Growing up in the city of Chicago, attending its public school system proved to be a challenge. But having an inner drive to want more, to overachieve, were obviously traits he gained from his father. Managing to graduate from high school at the age of seventeen garnered him much praise. Emilio was offered scholarships for his academic achievements statewide. Northwestern, Illinois, Illinois State and Wake Forest all wanted him to join their establishments. But he had chosen to stay with his mother until he was twenty-one. Rosa Mendez had been battling diabetes for the last ten years, so Emilio wanted to stay close. Being only forty-seven years old, Rosa Mendez was experiencing many difficulties with this metabolic disorder.

Rosa had told Emilio many stories about his father's rise to power in Colombia, never downplaying the risk or the death threats to his father or herself. These were the main reasons she fled, although Jose Gonzalez hadn't known at the time of her pregnancy. She had notified him secretly after Emilio's birth to let him know he had a son. But Rosa refused to go back to Colombia once on U.S. soil. Rosa Mendez used her wits and enrolled in Martin Luther King College and managed to graduate with a business degree. Working and going to school proved difficult during her pregnancy and after Emilio's birth. But determination pushed her, so Emilio would gladly sacrifice his future. Owning six coin laundries combined with their day jobs gave them independence. Rosa worked at Illinois Bell telephone company as the head of the billing department, while Emilio did accounting at the Federal Reserve Bank downtown. They both did everything they could to keep their ties to Jose Gonzalez secret so they could maintain the life they had built for themselves.

# Twelve

**Back at the hotel,** Lauren pulled the truck under the awning in front of the door and grabbed her overnight bag and purse. She watched as the valet came around the front of the truck and opened the door. As she stepped out the valet asked, "You need some help?"

"No, I got it, thank you anyway, I'll leave your tip at the front desk, OK? My hands are full."

"No problem ma'am," answered the valet.

Lauren walked into the building, heading straight for the front desk. She set her overnight bag on the polished tile floor and placed her purse on the front desk counter. Pulling her pocketbook from her purse, the desk clerk, a young white woman with long, brown hair tied back into a ponytail, spoke.

"Good evening, welcome to the Embassy Suites Hotel, how may I be of service?"

"Yes, uh, I would like to get a suite with a king-size bed on a floor with the least amount of occupants as possible."

As she spoke she thought of Derrick and his similar request when he paid for the room the night before.

"Let me see what we have available," said the clerk as she began typing on the computer in front of her.

Lauren reached into her pocket book for her driver's license and money. When the clerk looked up from the computer screen she said, "We have a suite on the fifth floor, you should be pleased that the floor is unoccupied."

Lauren found this fascinating because just the night before the hotel was full. Being the day after New Year's made a big difference, she reasoned.

"That's perfect," Lauren said, handing the clerk her license Then she paid and signed for the room.

The clerk waved to a bellhop, who immediately came to the desk. The clerk instructed him to assist Lauren with her things. Before walking away from the desk Lauren gave the clerk an extra twenty dollar bill saying, "This is for the valet who parked my truck. It was the dark blue Denali."

The clerk smiled at Lauren as she took the bill saying, "I'll make sure he gets it."

At the elevator the bellhop pushed the up button and the doors opened almost immediately. Getting in with Lauren trailing him, the bellhop pushed the fifth floor button, closing the doors.

As the elevator moved upward Lauren thought, *I can't wait to get a hot bath and relax and wait for Derrick to come through. I really dig the way he handles himself. He's focused, sure of himself. I like his confidence, and people seem to respond to him well. I wonder what exactly I done got myself into? Almost overnight I got a new place to live, a truck and a man, what the fuck? It's like a got a full-time job with the best benefits ever.*

The elevator chimed, snapping Lauren back into the moment and away from her thoughts. The doors opened up to the fifth floor with the bellhop leading the way and Lauren close behind. As she reached the room at the far end of the hall, Lauren looked at the panel with the key-card. He held the door open for her to enter and then followed, setting her bag on the bed, and then extended his arm to her, handing over the card. The bellhop, a young white guy barely out of his teens, held onto the card a little too long when she grabbed it. The look he gave her was expectant and flirty, which she found amusing. Flattered, she dug into her pocketbook, taking out a ten dollar bill and handing it over.

"If you need anything just call downstairs. My name is Tom and I would be pleased to move mountains for you," he said, still giving her the eye as he backed toward the door.

"I think I'm good, Tom, thank you though," she said, then walked over to the bed and kicked her shoes off. Reaching into her overnight bag, she pulled out her slippers and dropped them on the floor. Sliding into them she picked up the cell phone and pressed the number four twice, then waited.

~ ~ ~

Hearing the phone ringing in the next room brought Soltan out of the semi-consciousness he was in. Looking up at the clock on his wall, he realized he had dozed off for an hour on the couch watching videos. In his bedroom, he plucked his phone from the charger on the fourth ring. Pushing the button to receive the call he said, "Yeah."

"I'm sorry, did I wake you?" Lauren asked seductively, hearing the grogginess in his voice.

"Naw, I just dozed off for a minute, what's up?" said Soltan, now laying back on his bed. He already knew who he was talking to, letting her sultry voice stimulate his brain.

"The room number is five-ten. You told me to call when I got here."

"Ok good, I'll see you later tonight, thanks for the wake

up call," he laughed into the phone.

"I thought you said you weren't asleep," she asked teasingly.

"I'm not," he said before ending the call.

Soltan dropped the phone and stretched hard, relieving as much tension as he possibly could. Laying there for another ten minutes, he ran a mental checklist of to-dos for the night. Afterward he took another shower, getting rid of the light sweat that sleep brings and then got dressed.

Before he could walk out the door his phone rang again.

"Yeah."

"Derrick, Donte's on the line," said Lori.

"What's up D, what's the business?" asked Donte.

"What's up black, you bout ready to get off the bench and play ball or what?"

"More than you know man. Hey listen, I need your help."

"I'm listening."

"I need you to move my babies for me. I need her moved by this weekend to a new spot."

"Is there a problem?" asked a concerned Soltan.

"No, no, nothing like that, ease up. The lease is up on the apartment, plus she wants to move closer to the school anyway."

"Yeah no problem, I got you, just tell her to hit me when she's ready."

"Baby, you hear him? Baby...?" Donte called into the phone.

"She must have put the phone down so we could talk, but I'll let her know."

"Alright, I'll get at you later, you hold down in there, you know I got your back out here. Holla at me if you need something else." Soltan said, ending the call.

# Thirteen

**Walking out his front door,** Soltan decided to drive the rental Expedition that was parked at the curb. Starting the sport utility, he realized that he had the beginning of a headache, so he knew he needed to get something to eat fast, as he pulled away from the curb headed toward the zoo. B.B. and the others should already be there, no doubt waiting on him to show. Soltan knew he was supposed to have met with them earlier, but he had been too exhausted. His body needed rest. Now he needed food, so he figured he could grab something fast on the way. The only thing was he didn't know what he wanted to eat, so as he passed a Waffle House Restaurant, he let his stomach make the decision for him. Getting out of the truck he could see there was a nice crowd of people inside, but it didn't matter because he wasn't staying.

Walking up to the glass doors, Soltan entered the restaurant, walking into the smell of fresh brewed coffee, pork chops, eggs and potatoes. As he approached the counter he was greeted by an older white woman with an apron on, her name tag reading Stephanie. She looked to be in her fifties, but she also looked stressed out. She could have been younger, but stress had a tendency to make some look older than they really were. Stephanie had a fake cheerful look on her face; one that said, "I'm trying to be nice, but I'm also tired of being here. So I can't wait till my shift is over."

She asked Soltan, "What can I get you tonight?"

"Give me a Big Texas cheese steak with a double order of Hash brown, two slices of apple pie, and a large orange juice to go please."

She was punching keys fast as he gave his order, and when he finished she asked, "Will that be all?"

"Yeah, that's it."

"That'll be fifteen thirty eight."

Reaching into his pocket, Soltan fished out a twenty dollar bill, telling her to keep the change. She gave him his receipt and then stepped over to the juice machine and filled a cup with orange juice. Soltan stepped over to a stool and took a seat at the counter right in front of the door, waiting on his order.

Looking around the restaurant, Soltan noticed the people dining. They were from all walks of life, conversing while they ate. As he was surveying the room, he locked in on a couple in the far booth. The woman in the booth had her back to him, but the man seemed very familiar. The man was holding an intense conversation when all of the sudden he looked up and locked eyes with him. Meeting each other's gazes, Soltan felt his breathing collapse, like his heart had stopped. On top of having trouble breathing he was having trouble understanding what was going on.

The man in the booth spoke, "What's the matter Soltan? I bet you never saw this coming. Don't worry, I can't hurt you, yet. I'll see you when you make it to this side."

Soltan feverishly looked around the restaurant to see who was watching him but nobody seemed to be paying attention. Soltan looked back over to the booth to see the man still staring at him, not believing what he was seeing. As he focused more on the man's face he could see a grin spreading across it.

The man in the booth stood up and opened his shirt to reveal an opening in his torso that was all too familiar. The gaping wound was Soltan's work alright, and the man in the booth had it on display for all to see. Nervously looking around again, Soltan noticed the restaurant was now empty. He looked back at the man in the booth and asked, "What do you want?"

"I don't want anything, at least not right now, but she does," the man said, pointing to the woman in front of him.

At that moment the woman stood up and turned around, letting Soltan see the gaping wound in her torso.

At this point he was on his feet, shaking uncontrollably. He couldn't believe this shit, he was looking into the face of another one of his victims. She was holding onto what looked to be an unborn baby in her arms, still connected to its umbilical cord. With her body cavity open and the cord reaching back into her womb, she had a woeful look on her face when she said, "Did I deserve this Soltan, huh, did I? You used me then you killed me in cold blood. Is that what your going to do with the girl you're now using, are you going to kill her in cold blood too? You didn't know I was pregnant did you? You found out when you cut me open though. Well take a good look, Soltan, look at your son, your unborn son! You sent him directly to Samedi. Why? Don't you understand he owns you now, he fuckin owns you!" she said, holding the baby up in the air before she disappeared.

Soltan began shaking his head because he didn't want her to go, he needed to know what she was talking about. He reached out to her, but it was too late, she was gone. All he heard in the distance was Rome's laughter.

"Come back! Come back! I'm sorry! I didn't know, it was too late, it was too late." He said softly, then the ice flowed back into his veins "It doesn't matter now, I will have my revenge and I will not stop until they are all punished for what they did to me, to my family, I swear it! You hear me, I swear it!"

Blinking wildly, he tried to get himself together, putting things into perspective. Looking around the restaurant again, he noticed the waitress who took his order was looking at him while saying something to him. He immediately looked to the far booth and saw that the couple sitting there were looking at him along with everyone else in the place. When he finally turned back to the waitress, he could see a look of concern on her face. Her words finally became clear, "Sir, are you alright?"

"Yeah, uh, I'm fine," shaking his head, wondering what the hell was going on.

"Sir, are you sure? You were yelling and disturbing the customers. Looks like you seen a ghost, you're so pale." She said, genuinely concerned.

Gazing at the waitress with a confused expression he finally asked, "Is my order ready yet?"

"It's right here. Sir you look like you need some rest. I know I sure as hell can use some," she said, now back to worrying about her own problems.

The waitress handed Soltan his food. He took the bags and headed for the door. Before walking out of the restaurant he took one last look at the far corner booth to see the same couple he'd seen before back to enjoying their meal and conversation. Shaking his head again, trying to clear the cobwebs, Soltan walked out of the restaurant. Getting in the truck and setting his food on the passenger seat, he thought for a moment about what he had just experienced. Then he pulled off.

*That was some weird shit!*

# Fourteen

**En route to the zoo,** Soltan decided to call B.B. to let him know he was close.

"Yo."

"I'm on my way, who's there?"

"Everybody's here, we thought you would have been here earlier. Where have you been?"

"I went home to get some rest, I'll see you in a few minutes."

"You alright? You don't sound so good."

"Yeah I'm good, I'm just hungry. I'll see you in a minute.

Soltan began to run a mental list of everybody who needed more product and how much he was going to give them as he drove. When he arrived at the zoo, B.B. would brief him on who came up short and who didn't. Soltan had a mental log of everybody he supplied and how much was owed, but B.B. was the one who got the status updates from everyone.

He parked the truck, grabbed his food and walked to the door. Approaching, he distinctly smelled what he knew to be reefer coming from inside the apartment. This immediately made him angry, so with his food in his hands he kicked on the door, making sure to scare the shit out of whoever was there. Seconds later he could see someone come to the door to look out the peephole. When the door opened, he glimpsed a forty-five caliber handgun in Crow's hand. Straight ahead he saw two more of the guys with A.K. 47's, still crouched behind the counter in the kitchen.

Closing the door, Crow asked, "Where you been? We been waitin' on you all day to get this done."

Soltan shot back, "What the fuck did I tell you about smoking in here? When the police come in here because the neighbors smelled weed and bust up the operation, then what? You all gonna risk life in prison for stupidity, fine, let me know so I can get me a crew that fuckin' listens!"

As they all listened to Soltan they set their weapons down and looked back and forth at each other, wondering what had gotten into him. Before Soltan could continue, B.B. walked out of the bedroom saying, "Soltan, they weren't smoking. It was me, so calm down, I just got tired of waitin, yo."

Soltan looked at B.B. with a look so cold that B.B. couldn't hold his gaze. He knew that Soltan was very upset and when he got like this he was very unpredictable. "Get some air freshener or something and get rid of the smell." Soltan said, waving his hand in the air.

Walking over to the kitchen counter Soltan set his food down, then opened the container that held his steak sandwich. He ate fast because he was hungry. Soltan was not feeling any better as of yet, and his headache had grown worse.

B.B. came over to him while he was eating, saying, "We got everything pretty much set up and ready to go, but you might want to make a few changes."

Crow lit incense throughout the apartment. B.B. had retreated back into the bedroom. "Hey Crow, do me a favor. Go to the store and get me some Advil, I got a mean headache," said Soltan when Crow walked away.

"Yeah I got you," Crow looked around and said, "anybody else want anything while I'm out?"

"Naw, I'm straight" said one guy.

"Yeah" said Sammy, "bring me a gallon of Hennessy wit some cups and a bag of ice."

"Give me some money, I ain't buying that shit."

Sammy dug into his pocket, pulling out a wad of bills held together by a rubber band Peeling off fifty, he handed it to Crow.

"Is this it?" Crow asked, taking the money.

"Yeah, nigga, and hurry back," Sammy said, smiling.

Walking toward the door Crow shot back a "Fuck you," and then left.

Soltan finished his sandwich, drank his orange juice and found his way into the bedroom, speaking as he entered, "What's wrong wit you? You trying to go to jail? You setting a bad example of how to handle your business. B.B., you got something you want to tell me?"

"Man you had us waitin here all damn day and you bitchin' at me for smoking?" B.B. Said, now angry. "Let's get this shit done so we can bounce, I got shit to do yo."

Soltan realized his mood was contagious and didn't feel like going back and forth with B.B., so they agreed on who should get what quicker than usual so they could depart company and get back to whatever they were doing.

"So how much is this?" Soltan asked, pointing to the stacks on the bed.

"This is what's left after we packed the vases," said B.B. "It's a little over three hundred."

"Alright, take two hundred and split it, I'll put another hundred in Panama. You make sure the packages get out tonight, B.B.," Soltan stated sternly. Once they finished separating the money, Soltan asked, "Who came up short?"

"Everybody was straight except for Ford again."

"Oh yeah, again huh? What's this, his second go around? I guess he trying to test us and see if we let him slide. Don't worry about it, I'll take care of him. How much was it this time?" he asked.

"Ten grand flat," B.B. Replied, knowing Ford had sunk his own ship. He had tried to look out for him when he came up short the first time. But maybe he was trying to run game on them. Oh well, he had to deal with Soltan now. It was out of his hands.

In the living room Crow had just got back from the store and was placing the bag of ice in the sink. Setting the other bag he was carrying on the counter, he reached in past the cups and liquor to the bottle of Advil, and then started toward the bedroom. He reached the door and stuck his head in, saying, "Soltan, here's your Advil." Then he tossed him the bottle.

"Come in here, grab this stack, and tell the others to come get theirs." Soltan said.

He looked back at B.B., saying, "You can handle the rest, I'm going back home to lay down, my head is killing me."

Getting off the bed, Soltan looked in the closet and picked up a Pizza Hut duffle bag. After putting the hundred and change in the bag, he headed for the door past Sammy, who was in the kitchen fixing himself a drink. "Yo, ya'll get this shit together and get the hell out of here, and make sure you clean up before you leave. Don't take any unnecessary chances, you feel me?" said Soltan.

*Triple Crown Publications presents . . .*

"Yeah, I got you, but what's up with you? You ain't looking so good, man," asked Sammy.

Soltan looked at him before walking out the door with a blank stare, as if he had just heard something unrecognizable coming from that direction. Regaining his bearing, he turned and walked out the door.

Back in the house, B.B. and Crow were still in the room when Crow said, "Yo, Soltan don't look so good, he alright? He acting kinda strange, I ain't used to seeing him lose his cool."

"I don't know, just get this money and clean up so we can get the hell out of here," said B.B.

"That's one nigga that don't need no headaches," Sammy said seriously.

"He must have got some bad pussy or something, cause he uptight then eh muthafucka," Crow chimed in.

Crow looked over to B.B., "How much we got coming this week?" He was looking at the money in separate piles on the bed.

"You get fifty apiece. All the packages in the front ready?" asked B.B.

"Which one of you is going to make the drops tonight? Whoever it is leave your money here. You can get up with me later and pick it up cause I don't want you ridin with both." B.B. continued.

The guys all looked at each other, then Sammy spoke up, "I got it, I ain't got shit to do anyway, so hold mine."

With that they all got themselves together and cleaned up the apartment, getting rid of any evidence of them being there, and left.

~ ~ ~

Soltan headed toward the hotel to meet with Lauren. But as he drove he debated about what to do with the money he had in the bag. As he thought about it, he decided to go to the condo he had gotten Lauren and stash it there. It was right off the interstate, so he could make it to the hotel in no time once he left. While driving , his thoughts went back to what happened at the Waffle House. *Why had Rome appeared with the girl, and what was all that business about Samedi owning me?* Thinking he was crazy, he tried to tell himself all he needed was some relaxation, maybe some time away from this mess. But then he had a quick recount inside his brain. There would be no rest until they all were punished.

Trying to change his train of thought, he realized he would be with Lauren shortly. He thought she was going to be more than willing to help him relax. He sure hoped so, cause he needed a lot of relaxing right now.

# Fifteen

**Sitting in the corner office,** the one who called himself Region was in deep thought. Why was this task so difficult? All he had to do was convince Casi to open the shipping ports and they would all be rich. But Casi was a stubborn man. He practiced an outdated form of politics that put his life and his loved ones in danger. Region thought that if Casi knew his son was murdered because of Region then he would give in. But no, Casi didn't budge an inch - he actually he seemed more determined. Casi's reaction to his son's death pissed Region off.

Flipping open Gonzalez's dossier once more, he began reading. The dossier was furnished to him by the C.I.A. - unofficially of course. And reading now, he noticed a tab that he didn't see before, marking a separate section of the file. Turning to this section he read intently, not believing his luck. Here he was stressing about the constant pressure from Casi and he stumbles upon another chance. His luck had definitely changed for the better. Region couldn't believe that he had forgotten Jose's first wife. According to the dossier she now lived in Chicago with her son. But the question remained: was this Jose's child or not? Turning some more pages to find out, he came up with nothing. Thinking back to when Jose was just a fledgling enforcer he remembered something about their divorce, and how Jose's wife was definitely pregnant when she disappeared. It was time now to do some internal investigating to see what he could come up with. There had to be some other way for him to find out.

Picking up the phone, Region dialed his assistant's extension. Almost immediately the line came to life, "Yes sir?"

"Come to my office at once."

Moments later the door to his office opened and Philip walked in. A tall thin man, Philip could win a Gandhi look-alike contest. The only difference between the two was that Philip always wore suits.

"Is the pressure still being put on Casi for the results of the investigation?" Region asked.

"Yes sir, just today there was another inquiry from the Colombian's," Philip said, grinning.

"Good, I think we have another shot at breaking him. I just found Jose's other child." Region said while tapping the file on his desk.

"Another child, sir?" asked Philip, confused.

"Yeah, remember Rosa, his first wife? Well she was pregnant when she disappeared. Says here that she's in Chicago with her son."

"Yes sir, but I still don't understand."

"Philip, Philip, my dear Philip. You're not thinking. If we take out El Plaga's son it would take this situation to the next level. Casi is a stubborn old man who didn't care that his son was murdered by Colombian's. But El Plaga won't sit still for that. No, he would be devastated."

"But sir, the Colombian's didn't kill his son. Soltan did."

"Don't you dare question me, Philip! Do you want to be part of the future of this country? If so, you'd better mind your tongue!" Region roared.

"Sorry sir, but I just thought you were getting confused."

"Don't think, Philip let me do the thinking."

"Yes sir."

"Get me El Plaga on the line, it's time to light another fire," said Region.

"Yes sir. Anything else, sir?" asked Philip.

"Go!"

Philip bowed slightly at the waist, then backed out the door, keeping his eyes on Region.

Once he was alone, Region began to put his plan together mentally. He was going to convince El Plaga that Casi was targeting his son in Chicago. So that meant he would have to dispatch Soltan immediately. That way, by the time El Plaga sent his men it would be too late. If everything worked out as planned Region would be Casi's successor, and he would be doing beautiful business with the Colombian's. He would be making a mint.

# Sixteen

**When Soltan got to the hotel,** he was definitely in the mood for relaxation. The thought of enjoying the fine specimen of a woman waiting for him upstairs made it all the more enticing. He parked his truck, got out and noticed a flash of light in the distance. It seemed to be like some kind of reflection or something, like the sun off a mirror. But it was nighttime, so there was no sun out for that to be the case. Looking in the direction from which it came, he decided that it was nothing and proceeded to the front entrance of the hotel. He mentally prepared himself for the fun he was about to have. Reaching in his pocket he grabbed his phone and dialed the hotel's number to get the night clerk.

"Hello, thank you for calling the Embassy Suite Hotel. This is Amy, how can I be of service?" said the clerk. Soltan responded to the cheery voice with, "Room five-ten please."

"Just a moment."

Soltan heard muzak for about thirty seconds as he was placed on hold. Then there was a click as the room was being connected, and then the phone started ringing. The phone rang ten times as he walked through the door of the hotel, then was answered with, "You have reached Room Five-Ten. The occupant is currently away from the phone, please leave a message."

*She must have fucking left after all. Damn, what a waste.* Soltan hung up and kept walking to the room anyway, in case she was in the shower and didn't hear the phone. He reached the door and lifted his hand to knock.

"What are you doing?" asked Lauren from behind him.

Soltan jumped a foot in the air and came down with his gun drawn. "What the fuck!"

Lauren's eyes widened at the sight of the gun. "Dammit! Ease up! I just wanted to sneak up on you, since that's what you did to me before."

"Don't ever, ever sneak up on me. I almost shot yo ass."

"Well, if I'm dead you don't get no pussy, and that there is your own fault, but you don't want no sex no way right? You getting enough of that already from somewhere else anyway."

Hearing this upset Soltan to the point he wanted to do physical damage to something, anything. "Look, what the fuck is wrong with you? Is sex all you got to offer somebody? If all I wanted to do was fuck you, don't you think I would have by now? Don't be stupid. Open the door and let me in!"

"Jesus! Don't you even wanna know how I snuck up on you?"

"No, you keep your moment of glory. I'll just find a new way to check in."

Lauren opened the door and stood aside. Soltan walked in, and finally noticed she was wet with a towel wrapped snuggly around herself. After closing and locking the door he approached her, saying, "Sit down!"

Lauren sat down on the edge of the bed and looked up at him. She could see he was serious and was now thinking maybe she should have kept her big mouth shut and not pulled that stunt. "Do you think I brought you that truck or got you that condo just because I want to fuck. Are you stupid? I ain't in need of no pussy, let alone anything else, so don't get shit fucked up!" he said.

Recognizing he was upset, Lauren mirrored his attitude with one of her own. And she thought it strange that he was not even focusing on her sneaking up on him. He was talking about the sex comment outside. She began to rage at him.

"Nigga don't try me, I done ran into too many of you big willy nigga's to know that that's what you do. You buy pussy, plain and simple. Oh, don't tell me, you got me that stuff because of my good looks, right? Nigga please! You probably just want me for your side piece, your mistress, but ain't got the balls to just straight up ask! Shit, don't get me wrong, I ain't got no problem with it. I'll be your bitch on the side, but don't you stand there and act like it's more than what it is, nigga! You ain't gone plan on me and tell it's raining. I ain't no groupie bitch, and you better understand that!"

"Shut up!" Soltan said, pointing at her. "You listen, and you listen close, 'cause I'm only going to say this once. I don't need no side piece or someone fucking questioning me, period. You want a better life, or you want to keep struggling? If so, go back to where you came from. I don't know you and you don't know me, so if you want to be stupid and throw away an opportunity of a lifetime, be my guest, 'cause I got shit to do," Soltan said as he seated himself on the couch across the room.

"The opportunity of a life time. You're joking right?"

Lauren asked seriously. "What opportunity? All you've done, playboy, is bought a truck and paid for an apartment for a year. That might very well impress an uneducated hood rat, but you got me fucked up. My people got money too, asshole. You think you balling. Let me tell you, you ain't doing shit, muthafucka!" Lauren said, realizing that she had said too much.

"Is that right? So if what you say is true then why are you stripping for money, Ms. Rich Bitch?" Soltan asked. "And where are your people, that supposedly have all this money?" Soltan finished, making quotation marks with his hands in the air.

Looking at him now, Lauren knew that she had to do damage control. Her business was just that, hers. So she owed no one anything, especially no explanations. So now, blank-faced, she looked at him and said, "It's complicated, and I don't want to talk about it."

"Ok fine, that's your business. But don't tell me about what I'm doing 'cause you don't know, get it? You don't know shit about me, all I'm trying to do is help you. No matter what your people got, you don't feel me? At least not that you showed or told me, right?"

"Right," she said, lowering her head.

"Ok, so realize what's going on here for a minute, I just met you and don't even know your last name, but I bought you a truck and paid for a new condo for a whole year. You're smarter than you let on, I know," said Soltan.

Looking at Soltan now, she was curious as to what the hell was really going on here. *What is this nigga about. For real.* She said aloud, "So what's this all about, then?"

"Why did you leave wit' me from the party, why did you allow me to bring you to this hotel? Don't you think you were taking a hell of a chance with a complete stranger?" he asked.

"I thought about it a few times, but you don't necessarily look dangerous, so I guess I trusted you, I don't know." She paused for a second, then, "I just had a feeling about you the first time I seen you," as she was looking him straight in the eyes. "That's why I left with you, because I assumed it was sex you wanted, so I didn't think a one-night stand with you would be a big deal. I'm physically attracted to you and I can see that you definitely want me. But sex don't seem to be the reason you brought me here, so what do you really want with me?" she asked quizzically.

Soltan stared at her a moment and could see the edge of fear creep into her as he began to smirk.

Lauren saw the evil-looking grin on his face and it scared her, so she smiled herself, trying to hide her uneasiness.

"Look," she said, standing up, "I don't know what the price of all this is, but I'm going to go out on a limb and trust you. Whatever you throw at me I think I can handle it. I ain't got shit to lose, what the hell. I think this is going to be a life-changing experience. But I don't see you as the type of guy that's into some sick shit or something. I kinda figured you as a dope boy and that you was doing this shit for me because you wanted me to hold your stash or something. Am I right? You're a drug dealer, aren't you?" She asked, waiting on a response.

"Money isn't an issue wit me," is all Soltan said as he nodded his head at her while sitting on the couch, his legs crossed and his hands folded in his lap.

"My father was a drug dealer, I never cared about what he did for money until I seen what drugs can make people do. Until I seen how it changed people, turned them into animals. And I'm talking about both sides, not just the user. From the looks of it, I believe you are still in control. You haven't been overcome by the greed, as far as I can see. So that's why I'm trusting you, giving you a chance, but you got to tell me what the catch is," she now asked seriously.

"The catch is, I need someone who I can trust, someone who is going to be my right hand. Someone who is going to trust me as well, trust my judgment. I don't need no jealous bitch or someone who can't handle pressure. Because, not only is the world around you going to get better, it's also going to get worse. The world is going to apply pressure and so am I, so I need someone who can hold their own. I seen a glimpse of that type of confidence in you when you brought me that bottle of champagne, and then when you been calling me out here tonight. That's the same instinct I need you to have all the time, that aggressiveness, when you see something you want. I find that a priceless quality in a woman. So what do you think? Are you the woman I'm looking for? I hope so. I'm usually good with judging character."

"You still ain't told me shit. Fine, I'm the type of woman you like. I got that part. Yeah, I got fire and my own brain. I don't have to be remote controlled, so what? Why me? And what do you want from me? You need a woman, a companion, a 'Right Hand.' Spell it out for me as if I didn't make it past the third grade," Lauren said, getting aggravated.

"Look, calm down. I just want someone like you with me, in my life. I am not going to place you in harm's way or mistreat you. But the qualities I see in you are the qualities I want in a partner, is that so much to ask for? Are you wit me or not?"

Soltan was standing in front of Lauren, waiting on her response. Little did Lauren know, her answer was going to be the most important decision she would make

Her entire future depended on it. But with a bit of hesitation in her voice, Lauren began to say something. Then almost instantly, her whole demeanor changed. Her eyes hardened up and then she raised her finger and pointed it in Soltan's face, saying, "If you cross me nigga, I will be the last bitch you will see, understand?"

Soltan looked at her and couldn't believe what he was seeing or what he had heard. And by the looks of it, it looked like she meant what she had said. Even though this created that dangerous boiling in the center of his being, it amused him that this woman was definitely what he wanted, what he craved. *Yeah, she is going to do just fine, I can definitely use this one*, he thought to himself.

Out loud he said, "Hold up. I ain't sure, but I could swear you just threatened me, l'il mama. Is that what just happened?"

"I'm just letting you know that I'm gonna play along and be down wit you, and be down for you. But I don't want no shit out of you, you feel me? You keep your word, you understand?" she said, staring him square in the eyes.

With that, Soltan lowered his hands and started smiling at Lauren as if she was a pot of gold he had just stolen from a leprechaun. Extending his right hand out to her, he said, "You have my word l'il mama, and once this deal is made there is no turning back."

Lauren grabbed Soltan's hand, and as soon as their hands met flesh to flesh, Soltan pulled her in, giving her a hug. While hugging her he said, "Now that's out the way, can we relax? I'm exhausted and I could definitely use some quality R and R."

Lauren stepped back, smiled and said, "Don't worry baby," in a soft seductive voice as she unbuckled his belt. "You can relax now. I'm going to take good care of you from here on out."

Turning him around, she pushed him down on the bed. Kneeling down on the floor she untied and removed his shoes, then pulled his pants off. While she did this, Soltan unbuttoned his shirt and pulled it, along with his tank top, over his head. As soon as he was completely naked, he felt a warm and wet sensation on the crown of his member. Knowing instantly what was going on, he raised his body up on his elbows to see Lauren with him in her mouth. After a couple of bobs and a few lingering licks, she grabbed hold of his now erect penis and said, "are you relaxed yet - or you need more encouragement?" She said it with a smile, gently stroking his shaft.

Soltan responded with, "Don't stop." That was all he could bring himself to say.

Then Lauren stood up and said, "Uh-uh, not yet, come with me to the Jacuzzi" She grabbed his hand and pulled him off the bed.

Lauren pulled his now docile body toward the bathroom. Once there, she helped him into the already bubbling Jacuzzi and stepped over to the edge where a bottle of champagne was on ice in a bucket. Grabbing the bottle by the neck, Lauren picked a flute off the tray and filled the glass with the sparkling liquid. She handed it to Soltan and said, "Wait for me baby."

She filled another glass, then she stepped into the water and released the towel from around her body, making sure that Soltan got an eye full before she lowered herself into the water. Sitting next to him, Lauren held her glass up for a toast and said, "To my king. You have found your queen, may this union be eternal."

Hearing her words made Soltan feel like he had made the right decision, but there was still a situation he had to test her with. He had just met this woman, so the outcome of her so-called "Union" was going to be very interesting.

He said, "So anyway, how'd you sneak up on me like that?"

Lauren just grinned.

# Seventeen

**The next morning Lori** and her sister Rochelle were at Lori's apartment, packing the remaining items while talking about having Derrick help them move.

"How well do you know this guy? Just because he's a friend of Donte's doesn't mean it's safe for him to help us," said Rochelle.

"He's not just a friend of Donte's, he's got his back. Who do you think has been paying all the bills here? Who's been sending Donte money every month? I know you didn't think I was taking care of all that by myself. Shit, you ain't gave me much for the bills here, so how you think they was getting paid?" asked Lori.

"I don't even live here, plus you know I ain't got no job yet, I just graduated a month ago," said Rochelle, now aggravated.

"But all your shit is here right? You could get one of those so-called big dope boys you be messin' wit to give you money, but do you? No. All you do is let them run up in you and buy you jewelry and take you out to eat and jump up and down in you some more. Huh, I wonder, why ain't you got a place of your own, answer me that, Rochelle?" Looking at her, hands on her hips, "No, let me answer for you, all those dudes want from you is some pussy. They don't care about you, they care about that good head you got." Lori said, dismissing the conversation.

Rochelle had no response to her sister, because deep down she knew she was right. But in her defense she said, "It is good, how did you know? Shit, I can suck the chrome off a bumper," smacking her lips at Lori. "You jealous?" she said, laughing.

All Lori could do was shake her head at her insufferable sister as she picked up the phone to call Derrick to let him know she was ready to get this move on the roll.

~ ~ ~

Soltan confirmed a time and place to help Donte's girl move. He didn't want to do it – shit, it was a waste of time – but Donte had his back, and he would damn sure have Donte's. Even for something as shitty as loading a moving truck.

After hanging up the phone, Soltan looked down onto his chest and watched as Lauren's head rose up and down with his breathing. He had been awake, true enough, but wasn't up and about like he conveyed to Lori. At the moment he was just relaxing, enjoying Lauren's soft breath on his skin, the warmth of her body against his. He had spent the night having marathon sex. Lauren could not get enough, or maybe she was just determined to drain his body of all its strength. After their toast in the Jacuzzi last night, she had proven to be very athletic and insatiable. He hadn't lied to her when he said he like her aggressiveness. He thought about her and smiled as he lightly skimmed his fingers up and down the curve of her back. His fingers found their way to her behind eventually and Lauren surprised him when she spoke ever so softly, "You want more, baby?"

"No, I'm just enjoyin' your smell and the softness of your skin."

Moving slowly, she swung her leg over him, positioning herself on top of him without sitting up, all the while keeping her head on his chest. Crouched on top of him, she rocked gently back and forth on his already hard penis. She reached down, grabbing his solid member and placed him inside her already juicy folds. A low moan escaped her lips as she slowly, methodically, slid up and down on his shaft. All Soltan could do was lay there and enjoy it as he rubbed her back and caressed her firm ass while she tenderly took her time sexing him. Soltan knew for a fact that she could satisfy him sexually, but this was only one aspect of their journey together.

Twenty minutes later, they both found their peak with the soft sensual movement and rhythm of their bodies. In Lauren's mind she found this to be very good sign. She couldn't keep count of how many times in their lovemaking they climaxed together. She thought it to be a sign for compatibility and this made her very happy. *We're perfect for each other baby.*

Reaching down and grabbing Lauren, Soltan pulled her up further on his body so he could kiss her on the forehead. He said in a low baritone, "I got something to do today, so I probably won't see you until later tonight, alright, my little tiger?"

Lauren just nodded her head in compliance and moaned, "Unh-huh." Comfortable in her satiated state. "I'm gonna do some shopping today for my new place. Can't wait."

With that, Soltan kissed her once more on the cheek, patted her on the butt and said, "I gotta go."

Rolling off him, she grabbed hold of a pillow and

stretched out in the king-size bed, watching him get to his feet and head to the bathroom. It didn't take long for Lauren to doze off into a peaceful sleep again.

The next time she opened her eyes, she realized she had been out for longer that she wanted, because Soltan was already dressed and kissing her face.

"I'll see you later," he said.

"Ok," was all that she could come up with as Soltan laid five thousand dollars on the night stand.

He handed a glass of water to her. "If you need me, you know how to get in touch."

Lauren took a couple sips of the water and handed the glass back to him, then nodded her head before she laid back on the pillows. Placing the glass back on the nightstand, Soltan placed a final kiss on her lips, then walked out the door.

# Eighteen

**Soltan looked at his watch** as he hurried to his vehicle. It read nine o'clock. It was then that he noticed he was definitely pushing his luck. He had just enough time to go handle his business and get to Lori's on time. Soltan made it to his truck and noticed that the sun was shining bright, and he enjoyed the warm feeling of it on his skin. Also loving the smell of fresh air, he took a deep breath and smiled, deciding today was going to be a good day.

After driving for twenty minutes, Soltan parked the truck around the corner from Ford's house. Time to settle a debt. He knew Ford liked to party all night, so he should be sleeping his hangover off, lying next to a trick right about now. Soltan looked around to see if there was anyone in sight, then got out of the Expedition and walked around to the back. Once he unlocked the back door and had it open, he reached into the panel that concealed the truck's speakers. He felt around until he touched the bag hidden there, which contained his blade and a thirty-two caliber handgun. Feeling it, he pulled if free from its hiding place.

Unzipping the bag, he pulled the gun out first and then the blade. Untucking his shirt, he placed the gun in the small of his back, then picked up his blade. The knife had its own holster which he tucked into the front of his pants, the curved tip facing the inside of his thigh. Zipping the bag, he replaced it behind the speaker panel and snapped everything back together. Closing the door to the truck, he looked around again, seeing no activity whatsoever in this once beautiful neighborhood. This area had definitely seen better days, but the invasion of drugs and the criminal element had taken its toll. The houses needed roof work, and paint jobs. The front yards were just dirt mixed with gravel because of the constant traffic and neglect. The streets glistened with broken glass and abandoned cars lined up one behind the other. With no trees in sight or tall buildings to provide shade, Soltan wandered why this area seemed so dark and dreary. It was almost like a permanent rain cloud was hovering over. As it was, this was not a premier spot to live in - it was bad enough to double as a war zone if you were filming a movie.

Walking down the block with a strut like he belonged there, Soltan was hoping that he could do his business and still make his ten-thirty appointment with Lori. No matter, he was here now, so he would try to be as efficient as possible. Reaching the end of the block, Soltan walked past a man pushing a mountain bike. With a nod he looked at the man, but the man seemed to hold his stare as if expecting something. With a flip of his hand, Soltan waved the man off, signaling him to leave him alone. As Soltan walked down the street to Ford's house, he again took deep breaths of the morning air, still confident about the day to come.

But his thought's said, *Yeah, this is a beautiful morn-*

*ing and should be a good day, but too bad for you, Ford, you won't see it.*

Walking up to the door, Soltan tried the knob, but when it didn't turn he didn't force it. He tried popping the lock on the door, hoping to get lucky, but no luck. Soltan decided to walk around the side of the house where the garage connected. Walking up to the side door of the garage, he knocked lightly one time, then bumped the flimsy door open with his hip. Closing the door once he was inside, he noticed a 1972 Chevy Impala. Looking over the car, Soltan assumed that this was where Ford's money was going. With one of those fancy paint jobs and huge gold rims and leather top, the car looked pretty expensive.

After a brief inspection of the car, Soltan walked over to the house door. Turning the knob, Soltan was happy to find it was unlocked, reducing any further noise he would have to make to get inside. The door opened into the kitchen, showing Soltan that cleanliness wasn't on the top of Ford's priority list. There were empty pizza boxes, cans of beer and soda everywhere, along with trash bags overflowing and piled up in the corner. The floor was filthy with stains and food scraps, along with the sink being full of dirty dishes and cups. As Soltan made his way down the hallway to the bedroom, he could hear someone snoring. Pulling out his gun, he eased himself into the doorway and peeked around the corner to see Ford lying across the entire bed, spread out as if making a snow angel. Wondering if he was all alone, Soltan did a quick survey of the other bedroom and hall bathroom. Pleased that Ford was alone, Soltan walked back into the kitchen for some trash bags, finding a half-full box under the sink.

Returning to Ford's room, he set the box of bags at the foot of the bed and walked over to stand over Ford as he snored, ignorant of present danger. He watched Ford sleep as he screwed the silencer he carried in his pocket onto the barrel of the gun. Thinking quickly, he went back into the bathroom looking for a bar of soap. Not finding what he wanted, he checked the hall closet and voila, a new bar of Ivory. Going back into the bedroom Soltan decided it was time to wake Ford up. Tapping Ford on the foot with the gun brought Ford quickly out of his slumber. "Bitch, I told you don't wake me up! I'll get up when I'm good and goddamn ready!" Ford said, rolling onto his side and never opening his eyes.

"I'm not your bitch," Soltan said calmly.

Ford's eyes shot open as he sat up all in the same motion.

"Wha...wha, what's up Derrick? What you doing here?" asked Ford, now nervous.

"Grab that sheet there and rip it into strips," Soltan said, pointing the gun at the sheet next to Ford.

"What!"

"I'm not going to repeat myself," Soltan said, aiming his pistol at Ford's face.

Ford took a second to look into Soltan's eyes before grabbing the sheet next to him.

"Derrick, what's going on man? Is this about the money? I swear I'll make it up on the next go round."

Ford spoke nervously as he began shredding the sheet into long lengths. When Ford had four long strips Soltan spoke again.

"Now tie your feet together at the ankles, tight."

With no hesitation, he wrapped his ankles with the cloth and tied a tight knot, to Soltan's satisfaction. Ford began to think that he might not make it out of this situation, but his fight or flight reaction was dulled with the probability of certain death. Looking at the silencer pistol confirmed his fears.

"Now take this," said Soltan, throwing the bar of soap at Ford. "And put it in your mouth and tie one of those strips around your face to hold it in."

"Fuck you, I ain't putting that in my mouth! You gone kill me, then get it over with. But I ain't going to help you do it!" Ford spat out as fear turned into anger.

Soltan lowered the gun and shot Ford in the shin.

"Aaargh, you piece of shit! You fuckin' shot me!" Ford said, spit flying out of his mouth.

"Put the soap in your mouth now!" Soltan growled.

Ford unwrapped the bar and stuck it in his mouth as tears rolled down his face.

"All the way," said Soltan.

Ford couldn't believe it, he was in so much pain that he just pushed the bar inside his cheek, crushing it past his teeth to get it horizontally in his mouth.

"Now tie the strip around your mouth to hold it in."

With saliva running out of the corners of his mouth mixed with tears, Ford reached his shaking hands over to pick up another length. He wrapped it around his head and his open mouth. It took what seemed like an hour for him to tie the knot.

Soltan now took aim again, this time at Ford's shoulders, placing the first bullet in his left shoulder. A muffled crack came from Ford as the force of the impact laid him flat on his back. Soltan walked around to the left side of the bed and shot Ford again, this time in the opposite shoulder. Blood had begun to pool onto the sheets and began spreading across the bed, turning it crimson. The strong smell of copper was in the room now, drowning out the staleness of the bedroom. Grabbing the two remaining strips of sheets, Soltan tucked the gun in his waist and pulled Ford's immobile arms together, tying then at the wrist. Then he pulled them back behind Ford's head and tied them to the headboard. Ford's movements were minimal as Soltan tied his legs to the foot of the bed. Ford was still alive but he was bleeding pretty well, so Soltan knew he had to hurry.

Soltan now stood over Ford, looking into his glazed eyes for recognition. He knew Ford was in pain but, he wanted to make sure he was still coherent - because the party had just begun.

"Was it worth it, Ford?"

All that came out was a whimper as Ford's eyes went wild, almost rolling into the back of his head. Reaching to the end of the bed for the trash bags, Soltan pulled out a couple and opened one up at the closed end, ripping the plastic. Then he opened two more holes, one opposite the other on both sides. Taking his time he pulled the bag over his head, sliding his arms through the holes on the sides.

Picking up another bag, he tore this one open at the closed end as well. He stopped through his hole one leg at a time, careful not to stretch the plastic further. When both legs were through, Soltan pulled the bag up his body to his waist. Satisfied the bag would stay in place, he pulled his blade from its holster.

"Finally," he said to Ford, "my favorite part."

~ ~ ~

Looking at his watch, Soltan realized he had spent too much time on Ford. It was now ten-fifteen, so he had to hurry if he wanted to be at Lori's on time. Stripping himself of his makeshift apron, he dropped the bags on the floor, knowing he would have to be quick if he wanted to make it. But this was business, and it had to be done first.

Wiping his blade off on one of the sheets, he took time out to look back at his handiwork and smiled. As

*Triple Crown Publications presents . . .*

his eyes poured over the desecrated body, he noticed the body was no longer Ford's, it was of someone he loved and cherished, and the image froze him, chilling him to the bone.

"Father?"

There was a knock at the front door that snapped Soltan back into the present.

"Ford, come on man! Open up! I got a hundred!" a voice yelled.

Quickly, Soltan put his blade back into its holster and darted back through the house to the kitchen. Taking a glance at the front door, he could see the shape of a man peeking through the window with his hands cupped on both sides of his face.

"Ford, wake up man, come open the door!" the voice boomed again.

Now standing at the garage door, Soltan stood there until the man gave up and walked away mumbling the words, "Fuckin' punk don't want to make no money."

Soltan went back into the garage and out the door he came through. Once in the backyard, he ran to the fence, hopping it with the agility of a cat. Running through the yard next to Ford's house, he hopped another gate and then slowed down to a casual walk. Working to get his breathing under control, he walked out of the yard and onto the sidewalk. Knowing he would have to walk all the way around the corner to get back to the truck upset him. That was more time wasted before he got to Lori's.

He rounded the corner onto the street he parked on and saw a man walking away from him in the opposite direction. Soltan immediately assumed it was the man at Ford's front door.

Reaching the truck, Soltan took a quick look around to see if anyone was watching him. He didn't turn his head or his body to let anyone know he was looking, he

just used his eyes and ears to tell him about his surroundings. He got into the truck and thought he should
call Lori to tell her he was going to be a little late.
Starting the truck and driving off, Soltan picked up his
phone and called.

"Hello?"

"Hey Easter Bunny, I'm on my way. You need anything before I get there?"

"Naw, I'm good. We're waiting on you though slow
poke, we wanna try and get the truck before twelve so
they don't charge us for an extra day."

"I'll be there in a few minutes, I'll call when I'm
downstairs."

"Alright."

"Bye," Soltan said as he punched off.

# Nineteen

**While sitting at his desk,** Jose Gonzalez looked out his office window, marveling at the lush landscape of Bogota. The trees were scattered strategically around his compound, providing plenty of shade, as well as fresh fruit. Being the number one cocaine producer in the world, he saw such fertile land as a blessing. Colombia was his, but he wasn't satisfied. He wanted to conquer other lands like Genghis Khan, or maybe even like Hitler. Getting rid of unwanted people who posed any kind of threat to his operation had never been difficult. But this Casi character has proven to be somewhat of a problem. Even though Colombia was a very poor country overall, Gonzalez made sure that he gave his people just enough to stay dependent upon him. But in his mind, Haiti was different, that country was extremely poor. If the two were compared, Colombia was wealthier by far, but if Casi would just submit to his demands Casi's country could rebuild a few resorts. One never knew. When money was involved, almost anything was possible.

Reaching for his phone, Gonzalez dialed his assistant's extension and spoke. Seconds later there was a knock at the door.

"Enter."

His assistant came in and closed the door behind him, found the plush leather chair in front of his boss' desk and sat down, crossing one leg over the other. Jose regarded his assistant Rico with the utmost carefulness. Rico was his personal bodyguard as well, standing at five-eight and one hundred and sixty pounds - he was nothing to trifle with. He was as deadly as the venom of a black mamba, trained in all the military and torture tactics in existence. Sitting in the chair, Rico waited patiently for the General to speak.

"I just received information that Emilio's life may be in danger," said Gonzalez.

"Ok," said Rico.

"Apparently Casi has located him and plans to kill him in retaliation for his son's death." Gonzalez said.

"But we had nothing to do with his son's death."

"Casi believes differently," said Gonzalez.

"General, I don't mean to question you, but as your bodyguard and advisor, I wonder what we are doing? Why don't we just kill the Haitian and be done with it? We could easily get what we want then." Rico said.

"It sounds, simple doesn't it? But unfortunately it is not, brother. If Casi dies we create problems for our American associates. Casi must remain alive until the Americans accomplish whatever they are after. I'm not going to create problems for my operation when money is flowing as good as it is."

"I thought the Americans wanted him out of the way as well?" Rico asked.

"They do, but you know the Americans aren't happy unless they acquire some sort of power or leverage in foreign countries. And from my understanding they are after more than just the Haitian government," said Gonzalez.

"So where does that leave us?" asked Rico, not taking the bait of asking about the Americans and what they really wanted. If the General wanted him to know the full story he would tell him when he was ready.

"I'm sending you to Chicago to protect my son," said Gonzalez, holding up a manila folder. "Everything you need to know is here. You are to find the boy and protect him at all costs. No exceptions. Nothing is to be held back. The boy is to live, he is my only son, do you understand? I will not except failure of any kind. Rico, your life depends on it." Gonzalez looked at him in the eyes.

Sliding the file across his desk, Gonzalez continued, "There is a plane waiting for you, take the helicopter to the airport. All the information is on the paper on the front of this folder."

Rico stood up, taking the folder off the desk. He bowed slightly at the waist and left the office immediately.

He craved action, it was in his blood. But he was going to be patient. He knew sooner or later his services would be needed and blood would run freely. He didn't like dealing with Haitians - he enjoyed killing them. It was Gonzalez who dealt with them, using them any way be pleased. It wasn't know he would do things, but he wasn't in charge. So for right now he would just follow orders and get a team together for his trip to Chicago.

~ ~ ~

Rico sat quietly in his seat on the chartered G-4, looking at the four men he had brought. He had chosen the best to accompany him on this mission. Rafael, a large muscular hunk of destruction was his demolition man. Renae, a small wiry blonde man was the best sniper he'd ever seen. Remi was his eyes and ears when it came to computer and surveillance systems. But Domingo was his rock, a quiet man who could always be depended on. He would come through when no one else could in a bad situation. He was a silent but very deadly man and was the only person he knew that made him nervous. He could probably use him on this trip. Being that near him made Rico nervous. If he could help it, he didn't want him near until it was absolutely necessary.

# Twenty

**B.B. had just finished rolling up** one of his blunts when there was a knock at the door.

"Yo, B.B. I gotta piss yo! What the fuck are you doing in there?" asked Crow.

B.B. flushed the toilet, pulled his pants up and opened the door. Staring right into Crow's face he said, "Enjoy, my brother," and then slid past him into the living room.

It took a second or two, but when Crow got a nose full of the stench, and then he responded. "A yo. What the fuck you been eating? You smell like something died in you. You might want to get yourself checked out."

Taking a deep breath and holding it, Crow finally walked into the bathroom and started pissing.

B.B., now sitting on the couch in the living room, lit his blunt and began flipping channels on the big screen TV. Not looking for anything in particular, he channel surfed for about ten minutes and then stopped and jacked up the volume to listen.

"... found dead in his home this morning by his girlfriend who had come home from work," the lady reporter was saying.

"Hey come check this out, Ford's on TV." B.B. said to the others.

Some of the crew came over to the TV. and stared. "... the victim was gruesomely mutilated according to initial reports, and the police are questioning witnesses at the moment and have launched a massive investigation into the atrocity, labeling it as a hate crime. According to reports the authorities have recovered a large amount of evidence so far, but are asking if anyone has any information about this terrible act they should call the toll free hotline number at 1-800-Crime-Stoppers. That's one, eight hundred, one, six, three, five, two..."

B.B. looked at everyone and noticed that they were all doing the same thing, shaking their heads from side to side.

"You won't be coming up short any more, will you?" B.B. said under his breath.

If the guys heard what B.B. said, they didn't comment. B.B. just continued watching TV.

Taking another long pull on his blunt, B.B. held his breath, trying to keep as much smoke inside his lungs as possible. In his usual clouded haze, B.B. reached inside his pocket and pulled out his phone. After dialing Soltan's number he grabbed the remote and turned the TV. volume down.

"Yeah," Soltan answered.

"Yo, I need to talk to you, where you at?" asked B.B.

"Meet me at OZ in fifteen minutes, I'm on my way there now."

"I'm on my way." B.B. said, ending the call.

Heading toward the door, B.B. was stopped short when Sammy, one of the guys, called to him. "Yo, you going to see Soltan?"

"Yeah."

"Yo, tell that nigga to calm down, we don't need this bullshit here, know what I'm saying? We getting a lot of money in this city, we don't need the extra heat."

"Yeah. I'll tell him." B.B. answered as he was walking out the door.

# Twenty • one

**The sky was shades of red** and orange when he arrived. B.B. could see Soltan's F-150 already parked in the lot. Pulling his rental beside Soltan's truck, B.B. got out and greeted him.

"Yo, what's up?" Soltan asked as they shook hands and then embraced. "Ford was on the five o'clock news just now," B.B. said, waiting for some kind of reaction but getting nothing.

"What did they say?" Soltan asked as he turned and started walking.

"Shit, too much if you ask me. They were talking about how gruesome it was, and they are calling it a hate crime and shit." There was a slight pause and then he continued, "You really didn't waste no time did you?"

Soltan laughed before saying, "I had some free time so I figured I'd drop in on him," with a grin on his face.

"Yo, they say they have evidence and witnesses, that can't be good," B.B. stated in a warning tone.

"It don't mean nothing, they always gonna say stuff like that to try and scare whoever did the crime to come forward with a confession. They can't have nothing, no fingerprints no nothing, I ain't in the system. They definitely don't have no witnesses cause the witness is dead. Let's be patient and see what they really have. But if we see them come around snooping, we know they made the connection, feel me? Then we will have to make some moves," said Soltan as they turned the corner of building H and began walking down the aisle.

"Won't it be too late then? If they start snooping, it means they have identified us, Soltan," B.B. said, concerned.

Soltan stopped and took a look at B.B., looking him in his eyes.

"What's wrong, brother? What's bothering you? This isn't like you to be so paranoid. We've been trained for situations such as these. You know how we will react to the police, why the sudden fear, brother?" Soltan asked.

"I have no fear, but I as well as the others feel that we are doing fine here. We are making plenty of money and we love the women. Everything is going so smooth, we just don't feel that we should be shaking things up like this," answered B.B.

"So you feel that I should have let Ford con us out of our money?" anger creeping through Soltan's veins now.

"No, he deserved what he got. But couldn't he have just disappeared instead of being put on display for all to see?"

Thinking about it, Soltan controlled himself, beating back his anger before he answered.

"Yeah, I guess he could have, but I just got a bit carried away. You're right, I was being kind of selfish. I'll try to control myself next time."

"Shit, I hope for everyone's sake there won't be a next time" B.B. said, laughing now.

Soltan joined in on the laughter as he turned and

began walking again.

"So anyway, what's going on? Why are we here? Did Region call?" B.B. asked.

"Yeah, he left me a message a little while ago, and I got a feeling things are going to get real interesting."

They walked another fifteen feet to the storage unit. Once they had it open, they began setting up the equipment in the darkness and cloned another phone. Once all this was done Soltan called Region.

"Hello?" Region answered.

"You left me a message."

"We have chosen a course of action continuing from the previous account. Instructions have been sent, you should be receiving them shortly," Region said.

"Who's the messenger?" asked Soltan.

"I'm sending Philip, he will be contacting you upon his arrival."

"Alright, anything else?"

"That will be all for now." Region said before ending the call.

Turning the phone off, Soltan looked at B.B., saying, "We're back in business, our target will be identified as soon as tonight."

"This is good, I have been kinda bored lately. I need a little excitement in my life to get my motor running again," said B.B. as he was putting the satellite back inside the unit.

Soltan started to lift a case to cover the generator but winced. B.B. noticed it and said, "What happened, my brother, did killing Ford take it out of you? You getting old on me?"

Soltan laughed. "No, nothing like that. I went to help one of my boys, you remember Donte, right? I had to help his girl move. The first goddamn thing I try to pick up, I hurt my back. So I said the hell with it. I'm gonna set her up with a mover instead."

B.B. laughed. "Yeah, that's what I thought. You're getting old."

As they were cleaning up a car drove past, down the aisle. When they heard it coming they tried to bring down the door in time, but it was too late. The car passed by before they could completely close it, and for Soltan, that's all it took.

Replacing the lock on the door he spoke, "Get Nell and move all this to another spot. I want this compartment cleaned out before the end of the night, but make sure to put the lock back on it. Have Nell get a new unit. No one has seen him before, and here," he said, handing B.B. the phone. "You know what to do with it."

"Why you trippin, it was just a damn car. And you was calling me paranoid, are you alright?"

Soltan's facial expression changed as he stared in B.B.'s eyes again.

"When was the last time a car passed by while we were here?"

"Never." B.B. threw his hands out.

"Exactly, so don't question me about why. I got a funny feeling in my gut that something about that car wasn't coincidental. Weird shit been happening to me all day. Even if it wasn't anybody to be concerned about, I want the shit moved anyway."

And with that they started walking back to their vehicles. Once there Soltan spoke, "You get Nell and handle the storage, I'll wait for the message and call you when I know something."

"Do you think that car could have something to do with Ford? Because if they're tracking you to here, we could be in some serious shit." said B.B.

"Naw, it's too soon for anything like that. But we still got to be careful just in case."

*Triple Crown Publications presents . . .*

"OK," was B.B.'s response as he got in his rental and drove off. But in his mind things were unraveling. Things seemed to be headed in a direction real fast, and whether the right or wrong direction was still to be determined. Although Soltan was usually right when he felt something, he hoped he was wrong this time.

# Twenty • two

**Sitting in their white department-issued** Ford Taurus, watching the two vehicles leave the parking lot, Detectives Smith and Clayton witnessed something they hadn't expected. They had been investigating Derrick Jones for three weeks now, trying to gather enough evidence to make a narcotics arrest. They received information Mr. Jones was shipping large amounts of money to a bank in Panama. The amounts supposedly shipped had been is excess of one million dollars. They had the account number in which the money was being deposited, but no name. Estimating the amount that had been sent so far made it impossible to know what the actual account balance was. While it was still early in the investigation, Smith and Clayton were confident they would eventually get all the information they would need. Right now they just were just trying to find out the ins and outs of his operation. They had a theory the money was drug related. That's why the investigation was started, but they had yet to see any drugs.

There was a house on North Summer Avenue their

department had under surveillance because of reports of drug activities. So far, they had multiple pictures of unidentified males and females that frequented the house as well as license plate numbers and vehicle descriptions. They haven't seen any concrete evidence of anything illegal yet, but what they just seen was different. What they saw could be the step closer to finding out what exactly Mr. Jones was up to.

For the past couple of weeks Clayton and Smith had been rotating on the home surveillance, seeing Mr. Jones come and go. They kept a revolving tail on Mr. Jones as well, following him everywhere he went. Today they had seen a suspected accomplice leave the house. All the while, Clayton and Smith had tailed Mr. Jones to the storage facility when they got the report that the suspected accomplice was headed in their direction. So they let the surveillance team know they were on location, and to fall back, that they would handle things from this point. The two detectives weren't surprised to see these two men together, because it wasn't the first time. But what was surprising was that the suspected accomplice couldn't be identified. His face didn't bring forth any kind of identification through local, state or nationwide databases. The rentals he drove were rented by out of state LLC's on which they couldn't get any information without a warrant. And anyone they talked to couldn't give him a name. They didn't want to call the feds because they didn't have enough evidence, so they concentrated on Derrick Jones.

The suspected accomplice met Mr. Jones in the parking area for an apparent conversation. Their listening equipment was useless as they pointed the microphone at them because of the constant traffic on the highway that the facility paralleled. But as they watched the two men walk toward one of the units they became quite curious. They wouldn't come all the way to a storage facility just to talk, would they? Their detective minds answered that question quickly. They wouldn't. They were here for another reason, but what? As the detectives kept them in sight, they watched as the two men came to a unit halfway down aisle H. To their surprise, the suspected accomplice came out the doorway with what looked like a satellite dish.

"What the fuck is he doing with that?" Smith asked.

"Don't know, but how about we drive down there and take a look?" Clayton responded.

"If we do that then they'll see us and we lose our cover," said Smith.

"We ain't got to pull up to them and say hi, we just need to drive by and get a good look at what's going on," Clayton said as if it was common sense. I want to get a closer look, but I got an idea about what's going on," he continued.

Detective John Clayton was a decorated Narcotics Detective with a large number of big drug busts, taking down some of the biggest drug dealers Charleston had ever seen. But John Clayton didn't always walk on the right side of the law. His street savvy, coupled with his intelligence made him an effective crime fighter. He had been on the force almost ten years and moved up the ranks at a pace the department didn't know existed. John Clayton was quite frankly a criminal-minded man with a badge. So the streets didn't stand a chance with him. Plus it didn't hurt to still have good contacts and resources in the streets, which made his job easier. Clayton being a man with few personal obligations, made it easy to pour himself into the role of crime-fighter. So to him the gloves came off when it came to the streets, knowing he had no worries of any form of retaliation, putting people he loved in harm's way.

As they began to move, it looked like the two men

were beginning to leave, so Smith sped up a little. As they passed, the two suspects pulled the door down to the unit. They almost didn't make it, but Clayton got a quick glance at what was inside before the door was completely closed.

"Shit, I couldn't see what was inside, but what I did see that whatever is in there they don't want anybody to know about it," Smith answered.

"Exactly, but I got a peek at what looked to be a lot of high tech electronic equipment. Now what is all that doing in a storage facility?" asked Clayton.

He looked at the screen on his digital camera. "I think I got a couple of good snaps as we went by," he continued.

"I want to see exactly what's in there," Clayton said, looking at Smith with a smile on his face.

"Don't start that shit John, we need to get a warrant first," said Smith.

Smith had been Clayton's partner for the past three years, and had grown to trust and like his partner. But that didn't help the fact that he was a straight by the book guy. He was always telling Clayton about procedure, procedure, procedure. But in the end he rolled with his partner anyway, right or wrong, because he believed in having your partner's back. With Smith having a wife and two kids and eight years left until he could retire, the decision to roll with his partner was not always an easy one. Some of the things they'd done had not only been questionable, but down right illegal and dangerous. But in the end, they always came out on top.

As his partner continued smiling at him, he already knew that John didn't need a warrant, or was even going to try to get one. He was going to the storage unit and there was nothing anyone could do about it.

"Fuck!" was Smith's only and final response.

# Twenty • three

**As Soltan drove off he** got a page. Checking the number he realized it had something to do with Philip. He dialed the number and a voice as cold as ice answered.

"I have something for you. I'm at Arrow Aviation. I'll be here until nine. How soon can you get here?" Philip asked.

"I'm on my way now, give me thirty minutes," Soltan answered.

"Very good, I'll be in the hangar bravo-one." And then the line went dead.

From where Soltan was it took twenty minutes to get there. After parking his truck, he walked through the entrance door and up to the front desk and asked for directions to hangar bravo-one.

As he walked toward the hanger he watched small G-4's and 5's, along with turbo props, taking off and landing on the spotlighted runways of this private airport. Because it was dark now, lights were on everywhere. Lights so bright they reminded you of the heat from the sun.

*For a private company, Arrow sure does have a lot of traffic,* Soltan thought.

Walking inside the hangar, he immediately saw Philip wearing a white linen suit with shoes to match. Soltan could see his bodyguard's jacket bulging just under the armpits, so there was no question he was armed. Philip had his back to him, standing in front of a small man, probably the pilot. Philip must have seen him out the corner of his eye because before he got too close, Philip turned to say, "Soltan, how have you been?"

"I've been living Philip, more than I can say for some," Soltan answered, pumping Philip's hand, ready for anything. "I see you are still running errands and delivering packages. You missed your true calling. If you hurry you could still apply for a job at the local UPS." Soltan joked with Philip.

"Easy Soltan, everyone has their talents, mine just happen to be non-violent." Philip smiled.

For the next few seconds they enjoyed a laugh together. "So what's up, tell me what I need to know."

Philip walked to the steps of the plane, turned and called out to a man who handed him a folder. Taking the folder he turned back to Soltan, holding it out to him. And at that moment Philip got a look at Soltan's shoes as he took a step toward him.

"Clean yourself up, you have blood on your shoes. You're getting sloppy Soltan. We can't afford to lose you to the authorities. You know your country needs you, and we depend on you Soltan, so don't let us down." Philip said sincerely.

As Soltan looked down at his shoes, he was wondering why he hadn't caught the stains earlier. He was wondering who all had seen the stains and how he could have been so careless. Thinking about what Philip had said, he drifted off into another place.

A service truck drove into the hangar, bringing Soltan back. He looked over at Philip and decided he was right, his countrymen needed him.

Without another word Philip quickly boarded his plane with a sly grin on his face. He knew Soltan was thinking now. To a lot of people Soltan was a hero - he provided opportunities for them they had never imagined. So a little more encouragement and acknowledge went a long way.

Soltan walked out of the hangar frustrated, excited and needing a release, because the weight of his responsibilities had just crashed home. But first, he had to get rid of his shoes.

~  ~  ~

Getting back to the truck Soltan called B.B.

"Yo," B.B. answered.

"I need you to bring me one of those mason jars I got in the fridge."

"I'm not at the house, so give me a few. Where you at?"

"I'll be at the Quick Clean, Rivers and James Street."

"I'm on my way."

A little over thirty minutes later, B.B. pulled his rental behind Soltan's truck and got out. Soltan was in one of the self service stalls, spraying the truck with soapy water, when B.B. walked over to him.

"Did everything get moved from the storage?" asked Soltan.

"Yeah, we got it out of there. We have to wait until the morning to get a new unit. What's up with you? What did the gopher say?"

"We have to go to Chicago from what I understand so far. El Plaga's got a son."

"Whaaaat?" B.B. asked incredulously.

"Yeah, he's not going to be happy to see us. Did you

bring the jar?" Soltan asked, dismissing the previous subject.

"Yeah, hold on," B.B. said turning back to his car. When he returned, he handed over the jar and took the sprayer.

Setting the jar on the ground, Soltan took his shoes off and placed them over the drain. Picking up the glass jar, Soltan lifted the metal latch, popping the sealed lid open, careful not to spill the contents.

"Spray the water that way," he said, pointing in the opposite direction.

Carefully Soltan began pouring the clear liquid directly onto his shoes, all the while being extra careful to stand clear so as not to get any on his bare feet. Within seconds the shoes began to disintegrate as bubbles foamed up while the hydrochloric acid ate and dissolved the solid shoes. They both watched the shoes disappear into almost nothing.

Soltan turned to B.B., "Spray the water over here now, so all this shit goes down the drain. I don't want to accidentally walk in this shit."

Spraying the soapy water all around, B.B. asked, "So when do we leave?"

"First thing in the morning, be ready. I'll secure the plane tickets online sometime tonight."

"I got a pair of old tennis shoes in the trunk, you want 'em?" asked B.B., looking down at Soltan's feet.

"Yeah," he answered as he took the sprayer from him and sprayed his feet to get the dirt off the bottoms.

Bringing the shoes back, B.B. watched as Soltan pulled them on and then put two more quarters into the machine, then continued to spray the ground. "Make sure you bring a good I.D., one you haven't used already. And don't tell anyone where we are going. We should be back in a few days so they shouldn't miss us."

"Alright, anything else?"

"No, I'll call you in the morning," Soltan said, walking around the other side of the drain.

B.B. turned, picked up the jar and walked back to his rental. Taking an old t-shirt out of the trunk, he wiped the outside of the jar carefully. Satisfied there weren't any prints on it, he threw it against the concrete. The jar shattered into thousands of pieces with a pop. He picked up the lid then, wrapping the cloth around it and slung it into the darkness of the nearby trees.

# Twenty • four

**At Ford's house the** Medical Examiner had been on the scene for thirty-five minutes, doing a preliminary time of death determination. Although it had proven to be tricky in the beginning because of the mutilation, she finally started to make some headway as she finally located a few livid patches of skin. Because Ford had lost so much blood, the points of lividity had been hard to find as she tried to pin down the time of livor mortis.

With livor mortis beginning immediately after death, it normally would take two hours before it would be visible. Between four and eight hours after death, the livor pattern is "unfixed" and can shift if the body is moved. And taking the temperature from the body's temperature would only be another preliminary guess, although possibly more accurate.

Ford's bedroom was overrun with crime scene technicians taking pictures and fingerprinting every touchable surface. They had already taken all kinds of samples and fibers that could possibly be used as evidence.

In the living room homicide Detective Ronald L

Trump was just about finished questioning the girlfriend. She had been so hysterical when they arrived that she was feared to be catatonic. After an hour and a half of coaxing, Detective Trump had finally gotten some basic information he could use to start his investigation.

"Alright Ms. Crane, let me repeat everything back to you to make sure I have it all correct. You came home about four thirty PM, to find Mr. Ford dead inside his bedroom, and then you called 911 from your cell," he said, pausing a moment as he flipped the page in his notebook. He continued. "You work at Renae's Beauty Salon, which is located at 3141 Ashley Phosphate Road from nine to four," Trump read from the notepad he used while he listened to her. Flipping another page, he continued, "You arrived home at approximately four thirty-two. You didn't go all the way in the bedroom, or touch the body? You don't know of any possible enemies he could have or anyone he owed money too, or would want him dead for any reason. Is all this correct?" Trump asked, looking up at Donna Crane's blank face, seeing her even more empty stare.

It seemed like it took a minute for the words to reach inside her brain, because she sat still like she hadn't heard the question. Customary as to how she answered all the questions, she blinked a few times and then said yes, like there was a sixty second delay between her and Detective Trump.

"Is there anything else you can think of or think we need to know?"

Again with the delay, "No, nothing," she said, shaking her head trying to get rid of the stain of the image of Ford's body. Then, with no warning her eyes became lucid and she began talking so fast Trump had to slow her down. She was rambling on and on about some guy.

When Trump finally got her to calm down, she said,

*Triple Crown Publications presents . . .*

"There is this one guy, I've only seen him a couple times. But I remember something striking me odd about him. He was very nice and smooth, and he'd always have a smile in his face. The odd thing about him was Danny would go out of his way to please this guy, you know? Danny would be at the guy's beck and call like a servant. Like the guy was royalty or something. One time, while we were having sex he got a phone call. At first he did-n't want to answer it, but when he looked at the incom-ing number he took the call. After a short conversation he got dressed and left, saying we would finish later. Who stops in the middle of sex and leaves without fin-ishing? Oh God! Danny!" Donna sobbed as another tor-rent of tears over took her.

After another few minutes she regained her compo-sure and continued.

"That struck me as crazy, because he loved sex so much I've had problems with him sleeping around on me. But then it hit me, it had to be that guy who called because of how Danny acted around him. And how he spoke into the phone. Danny was polite and mannered like a kid in the principal's office. If you knew Danny you would never think he would behave like that toward anyone. He was known to most as a bully or hard ass. Always pushing his weight around and giving people a hard time. Danny made sure everyone either respected him or was terrified of him. But not with this guy. No, this guy Danny respected.

"Can you describe this guy for me?" asked Trump.

Donna closed her eyes, trying to conjure up an image. "He's about six foot two cause Danny is six feet tall and he stood over him just a bit. He's also kind of skinny looking, but well built, like he's in shape you know. He has light brown skin and dresses really well, like he's right out of one of them GQ magazines or something. Oh, yeah, he wears expensive cologne also, at least it smells expensive," she finished.

"Is there any reason why you would think this guy would want to hurt Mr. Ford?"

"No, not that I can think of, he was always nice. But I just thought it odd the way Danny would act around the guy because he apparently just met him."

"Just met him?" asked Trump, a little confused.

"Yeah, he didn't know the guy but a couple of months maybe. At least I never saw him until a couple months ago."

"Are you sure?"

"Yeah, I'm pretty sure."

"Do you know the guy's name?" asked Trump.

"Rick... Rock... Derrick, yeah that's it. His name was Derrick, that's what Danny called him. I don't know about his last name."

"Detective, can I speak to you for a moment please?"

Trump looked up from the couch he was sitting on to see the crime tech with something in his hands.

"Would you excuse me for a moment?" he asked Donna. "Oh, could you give a description of the guy's face?" he asked as he was standing up.

"I guess so," Donna placing her hands on her face as she started another crying fit.

Trump waved over the department sketch artist and told him to get a description from her.

Walking over to the uniform, Trump asked, "What you got?"

"We found all kinds of drug paraphernalia: scales, baggies, baking soda, ceramic pots and glass beakers, with what we suspect to be cocaine residue on the pots. We're testing it now," said the officer. "We've also found signs of forced entry into the kitchen from the garage. And we have one good footprint on the kitchen floor, and we're taking photographs now."

"Good work, let me know if you find anything else. I want everything bagged and tagged and a full report ASAP."

"Yes sir."

Trump walked back over to Donna and interrupted her and the artist, asking, "was Mr. Ford dealing drugs, Ms Crane?" He was studying her reaction closely.

With wide eyes Donna looked up at Trump, then went into another crying episode.

"Ms. Crane, was Mr. Ford a drug dealer?" Trump asked with a little more force.

She stopped crying long enough to spit out, "I ain't never seen him with no drugs!"

"Ms. Crane, this information is very important to this investigation. I'm trying to find out what's going on here and find the monster who did this. If you know something that can help this investigation and don't tell me, I can charge you with obstruction. I want to put whoever is responsible for this behind bars. If Ford was selling drugs, which frankly I think he was, then this could very well be drug related." He stopped a minute to let his words sink in.

"How about this Ms Crane," he said, ignoring her tears now, "let me tell you what I know. We found all the materials needed to cook cocaine into its hardened form know on the street as crack. We have residue on the pots as well as the scales. Not to mention that nice car in the garage is easily worth thirty, maybe forty thousand dollars. Now, we know Mr. Ford doesn't have a job, and hasn't received an inheritance. So, Ms. Crane, are you sure you don't know anything about him dealing drugs?" he asked while looking her straight in the eyes.

She looked at him for a minute the said, "I told him not to be doing that stuff, but he wouldn't listen. He thought he would never get caught, but I never approved or participated. I made it clear I wanted nothing to do with whatever he was doing, it wasn't my business," she said to Trump, trying to distance herself from the wrong-doing.

Satisfied, Trump said, "Ok, Ms. Crane. You continue with the artist. I might need to talk to you again for a follow-up interview later. So don't leave, OK?" Trump looked at her with a stern face.

Leaving the room, Trump found his way back to the scene of the crime and stood in the doorway watching as the M.E., the latent fingerprints examiner, the forensic photographer and the trace evidence examiner buzzed around the room.

Standing in the doorway of the bedroom, Trump watched as the M.E. examined the body. Looking at it, Trump imagined that if he stared too long the image would be that much harder to rid out of his memory. The victim lay flat on his back, arms tied to the headboard above his head. His feet were tied spread apart at the ankles and anchored to the bed's legs. From the look of it, the body's extremities were secured by strips of torn bedsheet. The victim's viscera and innards were on display across the collarbones forming a "Y". The body looked as if it was a wetsuit unzipped down the front. But it wasn't lycra off to the sides, it was skin.

The vision left Trump with not only a bad feeling, but also a horrible taste in his mouth. A taste that told him that his lunch wasn't too far off from being rebirthed into the world. Trump had seen plenty of death, some cases stranger than others. But never had he seen something like this. This made his stomach turn and his heart ache.

Trying to blink the sight away without any luck, his brain kept processing the scene. The bed sheets were stained and splattered with blood, as well as the headboard and wall behind it. The messy bedroom was fairly undisturbed as far as he could tell. No apparent signs of struggle, the scene looked confined to the bed and its immediate area.

The M.E.'s sixth sense must have told her she was being watched, so when she looked up she saw Trump standing in the doorway. She stopped what she was doing. "Hey Ronnie, you don't have to keep checking on me. I think I got enough experience to know what I'm doing," she said teasingly, with a smile on her face.

Trump was grateful at the distraction of the M.E. speaking to him, because he had become transfixed on the victim.

"Now Monica, you know I get jealous when I see you with other men," Trump said with a sly smile on his face.

Monica Star continued staring at Trump through her glasses. She was a very attractive woman who could easily be mistaken for a model. With her toned shapely body and angelic face she turned heads all through the department. But no one but Trump had ever had a chance with her. Some cops called her bisexual, she called herself a lesbian. Even beneath her lab coat and the booties she wore on her feet, there was no mistaking the sexuality that she emitted. When people found out that she was a medical examiner their jaws dropped. No one understood how someone with that much sex appeal made their living off of dead people.

As she looked at the only man she had ever loved, Monica remembered why they weren't together anymore.

"Please, the only thing you're jealous of is my girlfriend's tongue," she said with a husky laugh.

Dismissing the comment with a wave of his hand, Trump stepped outside the room. The truth was that he was jealous of her girlfriend's tongue. But that was something that he wouldn't admit openly. The day he found out that Monica was seeing someone else he became enraged. But when he confronted her about her affair, Monica openly told him the truth. His rage turning into shock, Trump would have felt better to lose her to another man. But to lose her to another woman made him feel inadequate. It took a long time to come to grips with the truth. A part of him thought they still had a chance together, the other part of him was still confused.

"So what have we got?" he asked, stopping to stand at her side.

Back into Medical Examiner mode, she responded, "Well, the only time I usually see this much of a body is on the table back at the office. Whoever did this has got real issues, plus a knowledge of autopsies. I'm not a psychologist or a detective, but I'd say the individual doesn't have any respect for the human life."

"The cutting was done with a razor sharp object, probably a knife or box cutter, could have been a scalpel. From the look of some of these cuts the victim was still alive when the cutting started between the legs. Whoever did this worked meticulously and it wasn't his first time. Cutting from anus to sternum, I believe this to be the work of a psychotic individual."

"That would be an understatement," said Trump, still not happy at what he was seeing.

"But there is one thing that stuck me as odd," Monica said, moving closer to the front of the bed.

"Take a look at this," she said lifting a flap of skin. "What does that look like?"

Trump moved closer to her to get a better look. What he saw was a small entry wound from a bullet.

"That's a bullet hole." He said, stunned. "He was shot also?"

"Apparently so, Detective," Monica answered.

"What the fuck are we dealing with?" he thought out loud.

"Hold on, I'm not done yet, it gets better. Look right her," she said pointing to the middle of the victim's chest. "You see the difference in the color of the blood?"

"Yeah, OK What does that mean?" Trump asked.

"Well, when I saw it myself I was a little taken back. The thing is, that the blood inside the heart is darker than all the other blood in your body. It's enriched with oxygen before it's distributed through the arteries and veins, hence the dark color. You following me?" she asked, looking over her glasses at him.

"So far," he said

"Ok, so when I saw this I probed around the heart and found that it had been pierced. This man's heart has been stabbed through the left ventrical with a sharp object. I can't tell whether or not it was done while it was still beating, but initial thought would be no." Monica finished.

"You got to be fucking kidding me?" You are telling me that not only was this man cut open like a fish, he was shot and stabbed through the heart? Who is this guy, Dracula?" Trump asked, unbelieving.

"So far, that's what I'm telling you. I don't know about the Dracula thing though." She answered.

"Someone really wanted this guy dead," Trump said.

Monica shrugged her shoulders, "Whoever the suspect is has definitely performed this act before, because it's neat and to the point. Not sloppy like someone who's been blinded by rage. This guy took his time and from the looks of these trash bags," she continued as she pointed to some evidence bags close by, "He used them as a makeshift apron, so as not to get himself too messy. We definitely dealing with a professional."

"Do you have a time of death?"

"I haven't nailed it down absolutely because of the massive loss of blood, but I have an idea. Typically a body losses temperature at a rate of one and a half degrees during the first eight hours, then one degree an hour until the temperature of the body is at equilibrium with the surrounding environment. It's seventy eight degrees in this room, the body's temperature when I checked it upon arrival was at ninety-one degrees. So my guess right now is he's been dead about seven to eight hours. That make his time of death occurring somewhere from around nine to eleven o'clock this morning. I'll know more and could possibly give you a more definite time when I get him back to the lab." Monica finished.

Trump shook his head, trying to process all the information he had just received. It was too much, he had to take his mind to a better place. So when he looked at Monica's green eyes he decided to take a shot.

"Ok, I can't take anymore of this. How about dinner tonight?" he asked as he was turning to leave.

"Can my girlfriend come?"

"Not a chance."

"Then get lost freak. I don't get you, what kind of man doesn't want to entertain two woman at once?" she asked seriously.

"I guess I'm old fashioned," Trump shot back and disappeared down the hallway. Monica shook her head and got back to her work.

"I don't mind two women," the young forensic photographer spoke up.

Monica looked at the young man saying, "Get back to work," as she stifled a small laugh.

~ ~ ~

"Detective," a uniformed officer called out to Trump as he was making his way back into the living room to check on the progress of the artist.

"Yeah, what's up?" Trump asked.

"I got a guy outside says he seen a guy earlier that looked out of place around here."

"Where is he?"

"My partner's got him outside."

"Let's go," Trump said, letting the uniform lead the way.

Outside the house, Trump followed the officer over to his partner who was taking the witnesses statement.

"What do we have?" Trump asked as he was walking up.

"This man says he saw what could be our suspect around here this morning." said the uniform.

Turning to the man holding the ten-speed bicycle, he said, "I'm Homicide Detective Trump, how about you tell me what you saw."

"Well, this is the same thing I just said to this fella, I seen a guy looked like some kind of model or some shit, lookin' all movie star-ish, feel me? Ain't no stars round here," the man spat out through his blistered lips and missing teeth.

Trump looked him over and knew the man had a drug problem immediately. With battered and dusty clothes and disheveled hair that was disappearing in random spots around his head as if he had the mange, the man had seen better days. His face was sunken in at the cheeks with huge pock marks, making his skin look like worn leather. It was very obvious this guy was down on his luck and possibly lived on the streets. "Do you think you can identify this guy if you saw him again?" asked Trump.

"Yeah sure, I walked right past him, I got one of those, what you call it?" He said this while tapping a finger on the side of his head.

"Photographic memories?" Trump asked suspicious-ly.

The drug addict's face went from confusion to delight as he realized Trump knew what he was talking about.

"Yeah, that's what I'm talking bout, a photogentric memory," the man said.

Trump looked to the two uniforms, "Hold him here for a minute." Then turned and dipped back under the crime scene tape and re-entered the house. Walking back into the living room where the sketch of the suspect was still in progress, he asked, "How are we coming along?" to the artist.

Walking over to look over the artist's shoulder, Trump looked down at the drawing on the paper. He could see there was a man's face looking back at him. And by the looks of it, the artist was nearly finished.

"We're about done here Detective, what do you think?" the artist asked, handing the Trump the pad he was drawing on.

"It looks good, real good," Trump said as he inspected it.

"I need to borrow this for a minute, I'll be right back," he said before he walked off.

Back outside he showed the addict the drawing and asked if the guy looked anything like the one on the paper.

"Yeah, yeah that's the guy, sure is. I seen him this morning. walked clean past him, sure did. He smelled all pretty and shit, like a French ho. If you asked me, it's like he poured the whole bottle of stink all over himself. I can still smell'em right now, all fruity and shit," the addict rambled on.

"Are you sure?" Trump asked.

"Yup, that's the guy alright, couldn't miss him in a barn," the addict smiled his best snaggle-toothed smile, then caught himself as obvious pain shot through him, the smile stretching his blistered lips.

"Good," Trump said to him, and then to the uniformed officers, "Take him to the station and get a formal statement, and give him a hot meal."

The addict looked back and forth at the officers and the Detective. "I don't need no hot meal, how about you just give me a couple dollars and we call it even?"

Trumped looked at him, all humor gone from his expression, "it's either some food or nothing, get it?"

The addict shoulders slumped before he bowed his head, avoiding Trump's gaze.

"Take him to the station." Trump said to the uniforms.

"Yes sir," they said in unison.

"What about my bike?" asked the addict.

Trump walked away, thinking now that he had a suspect, he had to play it cool. Too much information to the public could run the suspect off. So he knew he had to handle this very carefully.

# Twenty • five

**A phone rings.** "Hello?"

"What's up?"

"Heyyy Baby Luv, you miss me, don't you?"

"You got company?"

"Nobody I can't get rid of for you. He's boring the shit out of me anyway."

"I'm on my way. I'll see you in thirty."

"Alright, I'll be waiting, just come on in, won't nobody be here but me. Momma and Cathy went to bingo, they won't be back until around eleven."

"Yeah, alright," he said, and then the line went dead.

Deb turned to face Marko, who was looking at her with a look of disbelief on his face.

"Who the fuck was that? What the fuck you mean boring the shit out of you? Bitch, you boring!" Marko spat out as he stood up.

"That was my man and he's on his way over, so bye, I'll see you another time," she spoke to him dismissively.

"I got to go? What the fuck you think, I'm some kind

of chump or something?"

"No, I think you boring, and you don't want no pussy. If you did, you could have gotten some by now. I think you probably wouldn't know what to do with this pussy anyway. You ain't made a move on me yet, and this the third time I done had you over here this week, nigga. What, you thought I like your company? Please ... So get your boring, no pussy wantin' bad breath ass out of my damn house!" Deb said, waving her hand toward the front door.

Marko couldn't believe how fast this seemingly sweet girl just transformed right in front of his eyes. He had actually thought she was different from all the other girls in the area.

"Fuck you bitch, I got something for yo ass!" Marko said as he headed for the door.

"Oh, now you wanna fuck, ain't that a bitch, too late nigga, I got a real man on the way over," Deb said, before she slammed the door behind him and walked to her bedroom to get some clean clothes, so she could take a quick bath before Derrick showed up.

~ ~ ~

As Soltan drove he was having a problem concentrating on the road. He kept seeing the image of his father's head just laying there with its eyes open, looking up at him. Burning a hole into his soul. He hated the way those eyes looked back at him, tearing him apart inside. Those eyes had haunted his dreams for too long. He imagined they would haunt him forever.

Looking into his rearview mirror, Soltan realized he was being pulled over by the police. As he pulled to the side of the road, he reached around to the small of his back and began to pull his pistol from its holster. Doing this, he noticed the police officer was already walking up to his window. Removing his hand from behind his back, he used it to press the button to roll down the window.

"Yes officer, what seems to be the problem?"

"Sir, I pulled you over because you were driving erratically, weaving from lane to lane and not keeping a steady speed. May I see your license, registration and proof of insurance, please?"

Soltan pulled out his wallet and produced the items.

"Sir, have you had anything to drink today?" the officer asked as he took the documents.

"No officer, I don't drink casually."

"Do you have an explanation for your unsteady driving?"

"Officer, I'm not feeling well at the moment, I have a migraine and I was on my way home to lie down."

The officer didn't seem to buy the story, but listened as he scanned the interior of the truck.

"I'll be right back, sit tight," said the officer as he walked to the back of the truck and spoke into the microphone at his shoulder, "Four-one to dispatch."

"Go ahead Four-one."

"10-4 dispatch. I'm 10-60 on Roberts and Five mile road. I need a 10-28 and 10-29 on a red Ford F150, license number, Juliet-Lima-Kilo-three-four-niner," the officer said, asking for registration information and a stolen vehicle check.

"10-4, one moment four-one."

Soltan watched the officer in the side view mirror and was waiting for any sign that something was wrong. He knew taking out the cop wouldn't be a good idea, but if he had to he wouldn't hesitate

"Dispatch to four-one," the officer's radio came alive.

"Four-one, go ahead dispatch."

"The vehicle is registered to one Jones, Derrick, and is 10-80," which meant it was a privately owned vehicle.

"10-4 dispatch. Could you also give me a 10-44 on

the said subject."

"Jones, Derrick, black male, six foot one, delta-oscar-bravo, zero-six-one-five-one-nine-seven-six. No priors, no warrant's."

"10-4 dispatch."

As the officer returned to the driver side window he asked, "Sir, would you mind taking a blood alcohol test for me?"

"No problem officer," said Soltan.

"Good, could you exit the vehicle and follow me back to my squad car?"

Soltan did as he was asked, the whole time taking a survey of the area.

With the trunk of his squad car open, the officer retrieved a little black box and opened it. It contained a blood alcohol register meter in the center and disposable straws in a side pocket. Pulling both items out and putting them together, the officer turned to Soltan. "Now take a deep breath and blow until I tell you to stop," he said, bringing the straw to Soltan's face.

Soltan blew through the straw and when he was finished the machine registered all zeros.

Seemingly satisfied, the officer packed up the device, logged the test and closed the trunk.

"Sir, the breathalyzer registered a zero point zero blood alcohol level. Confirming the fact that you don't have any alcohol in your system. Are you under the influence of anything else?"

"No sir."

"Do you mind taking a field sobriety test?"

Frustrated and getting upset now because he felt like the officer was going too far, Soltan responded.

"Officer, I'm not under the influence of anything, I told you I'm not feeling well. I would like to go home and lay down."

Completely unaffected by Soltan's response, "Sir this will only take a few minutes."

"Fine, let's get this over with."

As the officer took Soltan through a battery of tests to determine if he was intoxicated, the fire inside of Soltan started to consume him. He began to wonder how much longer he was going to be able to control himself. Finally finished, the officer handed him back his license and insurance card, then said, "You need to be careful how you drive. You go home and get some rest, you're free to go. Thank you for your cooperation."

Soltan took his documents and walked back to the truck in a nearly uncontrollable rage.

After driving off, he thought, *That was thirty minutes I could have done without.*

Minutes later he was at Deb's. He let himself in to find her in the bedroom waiting for him. Not wasting anytime, he got undressed and jumped on Deb. He could tell her later that they were through.

~ ~ ~

Lauren had been shopping the day away, feeling good about herself and her new boyfriend. She had bought herself clothes, a new living room suite, and a few other necessities. She wasn't worried about the money any more, so she charged everything to her "emergency" credit card. While she shopped, she had eaten a slice of pizza from Sbarro's in the mall food court, being careful not to get full because she wanted to sit down and have dinner with Derrick later. Once back at the hotel she took a bath and called to see what he had planned for the night. Lauren was dying to wear the new dress she had bought for him, just to see his mouth water with lust. As she bathed she let the CD player soothe her with the music of Ciara's "Love, Sex and Magic."

This thing that was going on with Derrick had finally turned sexual, but she wanted to also keep her head on straight. He still wasn't giving her any information, and she still didn't know what the cost was to be in his life. But she was willing to go along for a little while longer anyway. This was turning out to be the best job she ever had. And the best time she'd had since she got to the United States. *No,* she thought to herself, *I don't want to think about that stuff. Happy thoughts tonight only.*

~ ~ ~

Getting dressed, Soltan looked over at Deb as she lay there in bed in a post-coital daze. He was pulling on his pants when she spoke, "You're leaving? Come back over here and hold me for a while," she said in a exhausted whisper.

"I've got to go. I'll check in with you in a couple of days," Soltan said.

While he was pulling on his shirt and heading for the door, Deb spoke up in an even softer whisper, "I love you, Derrick."

Stopping in the doorway, he looked over at her, meeting her eyes. For a moment Soltan didn't know what to say, so he said nothing. When a little smile crept across her face, Soltan gave a slight shake of his head and said, "Deb, we gonna have to call this off. I think we need to cool it off, just focus on the business side of our relationship."

Deb's eyes got big. "Nigga, what? What the hell you mean? Ain't I your girl?"

Soltan didn't want to deal with this. He started to lose his temper. "Girl, you just someone I fuck. Ain't nothing more than that. Never was."

Deb jumped out of bed, titties flying, and walked over to her dresser. She opened the top drawer and pulled out a roll of cash. "Just business, then. Fuck you, Derrick.

Take your fucking money and get out!"

She threw the wad of cash at him and then stomped into her bathroom. Soltan picked up the roll and thought, *Damn she sure can sell that coke fast.*

Soltan grinned to himself at her drama, and then walked out the door. When he got back to his truck, he glanced at his watch. It was almost nine o'clock. "Shit," he said to himself. He knew he didn't have much time.

Inside the house, Deb was on her phone. "Marko, baby, I didn't mean that shit earlier. You wanna come back over?"

# Twenty • six

**Leaving the station,** Smith looked over at his partner and wondered what was going through his mind. While at the precinct they had gathered all the information they could find. The truck was registered to the suspect Derrick Jones. The storage unit was rented to a David Smith, who was also clean as a whistle. But his partner seemed to be disturbed and off balance. Maybe it was the murder that happened earlier on the east side. From reports, a man had been gutted like some kind of animal. But why would that concern Clayton, it wasn't like he knew the guy, or did he?

"What's up partner? How you doing over there?" Smith asked while he was driving.

"I'm good, what's up?"

"You ain't said too much of anything since we heard about the one-eight-seven out east. That's why I'm asking."

"I don't know man, I've just been thinking. I got a funny feeling and I don't know what it is," Clayton said, staring out the passenger window.

"What do you mean funny feeling? A funny feeling about what?" asked Smith.

"I don't know, but something ain't right. Let's go back to the storage, I wanna see what the hell all that stuff in there was. Maybe that's what my problem is. I've been thinking about it all day," Clayton said, trying to throw his partner off the subject of why he was so distant now.

He knew his partner was smart and it was only a matter of time before the rest of the department figured out the man found dead earlier was his brother. Clayton had done his best to conceal that fact, but there were already a couple people who knew. They didn't have the same mother so there was little resemblance and of course they had different last names. Knowing Danny sold drugs made their relationship hard.

Clayton was a cop, and his job was to take people like Danny to jail. But that didn't happen. What did happen was Clayton turned a blind eye to Danny's activities. Clayton also did his best to keep his brother informed of any and all information the department had on him so he could avoid being arrested. But this didn't always work for Danny, because of his arrogance. Clayton remembered the time that Danny had been pulled over while trafficking nine ounces of powder cocaine. He wound up in the county jail on trafficking charges with a hundred thousand dollar bond. By the time the case made its way to court, the evidence had mysteriously disappeared. The defense attorney asked for a complete dismissal and the judge promptly granted the motion. The prosecutor went nuts, and vowed to have the head of whoever was responsible for costing her an open-and-shut case. So much hell was raised that an internal investigation had been launched in the department. No one was ever found responsible but Clayton knew his brother was just too cocky and it was only a matter of time before something happened to him. Even though Clayton never expected this, he knew that he would one day have to face the facts and reality of his brother's chosen occupation.

Someone had brutally murdered his only brother and he wanted to know who. The law was not for the person who took his brother from him. He would move heaven and earth and bring down the wrath of God upon that person. Even if it cost him his own life.

At the storage, Smith pulled the squad car in close to the door of the unit they wanted. The aisles of the storage compound were well lit with bright spot lights on every corner of every building. But in the middle of the aisles the lights were more spaced out, making the breaking and entering they were about to do almost invisible at a distance.

Clayton got out of the car talking to his partner. "Pop the trunk," he said, like a man on a mission.

"You always got to put me in compromising situations, don't you partner?" Smith said, meeting Clayton at the trunk.

"Only when I'm trying to catch the bad guys."

Reaching inside the trunk, Clayton pulled out a pair of bolt cutters that he kept their for special occasions just like this.

"So what do we do when we find out what's in there?" asked Smith.

"Shit, I don't know. I just want to know what the hell it is. I'll figure out what to do about it later," Clayton said, cutting the lock off.

Once he had the lock free, he pulled the door up and hit the light.

"What the fuck is going on?"

The place was empty, the only thing left inside was the sound of roaches scattering around on the floor, trying to get away from the light.

"Looks like someone didn't want us to know what they were storing," Smith said.

"Ain't this a bitch. We got us one that thinks he's smart," Clayton said, a little surprised.

# Twenty • seven

**After leaving Soltan,** B.B. went to his apartment and packed some clothes and identification. He lived in a two bedroom apartment in an expensive neighborhood near Eagles Landing, which was where the who's who of Charleston lived. Having no regular girlfriend or any family in the states enabled his comrades to be his family. They were brothers of the same struggle, and he existed purely for that struggle. Being alone in his personal life prevented any kind of servitude or attachment to anyone but his comrades and their struggle.

Leaving his apartment he went to the junkyard to unwind and think about what lay ahead. Arriving, driving his vehicle into the yard, he noticed no one was there. The place was actually empty for a change. Letting himself in B.B. turned on the TV and sat on the couch and rolled a blunt. Happy to be alone, he knew he could nurture his thoughts better. The blunt lit now, he took deep pulls, letting the smoke find its way through his lungs. When the THC reached his brain he began thinking about Soltan and what kind of future they were headed for.

He'd known Soltan his whole life and always trusted him without question. Soltan seemed always to be in control and always knew what to do in any situation. Both born and raised in St. Louis Du-Nord, a small city in Haiti, six hours from the capital city Port au Prince, they grew up poor and fought for scraps in the street. As they got older, things changed though. B.B. remembered how all of the sudden Soltan didn't have to do the same kinds of scams they had grown accustomed to in order to get by anymore. Soltan wasn't doing exceedingly better than anyone else, but he seemed to definitely have it easier than the rest of them.

If his memory served him correctly, one night they were at their regular hang out, club Big Up, when he had seen the change. Soltan was buying drinks for everyone all night, but wasn't drinking.

After getting fairly drunk, he had gotten into an argument with a club regular. Soltan was watching the whole time and when he saw things were going to get out of hand he intervened to diffuse the situation. But as Soltan began pushing him toward the door, the not-to-happy club-goer grabbed Soltan by the shoulder to spin him around. What happened next caught the drunk off guard.

Soltan allowed the drunk to turn him around. Having unsheathed his blade he struck with absolute speed and accuracy. It took a few seconds for the drunk to realize what happened, but as Soltan stood still staring him in the eyes, the realization that he had been stabbed sunk in. Just standing there, Soltan held the blade steady as blood dripped and oozed down the drunk's pants legs. When enough blood had drained from the man's body to create a pool at his feet, Soltan pulled the blade out as quickly as he had inserted it. Satisfied, he turned and

*Triple Crown Publications presents . . .*

walked out the door while the drunk fell to the floor.

This memory reminded B.B. that Soltan was nothing to be trifled with and could strike with the surprise and deadliness of a cobra. But now he began to question their cause. There was never any doubt that Soltan was the one who found a way to get them out of Haiti and set them up with a good life here in the States. But it seemed no-matter how much money he and Soltan made, or how much freedom they seemed to have, they were nothing but puppets. Soltan was Region's puppet and he was Soltan's. It was almost as if all their freedom was just an illusion. In his belief, real freedom didn't consist of any form of hierarchy. Soltan was undoubtedly the one in charge, and he was a trusted and loyal friend. But for some reason B.B. felt as though something was amiss. His feelings were something he would definitely convey to Soltan if for nothing else, to ease his fears. Taking another pull on his blunt and blowing the smoke skyward, B.B. continued trying to fit the puzzle pieces together.

# Twenty • eight

**Soltan came out of the** hotel bathroom, finding Lauren laying on the bed and watching TV. He walked over to her, fell back on the bed and stretched his arms outward. Comfortable now, Soltan let his hand fall on Lauren's back, caressing her as she watched TV. He couldn't help himself as he slid his hand between her legs and began kneading her inner thigh. Lauren turned around, looking at him and saying with a smile, "You are insatiable. What is it going to take for you to stop molesting me?"

Repositioning herself so she was in the cowgirl position, she settled down on him and began to lick around his nipples. "I can't help the fact that you turn me on. You should be happy, it's hard to keep my attention," Soltan said as he enjoyed the warm feel of her soft lips and tongue against his skin.

"I miss you too, I even bought a dress today and if it doesn't give you high blood pressure when I'm wearing it, I'm going to get you some Viagra," she said as she ran her hand lower on his body, copping a quick feel. "Apparently, your blood flows very well," she continued as she stroked the length of him. "But… unfortunately, big boy, no more for you until later," she said as her head craned, looking down between her legs as she spoke to his penis.

"Well then, on that note, get your things together cause we're going to Chicago in the morning."

"What do you mean Chicago? What for?" she asked, stunned.

"We have some business to take care of, so get your things together. Everything you don't want to take, we'll drop off at the condo."

"What do you mean, we?" she asked.

"You don't want to go to Chicago?"

"Well, yeah, I want to go, but what's this business stuff you are talking about?"

"I would like you to meet someone there. Have you ever been to Chicago?"

"No."

"Then what's the problem? Do you want to go or not?" he asked, hoping the psychology tactic would work, because if it didn't, he was going to have to come up with a new plan.

"Oh, alright. Since you insist. And you're the boss," she said smiling. "When are we leaving?"

"Glad you recognize. First thing in the morning."

"Well then, in that case, I guess I can feed the monster again."

Biting Soltan's bottom lip, she kissed and licked a trail down his freshly-washed body. When she had gotten down to the towel, she unwrapped it to gain better access to his already hard penis. Without hesitation she took if full into her mouth and as far down her throat as possible.

Soltan couldn't help but moan in delight as Lauren proceeded to occupy herself. He enjoyed the pleasure he was enduring, knowing the next couple of days were going to be tricky in more ways than one.

# Twenty • nine

**Walking down the hall he** came to a door, his instincts telling him it was the right one. He heard noises coming from the other side, so naturally he tensed up. As he grabbed the door knob and turned, the door opened easily. A cloud of thick white smoke seemed to be hovering in the empty room. In a blink of an eye, the smoke disappeared to reveal an empty room with partially rotten wooden floor boards. The flooring had gaps and spaces in it everywhere. He had to be careful not to fall through the floor, taking tentative steps forward when the door closed behind him. Turing back toward the door he almost lost his balance. He couldn't get to the door anyway because that part of the floor disappeared. His gun already in hand, he pressed the clip's eject button to see how many bullets he had left. All of the sudden he heard a parade of voices talking all at once to him. One voice in particular scared him.

"Soltan!"

This caused him to stumble again, and this time his left foot fell through the floor. Stumbling caused him to drop the clip, with it falling through the floor boards to the ground beneath. When he bent down to retrieve the clip, bullets burst up through the wood, hitting him in the chest, leg and arm. The impact of the assault forced him to straighten up and stand tall, gritting his teeth as he fought the pain. Despite the agony of his wounds, he tried to again to pick up the magazine, again receiving a barrage of bullets that ripped into the flesh of his body. Unable to take any more he stood up once again, and again the bullets stopped coming. Bleeding heavily from the wounds the slugs produced, his pain turned into anger. Determination set in, and he believed if he could pick up the fallen magazine the gunshots would stop. The clip he dropped he believed to be the source of the bullets. Unable to see anyone or anything, he had an idea of where the voices were coming from.

Looking at the floor he yelled, "Samedi, I know you are down there! Show your face you coward, you exist because of me. Without me you are nothing!"

He believed that since the bullets were coming through the floor, his enemy was under the floor as well. With two failed attempts and countless bullets holes in his body he continued to lash out with angry words. "Fuck it, you want to kill me, is that it?! You want me dead?! Well here I am, take my life!"

Out of nowhere a barrage of bullets burst through the floor - this time with so much intensity that all the gunpowder produced a cloud of smoke so dense you couldn't see through it. The projectiles tore into Soltan's flesh, ripping him apart. Lasting all ten seconds the smoke cleared away as fast as it appeared, to show Soltan still standing despite the physical damage to his body. "Fuck you, you hear me! I am eternal, you hear me, eternal!"

The floor exploded in gunfire again, engulfing the whole room. This time Soltan let out a laugh of his own,

*Triple Crown Publications presents . . .*

stretching his arms away from his body. His body shaking and twisting at the impact of each bullet. "Is this it? Is this all you got? I told you I am eternal. I am Soltan, I will not die!"

But the bullets kept coming, hitting their target over and over. "You are eternal Soltan, but only because I say so. You serve me and not yourself. You are now ready. The passage way for me has been cleared now, I am you and you are me." Samedi said eerily.

~ ~ ~

Not knowing he was shaking his head from side to side, Soltan woke with a gasp of air.

Lauren woke immediately, "Baby, what's wrong?" she asked, scared, "Are you hurt? Baby wake up!" she continued as she tried to shake him awake

When Soltan opened his eyes, he saw the hotel room they were in and some rays of light creeping in from between the curtains. He could feel Lauren's touch, but he could also still feel the sting of all the bullet wounds he received in his dream. His skin felt like it was on fire, and the smell of gunpowder, mixed with burnt flesh and the coppery smell of fresh blood was heavy in his nostrils.

Turning back to look at Lauren he said, "I'm okay, just a bad dream, go back to sleep." He sat up, rubbing his arms and chest.

"You want to talk about it?"

"No. Go back to sleep, you need your rest."

Skeptical, she lay back down. When her head hit the pillow, he leaned over and kissed her on the forehead and ran his thumb down the side of her face. "Everything's fine, go back to sleep."

She looked at him confusedly, but said nothing. Soltan got out of bed and went to the bathroom, checking his watch on the way. It was three o'clock in the morning. Sleep was out of the question now, so he was going to have to make the best of it. Once inside the bathroom, he closed the door and turned the water on in the sink, cupping his hands together and catching enough to splash on his face. Doing this a few times he tried to gather his senses, and then reached to the towel rack and dried off.

In his mind, his demons were his and his alone. There would be no sharing, because he knew they would torment him worse for sharing with anyone. He also realized they were getting stronger, this surprised him. It had been a long time since he couldn't control his dreams or their outcomes. But this time when he fought, it seemed like he was going through a trial or some sort of cleansing. He felt weird now. Almost as if he had gained some kind of otherworldly power. His body continued to buzz all over. He continued looking at his reflection in the mirror, looking into his own eyes and seeing something that wasn't there before. It was unexplainable, what he saw, but never the less it was there. Something had changed.

Coming out of the bathroom, he looked at Lauren, who had fallen right back into her slumber. She looked so cute and peaceful lying there wrapped in the sheets and blankets. Soltan walked over to the night stand and picked up his phone, then walked to the far side of the suite near the window and sat down on the love seat.

"Yo."

"Meet us at the airport at six, our plane departs at seven."

"Yeah, alright, you bringing someone with you?" B.B. asked, picking up on the word us.

"Just a little help, why?"

"No reason, see you then," B.B. answered.

Ending the call, Soltan began to wonder if B.B. had

the same problems when he slept. When he'd answered the phone, he sounded wide awake as well.

It didn't matter, Soltan reasoned, as long as he was ready when he needed him. Soltan sat on the love seat and mentally pieced together every step he was going to take next. This type of meditation was normal because sleep had become too hard to obtain. Glancing back over to Lauren, he knew his next move was definitely going to test her boundaries and character. He was going to be able to truly see what she was made of. He almost felt sorry for her because of what he had planned. But in this life, his life, it was all or nothing, and right now she was along for the ride.

# Thirty

**His mind wandering now,** Soltan began to think about the help he was going to need in Chicago. Knowing he couldn't bring the necessary equipment on the plane, he had to have someone in place when he arrived. So he called the only person he knew who had the type of connections he needed, a person he knew he could trust.

"Yo, this better be good because it's too early in the morning for bullshit," Jedi said, answering the phone on the first ring.

"Strictly business, mi amigo."

"Yo, my nigga, What's up? Kinda early for you ain't it? Jedi asked, recognizing the voice.

"I'm havin' a small bout of insomnia. What's your excuse? You still on the clock?"

"I'm always on the clock, I'll be on the clock until the day I die. It's the nature of the beast, but to what do I owe this honor? Is something wrong? I ain't supposed to hear from you until next month."

"I need your help, still got some juice in Chicago?"

"Of course, you know the brothers stick together like

sardines in a tin can. Why, who's your problem?"

"Nothing I can't handle, but I still need some tools and a tour guide. You know someone who can help?"

"When's the party?" asked Jedi.

"Tomorrow night."

"Say no more, I'm on my way. I'll make some calls and get the ball rolling."

"Good, I'll make reservations for you. You be flying out of Laguna, right?"

"Yeah."

"Ok, your ticket will be waiting on you, how's the Hyatt Regency sound?"

"Sounds like we've got a lot in common, said Jedi.

"Good, I'll book your suite as well, you know how to contact me when you get there."

"See you soon," said Jedi, ending the call.

As Soltan hung up the phone, he was pleased he had put another component of his plan together. Jedi could provide access to the necessary equipment and security he needed to get the job done. Jedi was a high ranking member of the Coalition, a group of ex-military specialists who help each other out across the nation. Their main purpose was the defense of their nation against domestic terrorists. The Coalition was strictly under the radar, and succeeded in funding their cause by not-so patriotic means. But their network was as strong as the government and if you could help it, you didn't want to be their enemy.

This organization was all about the empowerment, and protection of its people, the American people. This was something Soltan respected, because those were his own ideals for his people. Unfortunately, most Americans labeled the Coalition as a threat to its society because of their unity. Saying they were no different than the terrorists they claim to target. They were also said to be no better than any other group of organized criminals targeted by the Federal Agencies, despite their military backgrounds. Unbeknownst to the Government, their reasoning only made the coalition stronger and less likely to depend on what Americans called justice. The Coalition had its own form of justice, and when the time came, they dealt it out swiftly and without remorse.

Soltan knew what he had planned would be a walk in the park for them. He also knew he would be in very good hands once he arrived in Chicago. Jedi had always proven to be a loyal and trustworthy friend who lived life to the fullest. Managing to help Soltan make millions of dollars and provide the necessary connections like now also made him valuable. So he couldn't wait to see his old friend - he had no doubt Jedi was going to make this trip interesting.

# Thirty • one

**At five-thirty, Soltan and Lauren** checked out of the hotel and headed for the airport. By five-forty five, they pulled into the parking garage of Charleston International. Lauren followed Soltan in her truck, wondering how long they were going to be in Chicago. She still had a new place to decorate, and damn was she going to enjoy telling her roommates that. To her, it was early and she wasn't particularly a morning person. She had hoped she could have gotten a few more hours of sleep, but figured she could rest on the plane. As she was pulling her duffel bag full of clothes out of the truck, Soltan was already walking toward her to take her bags.

Soltan took her parking ticket also, and stuffed it into his pocket with his own. He could tell Lauren was a blink away from sleep walking. So he tried to hurry her along so she could get back to sleep on the plane. They left the parking garage and walked across the street into the airport terminal. The entrance was a wall of checkerboard-like windows encased by silver frames. The design curving around the corner created a dome-like structure.

Morning dew was the only thing visible through the glass as they walked through the door. At the Continental Airlines desk, they were greeted. "Good morning to you, Thank you for choosing Continental Airlines, what can I do for you this morning?" The desk clerk said cheerfully.

"I have reservations for two to Chicago."

"Ok great, and what would be the name on the reservations, sir?"

"Smith, Anthony Smith."

Soltan looked the clerk over. She wore a navy blue pants suit with a single row of large white buttons down the middle. Her hair was pulled back into a tight bun and her youthful face was clear and healthy looking. Glancing to her name tag, it read Becky. He should have known. She was probably captain of her cheerleader squad as well. Soltan decided it was too early for the amount of cheerfulness she exuded. The funny part of it was that it more than likely wasn't an act.

Lauren looked over at Soltan and didn't blink when she heard the name. She tried to fight through the fog in her mind to remind herself to ask him about it later.

"Ah, yes Mr. Smith, I have a reservation for two, first class. May I see some identification please?" the young lady asked to make sure the information was correct.

"Yes, that's it," said Soltan producing his I.D.

~ ~ ~

B.B. didn't bother getting up from where he was sitting in the waiting area. He sat still and watched Soltan and some woman at the ticket counter, wondering what her purpose was.

She wore a pair of loose fitting jeans and a T-shirt, but B.B. could see she was a very shapely woman. Her long black hair was pulled back into a ponytail, giving you a full view of her puffy face. It was clear that she wasn't fully awake, just going through the motions.

*Oh shit. That's the girl from the New Year's party.* B.B.'s eyes widened. *I know this motherfucker ain't thinking with his dick. Naw, maybe she fits into this job some kind of way. Soltan knows what he's doing. At least I hope so.*

~ ~ ~

"Mr. Smith," the young lady at the counter called. Soltan blinked a few times, coming back to the present. He had drifted back to his meeting with Philip, replaying the look on Philip's face after noticing the blood on his shoes. But it wasn't the ticket counter lady calling him that got his attention, it was Lauren's touch that reeled him back in.

"Mr. Smith, your tickets," the ticket clerk said again.

"Yes, Yes, thank you," Soltan said, taking them.

"Your plane boards at gate F, the boarding will start in twenty minutes."

Soltan made no other attempt to communicate, so he and Lauren slowly checked their bags and walked away. Walking toward the waiting area, Soltan made eye contact with B.B.

"You straight?"

"Yeah, what's up wit her?" B.B. nodded at Lauren.

"Later," Soltan answered.

Lauren could hear the disdain in B.B.'s voice but let it go.

Soltan had made arrangements for B.B. with the airlines using a password for the reservation. He could see B.B. was curious about Lauren's presence, but he knew B.B. trusted him so they would discuss the matter later. Not in front of her.

"Let's go get in line, the plane boards in twenty minutes," said Soltan.

No one said anything else as they walked to gate F carrying their bags.

Since 9/11, all airports had beefed up their security measures almost ten-fold. Armed TSA officers were posted at the metal detectors and the boarding terminal. Random bag searches as well as cavity searches were more common now than ever. They all had to show their tickets to enter the waiting area. Now through the metal detectors and the armed TSA men who, he noticed, carried Glock nine millimeters, they showed their tickets once more at the terminal entrance.

In line at the terminal the plane began boarding on time. Soltan, Lauren and B.B. proceeded down the tunnel and boarded the plane.

On the plane, Lauren was seated next to Soltan, and B.B. was right across the aisle. With little fuss, everyone else found their respective seat and settled in for the flight. After pre-flight announcements and the stewardesses passed out the pillows the plane took off.

Soltan was running through his mental checklist when Lauren leaned over and placed her pillow against his shoulder, getting comfortable. Once she settled, Soltan looked over at B.B. who was also wide awake. They made eye contact, passing the nonverbal question and answer about Lauren between them. Soltan knew that B.B. wanted to know what the deal was with Lauren. Looking down at Lauren now, he decided he also wanted to know. He felt something for her that he'd never felt before for a woman. But he was trying to convince himself she was just a tool which he would use and then discard. Leaning his head back, he decided to work and rework his plan on the two hour flight.

# Thirty • two

**Waking up and calling Derrick,** Lori was not happy she could not get him on the phone. She really needed to move into her new apartment today and Derrick failed to keep his word after trying to lift one single fucking TV and then giving up.

Rochelle spent the night with her sister so she could get the rest of the packing done.

She looked over and saw Lori looking frustrated. "What's the problem Lori?" she asked as she came into the kitchen.

"The problem is I can't get Derrick on the phone. We got to get this shit out of here today."

"I thought you said you could trust him, that Donte trust's him. Apparently he has more important things to do," Rochelle said.

"Not now Chelle, I don't need this shit right now," Lori said calmly.

Glancing at her watch, she said, "Eight fifteen, damn!"

Brainstorming now, Lori had to figure out a way to

get all her furniture and belongings moved. With Rochelle standing in front of her holding her baby, she stared at them, her mind drawing a blank. Then someone knocked on the door. "Shit, that's probably the manager wanting to know why we're still here," Lori said to her sister as she walked to the door.

When she opened it, she saw two men in green and yellow uniforms. "Good morning," they greeted her in unison. "We're looking for Ms. Lori Reed."

"I'm her," confused and curious. "Yes ma'am, we're from Mayflower Moving Company, we are here to make your move easy," the young man holding the clipboard said.

Lori looked him over. He was tall with a smooth brown face and soft smile. His uniform did little when it came to concealing how shapely this man was. His partner, though a little shorter, had the same soft smile and bulging muscles.

"I didn't call your moving company," she said.

"Is this sixteen hundred Village Parkway, apartment nine B?"

"Yes, but I didn't call you." ˆ

"Chelle, did you call a moving company?" she said, turning toward her sister.

"No, but hell, let them move this shit. They right on time in my book."

"I'm sorry, there must be a mistake, although we do need to move, I can't afford your services."

The man holding the clipboard in front of her flipped back the first page and read the second page. "A Mr. Derrick Jones retained our services to move everything from this address to wherever a Ms. Lori Reed instructed."

A Kool-aid smile appeared on Lori's face. He finished speaking. "He left you a message also, would you like it?"

"Yes thank you."

He handed Lori a sealed white envelope as Rochelle came walking up behind her. Lori opened the envelope and took out the letter which read:

*"Easter Bunny,*

*I'm so sorry I couldn't follow through with helping you. I had something very important come up, which is going to keep me out of town for a few days. The young men standing before you were hand-picked by me to do everything you need them to do. They were paid very well up front so it's no cost to you. They should prove to be very efficient and courteous. If they are not, I'm sure you'll tell me when you see me again. But rest assured they will be on their best behavior – and that means you should be too. Don't let your sister get at them until AFTER they moved your shit,(Smile)*

After reading the note, Lori turned around to look at her sister, who was sporting a Kool-aid smile of her own. "What?" asked Rochelle?

Lori turned back toward the young men saying, "OK, well, I guess you gentlemen can get started. Everything's pretty much packed and ready to go. You can start in the living room."

# Thirty • three

**Arriving at Midway International Airport,** Soltan had fine-tuned his plans mentally during the flight. He didn't sleep at all, unlike Lauren, who slept the whole way. B.B. didn't seem to have anything too important on his mind because he was quiet and casual as usual. They had talked for a minute about Lauren, and B.B. seemed satisfied about her – for now. Walking through the airport, which seemed to be very busy with check-in's and departures and frustrated people delayed by layovers, they went outside and found a cab already waiting. "The Hyatt Regency, please," Soltan said to the cabbie once all three of them got in.

"You got it," said the cab driver.

Soltan looked at the driver's identification which was posted right next to the meter. Yesef Akbar Muhammed was the name he read. Soltan made a mental note of the man who tried his best to hide his foreign accent and features with modern clothes and a Cubs baseball cap. He didn't know if he was going to have to see this gentleman again. He hoped not, for the cabbie's sake.

Soltan glanced over at Lauren who was awake and taking in the sites of all the high rise buildings and the hustle and bustle of this unfamiliar metropolitan area. She didn't say anything, but he could see the excitement in her face and body language.

It didn't take long for them to arrive at the hotel, and after pulling up out front, Soltan knew he made the right decision in picking this hotel. With a black marble and brass exterior surrounding the glass picture windows and doors, the hotel definitely looked high class. The trees in front gave the aura of seclusion, making the feel of the hotel stress-free and serene. In addition to being so close to Lake Michigan, it was an ideal location to hole up in because of all the ways to escape in case of trouble.

When the cab stopped, the car door was opened by a doorman under the awning of the hotel. He called over two bellhops to retrieve their bags as they exited the cab. Soltan and B.B. decided to keep their own bags, not wanting them handled by strangers.

Inside the Hyatt, they walked across the highly polished tiled floor to the black marble check-in counter. The overall theme of the building was the same - black marble with brass accents. There were even chandeliers hanging from the vaulted ceilings. Luxury was undeniable, and it went hand in hand with the 'Anything you need' customer service attitude.

Once the desk clerk was made aware of the proper information and identification for the reservations, Soltan was issued two electronic key cards. He and Lauren had a room on the tenth floor, with B.B. down the hall.

In the room was a king-size bed, a whole entertainment system and a complete wet bar. Across the room toward the window was a full living room set of the finest Italian leather couches and chairs you could find. Everything in the bathroom was sparkling marble with a standing shower and marble Jacuzzi. Large fluffy towels hung on racks with the Hyatt Regency Initials embroidered in them, with extras folded neatly on the counter top. The bathroom also had a mirror that extended the full length of the entire bathroom, floor to ceiling.

Soltan wasted no time settling in, and instead he told Lauren he would be back in a couple hours. She kissed him before he left, a kiss that had a lot of enthusiasm and excitement in it. "I'll be waiting," she said.

Soltan smiled and walked out the door headed down the hallway toward B.B.'s suite.

At the door he knocked once and B.B. opened it, letting him in after looking through the peephole. It seemed that B.B. didn't waste any time with unpacking either.

"You ready to go?" B.B. asked grabbing his coat.

"Yeah, but hold on. Let me run down how we're going to do this."

"Alright, shoot."

Soltan had memorized the dossier Philip had given him so it was easy to put a tentative plan together with minimal information. Unfortunately, the final plan was going to take some work. "Alright, the kid works less than six blocks from here. That's why I picked this hotel, so we would be close; makes following him and switching up easy. I brought the girl so we can use her to lure him to us. She should be able to help us get close to him."

"I figured something like that. I know your dick wasn't the one doing all of the thinking. At least I was hoping it wasn't," said B.B., relieved she just wasn't here for sport.

Soltan smiled and winked at his closest friend. "Ok, so then what? We use her then what happens? She ain't going back with us is she?" B.B. continued.

"Depends on how things turn out, I've been having a little trouble with that part," Soltan sheepishly admitted.

"Ah man, come on. You can't be serious, you're thinking with the wrong head after all. Soltan, we use her then get rid of her, are we clear?" B.B. said, assuming a father-like role.

"We'll see, but what we got to do now if find a spot to do some work. I called someone who's going to help us with transportation and equipment. If his flight is on time, he should be here in about two hours."

"Who's that?" asked B.B.

"The Jedi. I called him this morning."

"Oh great, may the force be with us," B.B. said sarcastically.

"I don't know what it is with you two, but we need his help."

"Yeah whatever, that guy is just too flamboyant for my tastes. But, I know we can trust him. What else?"

"We grab the kid and dispose of him and then get back to business," said Soltan.

"They sure are playing some dirty games, killing each other's family members like this. They should just meet up with each other and have it out themselves."

Soltan just shrugged his shoulders and headed toward the door. "Come on, there's some stuff I want you to see, and I'm hungry."

They both walked into the hallway and took the elevator down to the lobby and left the hotel.

# Thirty • four

**Jedi's plane landed at seven** minutes after four in the afternoon at Midway Airport. Exiting the plane and walking outside with his carry-on bag, he was met by a member of his organization. A tall and muscular guy with a deep parlor tan and goatee, who went by the name Junior. Junior possessed a penetrating stare that could rock you to the core. Some called it the thousand yard stare, which was the product of being in battle. Jedi standing five-foot eight and a hundred seventy pounds, walked up to him, saying, "Thanks for the welcoming party, you two haven't changed a bit."

He shook Junior's hand first, who responded with, "Glad to see you as well. And it's good to have you back in the Chi." Junior said

Junior turned away and started walking. "The ride's over here," said Junior, pointing at a black Escalade with tinted windows. They made their way to the truck and getting inside, Jedi pulled his door shut.

"A-yo, why the door so heavy?" asked Jedi.

"Since your last visit we've stepped up our game. The

whole truck is armored top to bottom," said Junior.

"Nice, I might have to invest in one of these back home," said Jedi. "I need to go to the Hyatt. I already have reservations."

Junior started the truck and pulled away, letting the V8 engine roar as it pulled the extra weight. As they were rolling, Jedi reached into his coat pocket to retrieve his phone so he could notify Soltan of his arrival. After texting him he dialed Frank, another member of their organization.

Frank owned an exotic car dealership in downtown Chicago. On the second ring he picked up. "Hey brother, happy you made it safe and sound, how was the trip?"

"It was alright, you know me, when I have the company of a good-looking stewardess the sky's always friendly." Jedi joked

"What would your wife say?" Frank joked.

"Nothing, cause she better not find out," Jedi said laughing. "Look, I'm en route to the Hyatt, can you meet me there, we got a lot of catching up to do."

"I'll bet. I'll see you soon," said Frank, ending the call.

Within twenty minutes time the Escalade had pulled under the awning in front of the Hyatt. Before exiting the truck, Jedi checked his weapon, a P228 Sig Sauer nine millimeter Junior gave him, complete with a shoulder holster. Once satisfied, he stepped out of the truck and entered the building. Junior drove off to find a parking spot in one of the parking garages nearby.

At the front desk, Jedi told the clerk about his reservation.

The clerk asked, "The name of the reservation please, sir?"

"The reservation is under the name Han Solo," he answered.

The clerk smiled and said, "Of course Mr. Solo, I have

instructions for your reservation right here. I have a message for you as well." The clerk handed a key card over the counter with a sealed envelope.

"Thank you" said Jedi.

Making his way up the elevator and down the hall, he found the room and did a quick sweep. In the coalition, Jedi was the equivalent of the soldier he'd been when he was enlisted in the Army's Special Forces, the same went for Junior. But the Jedi had achieved the rank of Lieutenant Colonel while he served in the army and that gave him the higher rank he deserved in the Coalition. Jedi was not only a ranking member, but a co-founder of their organization. So this entitled him to a high level of security as well.

When he was satisfied, he went inside and sat down. Getting settled, he texted the room number back to Junior, so he could join Jedi.

Jedi sat on the love-seat and opened the envelope.

*Jedi,*

*I hope you had a good flight, get yourself ready to have some fun, see you shortly.*

Once Jedi finished the letter he began to reminisce about how far both of them had come since their first encounter.

~ ~ ~

The night sky was clear, with the temperature in the mid-eighties. Jedi remembered their first encounter at the resort in Puerto Plata with uncharacteristic clarity.

Jedi was enjoying a beautiful night in the Dominican Republic, looking like a tourist, but really there on business. Coming back from the open air dance club at the resort, he had given his target a head start as he pursued him. Walking behind him now, he slowed down to make sure he wouldn't be seen right away. His target had gotten into a scuffle with another man, so keeping his distance was of importance. Then out of nowhere he saw his target snap the neck of the other man with a loud crack. Seeing the man's body go limp, it was obvious he was dead. His target then drug the limp body back to one of the outside lounge chairs lining the boardwalk. Upon placing the body onto the chair, his target looked up and saw him standing in the darkness, silhouetted by one of the many Citronella torches lining the walkway to keep insects away. He remembered the look in Soltan's eyes as they stared at each other for what seemed like eternity. The standoff was broken as a group of partygoers came their way.

"Yo, my man, I don't know and don't care, feel me? You hear those people? They're coming this way. It wouldn't be smart for either of us to be seen right now, get it?" said Jedi.

Soltan's face showed his anger and determination. Jedi had no doubt this man would do whatever he had to to get away. "We need to go!" said Jedi, hearing the people come closer. He was tired of standing in place, waiting to be discovered.

"Lead the way strange, I'm right behind you," said Soltan.

The party goers were coming in from behind Jedi, so they decided to walk in the opposite direction. As Jedi walked up to Soltan, he could see Soltan ready to strike. But to his surprise he let him pass, even though he had gotten close enough for Soltan to grab. Seeing Soltan snap the other man's neck made Jedi extra cautious, never turning his back to Soltan, despite his own military hand-to-hand combat training. With one eye on Soltan and the other toward his destination, Jedi made it back to his bungalow. With Soltan right behind him, they went through the door in a rush.

"Calm down, friend, you're safe here," said Jedi.

*Triple Crown Publications presents . . .*

Soltan said nothing as he stood at the door, unmoving. "Look, my name is Jedi, I'm here on business. I ain't going to turn you in so you can relax. What you did out there is your business. But the thing is if we were seen around that body we were both going to be held accountable. I don't need those kinds of problems, feel me?"

"So what do you want?" asked Soltan.

"Want? I don't want shit, at least not from you. I just don't want to go to jail, I got people that depend on me. Jail would seriously cramp my lifestyle."

Jedi walked over to the mini-bar and grabbed a glass, putting two ice cubes in it, and poured himself two fingers of whisky. Soltan watched closely, just in case the man tried anything. "What's your name?" Jedi asked, turning away from the bar and taking a seat on the couch.

"Why, so you know who to turn in?" asked Soltan.

"Listen kid, in my business, death is a way of life. Murder is usually the vehicle, so don't insult me again."

Soltan took a good look at this short bald headed man and was amazed at his arrogance as well as his nonchalance. "Have a seat, you gonna stand at the door all night?"

"Maybe. Maybe I'm a split right now."

"Is that right? Well, the way I see it, you need to stay somewhere right now, so why not here?"

Soltan thought it over for a minute then stepped forward to sit in the chair closest to the door. He was deciding whether he was going to kill this man or not. "So what business are you in" asked Soltan.

"The kind that needs no explanation."

The answer made Soltan think. It would be a safe assumption that whatever it was this little man did was not legal. Jedi spoke again. "But what does need an explanation is your escape plan. How do you plan to get off the island now that the man who was next in line to become president is dead?"

Soltan's mind went into overdrive. Who was this man? And how did he know who the man he just killed was? "Who the fuck are you?" Soltan growled, as he stood up, preparing to attack.

"It's not about me, it's about you and how you are going to get away with murder, Soltan."

With no more hesitation, Soltan lunged at the man and they both fell to the floor, Soltan on top. Quickly, Soltan was the one on his back. "I'm not the enemy, I'm here to help you escape, so calm down," said Jedi, struggling to hold Soltan down.

But Soltan said nothing as he swept his leg out, wrapping it around Jedi's neck, flipping him over, bettering his position. "Good move," Jedi said, surprised at the leg sweep. "I was told you were trained."

On his back again, Jedi reached around the stranglehold Soltan had on his throat, grabbing Soltan's left arm. Controlling the arm by the wrist, Jedi turned his body, relieving the pressure on his neck, and then threw his legs out, taking Soltan's head into a scissor hold as he fully extended Soltan's arm toward him. In this position Jedi had complete control of Soltan's arm, pulling it toward him and straining it at the elbow. He could easily break Soltan's arm, but he didn't want to hurt the man. He just wanted to talk.

"As you know, I could easily snap your arm right now, I don't want to. I just want you to calm down and listen to me. If you agree to do that I will release you."

Soltan was in great pain and knew what Jedi said was the truth. He could feel his arm giving under Jedi's effort. Thinking about what he should do didn't take long. He agreed to talk for two reasons, one, to stop the pain, and two, to get a better position on his opponent. "Let's talk," Soltan grunted.

"Play nice, OK?" Jedi said, releasing him.

Pulling his hurt arm to his chest, Soltan rubbed it, trying to get some feeling back. "You have good hand-to-hand skills, where'd you learn them?"

Jedi smiled, "I was Special Forces." He was bending down to pick up his whiskey glass.

"So how do you know who I am, and about my training?" asked Soltan, still looking for another opportunity.

"Let's just say that we have mutual interests and I think we can help each other," Jedi said, walking back over to the bar to pour himself another drink.

"Is that right?"

"Yeah, that's right," Jedi said, taking a seat on the couch again.

"Can we stop with the bullshit and get right to it?"

"By all means," said Jedi. "Relax." Jedi motioned for him to sit again.

Soltan backed up to the chair again, then sat down, no longer rubbing his arm.

"Alright, I'm part of a company of ex-military specialists across the world. We call ourselves "The Coalition." We are an antiterrorist group that functions outside the Government and its laws. Our responsibility is big, but our pockets are not. We have to make money by any and all means necessary to buy equipment, intelligence, vehicles, politicians and head of states. The man killed tonight was going to take office within the next year. He was promising to crack down on drug trafficking and corruption throughout his country. When we got wind of his intentions we used our network to find a solution. You were the solution. Your reputation is very good. You are good at what you do, Mr. Soltan. So through certain channels you were chosen for this job. I myself have been watching you since you arrived. It was no accident that I walked up on you. I took it upon myself to make sure that once you did the job that you get away safely. Now that I've done that I have a proposal for you. You make good money as a mercenary killer, but wouldn't you like to run your own empire? I know someone who could give you that opportunity. All he asks in return is that you do what you are good at when he needs you. You could be very wealthy man, Soltan."

Soltan was listening closely and everything he heard still didn't make sense, but now he was curious. "Doing what?" asked Soltan.

"You would be running his drug operation in the United States. Of course you would need some help, but I'm sure you could find your own people. But he wants you to control and run his operation throughout the states for him. You will have free reign to do as you please. All he asks is for you to coordinate with some of the people he already has in place. I am in control of the Northeast Region, and there are two others he would like you to meet. All of us are part of the Coalition."

"And who is this friend you are talking about? When do I meet him?" asked Soltan.

"First we have to get you back home. Once you get there you will be contacted by him if you accept," said Jedi.

"Getting home is nothing. Why do you think that I'm going to have a problem with that?" asked Soltan.

Jedi put the glass to his mouth, threw his head back, and swallowed the rest of the whisky. "There was a leak, so the authorities are looking for someone who fits your description. The Dominican government received an anonymous tip that your victim tonight was in danger. The only reason you were able to get close to him tonight is because he was such an arrogant bastard he didn't believe the threat was real. Didn't you notice that he didn't have security around him? He didn't think he needed any because he had yet to take office. Plus, he thought that because he was so popular with the people that no one wanted to hurt him. But now that he's dead, people are definitely going to be looking for you. We haven't gotten confirmation on the tipster but we have few ideas. We will find out. But what's most important is getting you home safely right now."

Soltan didn't know whether to believe this story. "How are you going to get me home?"

"All you have to do is trust me. Your escape is already set up."

"And what if I refuse to take this offer from your friend. Do I still get home safely?"

"Yes" said Jedi plainly.

"Well, let's go. I'll give you my answer later."

Soltan had proven to be very resourceful when he showed up at the Jedi's home in Bridgeport, Connecticut, two months later. He came into Jedi's bedroom as he read the morning paper. For a second Jedi thought that Soltan was there to kill him. But he had come in peace and offered his gratitude for helping him escape the Dominican Republic. After Soltan left, Jedi couldn't figure out how he had gotten past his security unannounced until they showed up at his door, guns drawn and really looking confused. Jedi couldn't help but to laugh right before he fired his whole security team. If Soltan wanted him dead, he would be. So the thought came - either Soltan was better than he thought, or his security team was just that bad.

~ ~ ~

Eating gyros as they walked North on LaSalle street past the Federal Reserve Bank, Soltan spoke in between bites. "This is the building. He works on the fourth floor," he said, motioning with his head in the bank's direction.

"You see all the traffic? It'd be kinda hard to snatch him here without drawing attention," B.B. said.

B.B. was referring to the lines of taxicabs and cars that were bumper to bumper in the streets. Not to mention the slew of businessmen and women walking the sidewalks and waiting on the corners for the pedestrian Walk signs.

"Right, but it makes it real easy to set up surveillance so we can time and track him and go undetected, feel me?" Soltan shot him a knowing grin.

Soltan's pager vibrated in his pocket. They were at the end of the street now. At the corner was a can. He threw his half-eaten sandwich and soda in before reaching in his pocket. Pushing the function button to bring up the display, the message read, "I'm here."

As he read those words his heart rate quickened and he felt a surge of adrenaline in his blood stream. "The Jedi has landed, let's get back to the hotel so we can get started," he said as he struggled to control his blood lust. He was getting anxious now just thinking about what he was about to do.

# Thirty • five

**"Damn girl!** You really like doing this don't you? It's like my dick is the most precious thing on earth, ahh," Crow said, gripping the seat cushions on the couch as Tasha deep-throated him, creating suction with her throat.

Ten seconds later she came up for air saying, "Baby, it's not just everybody I do this for, it's something about your dick. I just love to have it in my mouth," she said before wrapping her tongue around the head again. And then she tickled his balls with her left hand as she stroked his shaft with her right.

"Shit, suck that dick baby, I'm gone give you what you looking for baby, yeah," he said between moans. "Then I'm gone tear that ass up baby, umm," Crow continued as she worked her magic on him.

~ ~ ~

Domingo's men spread out, surrounding the house. They were as quiet and careful as death itself. With one at the back door and one at the front, they had both entrances covered. Two more were checking windows on either side of the house, looking in to make positive

I.D.'s on their victims. Domingo remained in a black nondescript van out front to keep an eye on any activity from the street. The last of the six man crew was posted in another black van at the end of the block, waiting and watching for anything on that end that was unexpected. "Positive I.D. on one of the occupant's sir, the other is an unknown female," spoke one of the soldiers outside one of the living room windows, kneeling in a crouch position and using a mirror.

Each one of the men wore black full length leather trench coats over plain clothes. They were all equipped with body armor and silenced 9mm Calicos in shoulder straps. Each one of them were also equipped with two-way communication devices so everyone was linked and functioning as one.

~ ~ ~

Crow was climaxing now, his body jerking in time to his ejaculations. Tasha didn't bother to slow down or ease up as she continued to suck for all she was worth. In fact, the moment she felt the first gush of sperm hit the back of her throat she squeezed his dick and began to milk it for the thick fluid. She gulped greedily as she swallowed the fluid, sucking harder and harder trying to get as much as she could. With her moans and slurps sounding like music to Crow, he knew his dick was going to stay hard enough for him to go another round. With his first nut out the way, he was quite sure Tasha was gonna be grateful of how he was going to beat her back out. "Mmm," Tasha moaned, licking her lips, then running her tongue across his head, lapping at what little come was left oozing out.

"Girl, you'll make a mutha-fucka marry your ass if you keep this up," Crow said, leaning back on the couch to enjoy the last little spasms of ecstasy.

"I knew I'd make somebody happy one day," Tasha

said, running her index finger across her bottom lip to the corner of her mouth, savoring the taste of him. "Looks like you want some more," she said looking at his still erect penis.

"Uh-uh, stand up," he said to her, turning her away from him and bending her over, her hands touching the floor.

Crow didn't waste any time lifting up her sundress and pulling her panties to the side, exposing her dripping wet core. Inserting two fingers inside her, he explored her with reckless abandon as she moaned in sheer delight. Removing his finger, he grabbed his penis and slowly guided himself inside her until the whole length of him disappeared. Enjoying the sensation, he let his penis throb and jerk in delight of the warm cavern it had been introduced to.

Tasha moaned as he slid himself inside her, biting her bottom lip with the pleasure of her first orgasm. When he began stroking himself in and out she didn't want him to ever stop. His strokes were long and strong, he was trying to go as deep as he could while she encouraged him by wiggling her ass. He had turned her toward the couch, something she appreciated because it gave her something to hold on to. While her hands had a death grip on the back of the couch, she squeezed his dick between her legs with all her might as he glided in and out. She could feel the death grip he had on her waist, but it didn't bother her as long as he didn't stop.

~ ~ ~

"Breach" was the command the soldiers heard through their ear-pieces, and simultaneously the front and back doors were opened slowly. The soldiers did their best to be as quiet as possible. Making their way into the house, the two soldiers stopped two or three steps in. They made eye contact from opposite ends of the house. They both heard Crow engaged in some hard-core sex, oblivious to his imminent demise. The soldier at the back door waited until the soldier behind him had taken his previous position at the door before he moved any further. His relief tapped him on the shoulder, letting him know he was in the clear. He then proceeded cautiously, gun in front of his body at the ready position, through the kitchen and into the living room.

The soldier at the front door came through the porch area the same way and slid into the hallway to check the other rooms in the house.

Crow just pounded away at Tasha as she cried out, "Yes, yes, fuck me, daddy!" in rhythm to the sound of skin colliding with skin.

When the soldier checking the rooms came back and shook his head to his partner, indicating the house was clear, the atmosphere changed. "Pfffttt," and Crow hit the floor grunting, grabbing his leg.

Tasha turned around to see what happened to Crow and noticed two men standing behind her holding guns. "Don't make a sound," one of them said as he walked over to her, grabbing her by the arm and putting the barrel of his gun under her chin.

Crow was trying to crawl toward the couch to his gun when the soldier that shot him grabbed him and pulled him into the center of the room, striking him in the face with the butt of his gun. "Where's the others?" the soldier asked.

"Fuck you!" Crow spat, as blood and saliva sprayed out with the words.

Tasha looked on horrified, not knowing what to do and wondering if she was going to live through this. "I'm going to ask you one time, where's the other motherfuckers?" Crow's only response was to spit blood in the soldier's face.

He knew he wasn't going to live through this and there was no way he was going to give up his brothers. So he made it easy on the soldier. He would die with honor, knowing one day he would be avenged. Once the soldier wiped his face clean, he fired three shots into Crow's face. His face exploded as he slumped backward onto the carpet, spraying brain and bone fragments against the ceiling and wall.

Tasha panicked and tried to free herself from the soldier's grasp. She began to scream but was stopped short once the soldier who shot Crow shoved his gun in her mouth, the hot barrel burning her lips. Tears staining her cheeks, she mumbled, "Please don't kill me."

The soldier eyed her then, and began smiling. "You look like a nice piece of ass, do you mind if I have a taste?" he said, running his fingers in between her breasts down to the neckline of her dress.

Hooking his finger in it, he ripped the flimsy sundress off to expose her fear-shaken body. He looped his finger inside her thong and ripped it off as well. Detached, Tasha couldn't help but to look at Crow lying in the middle of the floor, the pool of blood spreading across the carpet.

"Nice indeed, I think my friends and I should definitely have a sample, you don't mind, do you?"

Tasha could care less at this point what he wanted to do to her sexually, she just wanted to live, so she shook her head, "No."

"Good, but first you tell me what I want to know and I'll let you live. You lie to me and you end up like him," he said as he inclined his head toward Crow. "Deal?"

Tasha nodded at him as tears continued to roll down her cheeks. He removed his gun from her mouth and asked, "Where's the other guys?"

Her mouth free of obstruction, Tasha couldn't help

herself, she leaned over and vomited at his feet, her body convulsing in huge heaves. When she finished, the soldier holding her arm lifted her back upright and said, "Answer the question!"

"Sammy went to the store, he's coming right back, please," she said, rapid fire. "Please don't kill me." She pleaded.

"Where's the rest of them?" he asked, jerking her arm again.

"I don't know, I don't know!" Tasha sobbed.

Both the soldiers looked at her to gauge whether or not she was lying. A few seconds later the soldier that shot Crow touched the transmitter in his ear and spoke, "The girl said Sammy went to the store and is coming right back."

"Return to your positions and let's see if he shows up," said Domingo from the van outside.

All the soldiers heard the command through their earpieces and complied immediately.

Tasha was then yanked in the direction of the closed-in porch as the soldier holding her arm dragged her with him. "You better not be lying bitch, or I'll make you feel more pain than God ever intended for a human being."

"Please don't kill me, I just met them at a New Year's Eve party, please, I don't know what going on, what do you want from me?" she pleaded with the soldier, tears still running down her face. "I even have a video tape of the party to prove it, please, I don't want to die." She rambled on.

"What tape? I don't care about no tape whore!"

"Please, I'm telling you the truth. Me and my friend Lauren just met these people on New Year's. We came here to dance for them."

"Lauren? Who is this Lauren, whore?"

"My Latina friend, she came with me."

"Where is this tape? Give it to me!" the soldier growled.

"I have it at home, I can get it for you if you let me go."

"Nice try, but unfortunately you're not going anywhere."

"Please, please, if I get you the tape will you let me go?" she begged, now realizing his interest. She was thinking fast now, naked and in shock, that she was willing to do or say whatever necessary to live.

"Yeah, I'll let you go, get the tape," he lied.

"It's at my house, I'll get someone to bring it to you if I can make a phone call, please," she pleaded once more.

She was now on her knees begging for her life, hoping that she was getting through to her captor.

The soldier looked down into the pitiful face of the women. If the Lauren she was talking about is the General's daughter he would surely get rewarded. It was rumored that she was in this part of the U.S. so he hoped this was more than just a coincidence. Reaching into his pocket, he produced a cell phone and handed it to her. "Thank you, thank you, God bless you," said Tasha as she dialed a number.

The phone rang four times before it was answered, and the whole time Tasha was praying she didn't get voicemail.

~ ~ ~

"Hello?" Rochelle answered breathily.

"Chelle, I need you to help please!"

"What's wrong with you? You sound like you been crying, is everything OK?" Rochelle asked, concerned.

Rochelle had just rolled off of Detective Clayton, having just enjoyed another sweat-inducing bout of sex. He was lying on his back, looking at her as he caressed her thigh, rubbing his hand back and forth along the smooth muscle.

"I need you to bring me something. It's an emergency. Life or death."

"Life or death?" Rochelle repeated into the phone, raising her eyebrow as she looked at Clayton, her heart now racing. She could hear the urgency in her friend's voice and it scared her. Clayton was sitting up now, more alert to the conversation. "Slow down Tasha, tell me what's wrong."

"Chelle, just do what I ask you, and I'll explain everything later OK? Go to my house, there is a video tape in my top dresser drawer. It has a blue label on the front, bring it to me. I'm at three-two-two Summer Avenue, right off of south Rivers. Can you find the place?" asked Tasha.

"Yeah, I know the area, what's wrong Tasha, talk to me," Rochelle said, now with a tone of urgency in her voice.

"Chelle, just do it!" Tasha screamed before the soldier slapped her across the face with his gun, knocking two of her teeth out, and then took the phone.

~ ~ ~

When the line went dead Rochelle looked at Clayton with terror in her face. "I think my friend is in trouble," she paused, looking at him. "What are you doing?"

Clayton heard the address while Rochelle was talking and immediately knew something was wrong. He was standing now, getting dressed, not wasting any more time. "Chelle, that house is the place I have been keeping surveillance on. There has been some weird activity going on there. The people who hang out there are drug dealers and suspected murders. I think your friend is in a lot of danger."

He said this while checking the chamber of his police

issue Beretta and sliding it into his hip holster. "I'm going with you," Chelle said as she began putting her clothes on.

"No, it's too dangerous, you're going to stay here until I call you." But she kept dressing, not paying him any attention.

When she caught his eyes she said, "Look, it's my friend and I'm coming. Plus she needs something from her house you can't get, so I have to come. So let's go, I'll give you directions on the way."

Clayton shook his head as they headed for the door. He knew there was no changing her mind, so he went along with it for the moment. But he would have to come up with a way to get rid of her to keep her safe. He had a really bad feeling about this, hearing the stress in the voice on the phone sent a chill up his spine. But by Chelle knowing the location of her friend, she could always go there on her own if he left her by herself. So this was probably the best way for now, but he just couldn't shake the feeling something was terribly wrong.

~ ~ ~

Tasha held a hand to her mouth, trying to figure out why the hell she was bleeding. Then it came back to her, her captor had hit her in the face with something, his hand maybe, or was it his gun? Either way, she was still blinking, trying to refocus her vision, fighting back the pain of the teeth he dislodged.

The soldier from the back door heard Tasha scream, so he walked cautiously through the house to investigate. Seeing Tasha slouched over bleeding from the mouth he asked, "What the fuck are you doing? Keep the bitch quiet or kill her, do you understand?"

When Tasha heard this she looked up shaking her head saying, "Pleeth, pleeth, don't gkill me."

Her captor smiled at her, and she saw an all too

familiar look in his eyes. That one look sent an ice cold chill down her spine, paralyzing her body. Watching the other soldier walk away, she wondered what would be better for her; death or what she knew was on her captor's mind. Looking back at her captor, she felt a cold draft as if she was realizing for the very first time she was naked. The soldier grabbed her by the back of her neck and forced her face down on the bare wooden floor. She wanted to resist, but didn't want to upset him as she thought about her broken teeth. So she just laid on her stomach, terrified at what she knew was next. She could hear him unbuckling his pants and then she felt the cold steel of his gun pressing up against the side of her head.

"If you make any noise you die, understand?" he whispered in her ear.

Feeling his hot breath against her skin gave her goose-bumps as she whimpered, "pleeth don't do ghisss."

All hope had left her body when she suddenly felt his penis forcing its way past her labia, with one quick thrust he was all the way inside her. Her body rocked with each pump as she bit her bottom lip, trying to remain as quiet as possible, clenching her fists as he continued his onslaught. The violation seemed to take hours, but had only taken a few minutes. The smell of his rotten breath coupled with the dried blood in her nostrils and made her want to heave again. When he pulled out, she was thankful it was finally over and still alive. But all of the sudden excruciating pain exploded in her lower back as he bulled his way inside her anus. She couldn't help herself at this point as a half scream, half grunt slipped out of her mouth. Her captor hadn't noticed though, because he was too caught up in violating her. Moments later she felt the pressure of something penetrate the white noise in her ears created from the pain of her rape.

With a loud thump, her captor hit the floor next to her, a blank stare on his face as blood began oozing out a dime-sized hole in his forehead. She was in so much of a state of shock that she couldn't do anything but stare at the dead man's face, thankful he had stopped. The same pressure as before flowed through the room a second before her sight dimmed, the white noise fading off into the distance.

~ ~ ~

"There's a car approaching, the driver could be Sammy, but I couldn't make a positive I.D." said the soldier posted at the end of the block.

"I've got him, he pulled into the yard out front, all position's ready?" asked Domingo.

"Everyone's in position, sir," said the point man standing over the two bodies, as he waved at his back-up man at the back door to come further into the house.

"It's Sammy, I repeat, positive I.D. on Sammy, take him once he's inside," said Domingo.

~ ~ ~

Sammy drove right past the black van parked on the corner, never giving it a second look. He was more concerned with getting back into the house so he could satisfy his sexual craving with the freak Tasha. He had gone to the store and bought four boxes of Magnums and a fifth of Hennessy, along with a bag of ice and plastic cups. As he pulled his rental Chrysler 300M onto the grass in front of the house, he noticed the black van with tinted windows across the street. Not thinking much of it, he grabbed the brown paper sack and bag of ice and made his way to the front door with the anticipation of the pleasures to come.

# Thirty • six

**Rochelle and Clayton stopped by** Tasha's house and picked up the tape. There were let inside by Stacey who was not at all concerned with why she had to get something from Tasha's bedroom. She seemed more concerned with the television show she was watching, just waving her hand in the direction of the bedroom. Rochelle always knew Stacey to be somewhat distant, but at this point Rochelle was totally unconcerned with Stacey's behavior.

Clayton had followed her into the room and watched as she picked up the tape with the blue label. It was right where Tasha said it would be. Without caring what was on the tape, Clayton and Rochelle left the house in a mad dash to save someone's life. Stacey didn't even blink as they blew by her as she sat on the couch in the living room. Clayton steered his vehicle onto Summer Ave., noticing immediately the black van at the corner.

As Clayton continued down the street, he noticed a similar van sitting right across the street from the house he had been watching for the past month. The hairs on the back of his neck stood up now, because he definitely knew this was not a police department surveillance team. Looking over at the house he could see a man carrying a grocery bag approaching the front door. "That's the house right there, where are you going?" asked Rochelle.

"I know, but something's wrong, see that van there," he nodded with his head across the street. "It's not from my department," he said as he tried to smoothly drive down the street passing the house.

"So what are you doing?" asked Rochelle.

"I'm going to circle the block and park so I can check out what's going in on foot. I'm going to leave you at the gas station in case something happens," answered Clayton.

~ ~ ~

"Sir, there is another vehicle approaching; male driver; female passenger," said the lookout at the end of the block, alerting the whole team.

"Is it a target?" asked Domingo.

"Negative, it is not a target," answered the lookout.

"I have a visual, everyone maintain your positions, and when Sammy gets inside, secure him and wait for further instructions," ordered Domingo as he watched the car creep slowly past him.

The soldiers inside the house were set in their positions; one directly behind the front door; one crouching behind the wall that led to the porch entrance. The dead soldier and Tasha had been pulled over to the side of the front door entrance. Crow still lay in the center of the living room floor, but it didn't matter, because by the time Sammy saw him it would already be too late.

~ ~ ~

Sammy opened up the front door of the house and walked into the porch area. Immediately seeing blood on the wooden panel of the floor, he dropped the bags he was carrying and began reaching at his waist for his gun.

Before the groceries hit the ground he was hit with the butt of a gun from behind the door. Sammy fell to the ground face first and was grabbed by both soldiers occupying the house and was drug into the living room. With one soldier standing over Sammy's unconscious body, the other frisked him for the weapon he reached for and any others he carried. After throwing Sammy's gun across the room, the soldier touched his earpiece. "Sammy is secure, what are your instructions?"

"Standby, we have some activity out here," said Domingo.

He could see the end of the block from where he was parked and noticed the same car that just passed him turn the corner.

~ ~ ~

Clayton pulled his car into the parking lot in front of the Quick Mart convenience store on the corner of Summer Ave. Without a word to Rochelle, he reached for his CB microphone under his dashboard and called for backup. "D-T 614 to dispatch."

"Go ahead 614."

"I'm requesting backup at three-two-two Summer Ave, possibly a two-eleven in progress and possible hostage situation," Clayton spoke into the mic.

"Copy 614, alerting all available cars in the area," came the dispatcher over the radio.

Putting the mic back under the dash, Clayton looked at Rochelle and said, "Don't leave this car, you understand? I'm going to check on your friend, I'll be right back."

"Baby I'm scared,"

"Don't worry, I'm coming right back, OK?"

"Be careful baby," she said in a shaky voice. She could now feel the seriousness of the situation and feared the worst.

Clayton leaned over and kissed her briefly, slipping his tongue in her mouth and without warning broke loose and exited the car.

Clayton straightened his shirt as he walked toward the house so that his gun at his waist was not visible. He was going to attempt to nonchalantly walk up to the house to get a better look.

~ ~ ~

"We've got company, the driver of the car that just passed parked at the gas station and is on foot heading in your direction," said the lookout on the corner. "I believe he is armed, and he used a radio before he got out the vehicle."

"Ok gentlemen, we have a possible cop coming. Dispose of him as quickly as possible. There could be more on the way, so take care of Sammy. Eagle Eyes, is the woman still in the car the cop got out of?"

"Yeah, she's just sitting there."

"Take her out, do you copy?" asked Domingo. "Copy?"

Domingo watched the man walking up the street wondering to himself of the man could feel death in the air.

*Triple Crown Publications presents . . .*

# Thirty • seven

**Sammy's head hurt like he** had been hit with a sledge-hammer. He opened his eyes, trying to regain his focus, finally putting the image in front of him together. He was lying on his stomach with his head to the side when he realized he was looking at Crow in a pool of his own blood. *Am I dreaming? Damn head hurts. Crow? Fuck, Crow what the fuck is going on? Shit... Who the fuck is that moving around? Don't move, don't move, I don't need them knowing I'm awake. Fuck, these motherfuckers are going to kill me too.*

Out of the corner of his eye he could see someone standing over him holding a gun. *Naw, this ain't no dream, this is real shit. What to do? What to do?* were the words flashing like neon lights in his mind's eye. He tried to get a handle on his racing thoughts, but his throbbing head made it difficult. *I gotta do something.* He knew if he didn't come up with something fast he wasn't going to make it.

~ ~ ~

Eagle Eyes slipped out of the van's passenger door so that no one on the opposite side could see his exit. As he walked around the back of the van, he placed his silenced PK-9 in the right side pocket of his trench coat. Then casually, he walked toward the car where Rochelle sat unsuspecting.

~ ~ ~

Beep Beep, Beep Beep."Fuck!" said Rochelle as her phone died. "Ain't this a bitch, of all the times you could fuckin' go dead, you do it now!"

Rochelle got out the car and walked into the convenience store. Eagle Eyes paused for a second because he hadn't gotten as close as he wanted yet. He knew he couldn't just walk up and shoot her, he would have to be a little more discrete. So he kept walking as if he was just another person headed to the store.

~ ~ ~

Clayton approached the house, noticing the area possessed an unsettling calm. Things were very quiet for his tastes. Nearly walking past house three-two-two he decided to go around the back to get off the street and hopefully find a window to get a better look at what was happening inside.

The perimeter heard Clayton coming in his direction as Clayton's feet crushed dirt and grass underneath. He was going to wait until the man walked past him in the darkness to put a bullet in the back of his head, with his victim being none the wiser. "He's coming around the back, perimeter," Domingo said as he watched Clayton disappear on the side of the house.

Hearing this, the soldier guarding the front door left his position to render any kind of aid to his comrade out back, knowing they were one man short. It wasn't the thought that one man would be a problem, it was just insurance against all eventualities. It was better to have the odds in your favor, making for less mistakes, and also getting the job done more efficiently.

*Triple Crown Publications presents . . .*

Passing Sammy in the living room, the soldier gave a nod to his comrade who stood over him. Without hesitation, two slugs were shot into Sammy's back, making his body spasm at their impact.

Falling in step behind his comrade at the backdoor, the point man decided their mission had been accomplished as he touched his earpiece. "Sammy has been eliminated."

With no one responding to the transmission, the remaining soldier knew where their focus was now directed.

~ ~ ~

Clayton crept toward the back door of the house, then noticed a shadow pass by the window he just looked through. What he'd seen inside had frightened him. There were two bodies on the living room floor, one lying face down in a pool of blood, the other was crumpled backward, missing half his head, as if he was on his knees when executed. He did what he could to regain his composure and proceeded to the back of the house, gun out and in the ready position. Rounding the corner behind the house, his peripheral caught something move in the shadows. Spinning around, he was confronted by man in a trench coat aiming a gun at him.

He spun just in time to grab hold of the man's arm as the pistol jerked twice in the assailants' hand. Head-butting his attacker in the face, then kneeing him in the groin provided Clayton with opportunity to knock his attacker's weapon from his hand as he doubled over in pain. Incidentally, Clayton lost his weapon when he went on the attack. Hearing the footsteps of someone else coming, he wasted no time turning and hopping the nearby fence. Landing on the other side he heard the sound of muffled firecrackers, knowing instantly he was being shot at. It took a full hundred feet to realize he had been hit as the warm blood poured out of the wound in his side.

# Thirty • eight

**Rochelle closed the door of** Clayton's car after getting back in, the feeling that something was wrong getting stronger and stronger. She went inside to use the phone, asking her sister to come and get her. With Lori now on the way she knew she would soon be safe and sound at her sister's. She had let Lori know that she was with Clayton, but something wasn't right. She picked up the VHS tape and put it in her lap when she noticed a strange smell. Before she could turn around to look into the back seat she was shot twice behind her left ear. Blood and bone splattered the windshield and dashboard as her body slumped forward. Eagle Eyes, now rising up from the back seat, reached across the seat, pulling her back into the upright position. He noticed the bloody tape in her lap and decided to take it, wondering why it seemed important to her. And without another thought, he got out of the car and walked back to the van.

~ ~ ~

"The cop got away," the point-man said into his

transmitter. "He's running behind the house toward the corner, you should see him in a minute, Eagle Eyes. I believe he's wounded, there's blood on the fence," the soldier said, trying to stop the blood flowing from his nose.

"Forget him, the cops are arriving, get back to the van, we're done here," said Domingo.

By the time all three of the soldiers were in the van across the street, Eagle Eyes drove past them going in the opposite direction.

"We ditch the vans and meet at the rendezvous point," Domingo said to Eagle Eyes as he passed.

"Copy."

Back inside the house looked like a massacre, the walls and carpet stained with blood as the four bodies lay still and unmoving.

Leaving Sammy for dead, the soldiers never bothered to see if he was still breathing. Even though it wasn't simple, Sammy still had life in his body. The pain he felt was like the weight of an elephant sitting on his chest.

Sammy figured one of the bullets had punctured at least one, if not both, of his lungs, and knew his life was coming to an end. Reaching in his pocket and digging out his cell phone took everything he had left in him. Finally having phone in hand he pressed in the code Star-5, to speed dial Soltan's voicemail. Once connected, he gasped out the words, "Dead ... Crow ... hit ... squad ... won't ... make it..." as blood and saliva poured out from his nose and mouth.

Breathing was just too hard to do now and he could feel his heart's pace slowing down until it came to a complete stop. The phone fell out of his hand onto the carpet as the last attempt his body made to live went through his mouth in a hiss of hot air.

~ ~ ~

Clayton was forced to stop running and was now walking at careful pace, with his hand clamped over the wound at his side. He had lost a lot of blood and he could feel his body temperature dropping as he fought the urge to stop and catch his breath. The only thing on his mind now was getting back to the car and getting Rochelle away from drama. He could pretty much guess her friend Tasha was dead, even though he hadn't seen her in the house. But what he had seen made it awfully clear as to what the situation was.

Clayton now stumbled through some bushes and proceeded at his slow pace as he heard sirens and saw red and blue flashes lights up ahead. He was directly behind the convenience store when he paused for a quick second, putting a bloody hand on the wall in an attempt to gather himself. Hobbling until he was back in the parking lot, he was determined to get back to where he left Rochelle sitting in the car. He couldn't help but to wonder what the hell all the police cars and ambulance were doing here when the people needing the assistance were down the street.

No one paid Clayton any attention as he made his way to his car. He saw officers taking pictures of someone inside. His worst fears were realized as the officers blocking his view moved, giving him a clear look.

Rochelle was slumped against the passenger window with what was left of her face. Blood and brain fragments obscuring the windshield. It was the last thing he saw right before he collapsed onto the ground and passed out. A nearby officer ran over to Clayton, then recognized who he was, yelling, "OFFICER DOWN, OFFICER DOWN, WE NEED SOME HELP OVER HERE!"

# Thirty • nine

**Soltan and B.B. made it back** to the hotel when Soltan's pager began vibrating again. It had taken them almost thirty minutes to make it back to the Hyatt. The traffic had congested to the point where it made the journey back frustrating, moving at a snail's pace, not to mention the traffic lights at every corner making the taxi stop every thirty seconds.

Pulling his pager out his pocket as he and B.B. stepped into the elevator, Soltan read, "1 VOICE MAIL," on its LCD display. He decided to use the phone when he got to his room, sliding the pager back into this pocket. "Region?" B.B. asked.

"Yeah, I think so, but something's wrong, he usually waits to hear from me when we're working," said Soltan.

For that reason alone Soltan caught a slight chill. His instincts were telling him something was terribly wrong.

Arriving at Jedi's door, Soltan knocked and stood there with B.B. as his imagination took over, showing him images of blood and dead bodies. Someone came to the door and looked out the peephole. The door opened a second later, a large Hispanic man, holding a gun at his right thigh, filling the doorway.

"What up?" greeted Soltan as he walked into the room and gave him a hug. "I see you still trying to pop a blood vessel," Soltan said to Junior as he stepped back out the embrace.

"Muscles don't go out of style, papa," Junior shot back, flexing his bicep.

"Neither does killing," shot back Soltan.

"Junior," B.B. greeted, following Soltan inside.

"How's life treating you?" Junior asked B.B. while shutting the door.

"Can't complain."

Jedi appeared from around the corner with a drink in his hand. "My brother, how are you?" he asked while walking up to greet Soltan. "Been a minute, you look well. Hey B.B., you ready to party? I got a feeling we're going to have a lot of fun this trip," Jedi continued.

B.B. gave a nod as he walked over to the picture window and leaned against the wall. "That's funny, 'cause I got a bad feeling," said Soltan. "That reminds me, let me use your phone," he said, walking over to the nightstand where the phone sat.

He dialed the number to his voicemail and Jedi picked up the conversation with Junior while B.B. listened. After dialing his access code and pushing the appropriate number to retrieve the message, he froze stiff as he listened.

Soltan turned around to face the room as he looked at B.B. and then dropped the phone back in its cradle. "They're dead," he said to B.B. "Dead!"

B.B. stiffened at those words, asking, "Who's dead?"

"Crow and Sammy are dead. That message was Sammy, he said that a hit squad was there and he probably won't make it. It sounded like he was wounded," Soltan said, his demeanor changing as he spoke.

B.B. eye's narrowed into thin slits at Soltan's words as he asked. "Who sent them?"

"I don't know, but whoever it was is going to need Jesus in the flesh to save their souls."

"Who would send a squad for us? Whoever it was must have thought we were going to be there. But who knew where we were?" asked B.B.

Junior listened to the conversation in just as much shock as B.B. and Soltan. "It's gotta be that fucking Rico. Maybe he was trying to get at me before I got to the boy, trying to take me out before I made the trip. But how did he know what we were doing? Someone on the inside leaked the information, that's the only thing I can come up with. We wasn't there so he didn't want no one to warn us that he came. But somehow Sammy sent me a message."

Soltan started pacing the room as he thought out loud. "I knew I should have killed that piece of shit a long time ago! It's gotta be him, no one else would be stupid enough to fool with me. He's the only one dumb enough to try." Soltan continued as he paced the room.

Everyone watched as he put the pieces of the puzzle together, then Jedi's phone rang. "Hello?"

"I'm out front," said Frank.

"Ok, I'll be there in a minute, I'm sending Junior down," said Jedi, not wanting to talk on the phone.

"Alright."

Hanging up, he looked at Junior and said." Go downstairs and tell Frank to hold on, and we'll be down in a minute. Let him know we got Soltan here."

With a nod, Junior walked out the room of his mission. "Or, he was trying to get rid of them before he got to me. He could know that you're with me," he looked at

B.B.

"Yeah, he knows, he wants to cut us out clean and surgical," he rambled on. *But where's the other guys?* he asked himself walking over to the phone.

He dialed the first guy he could think of, Nell. He was hoping to hear his voice, but the phone just rang. Without hearing Nell's voice, he feared the worst.

B.B. looked over at Soltan, but Soltan shook his head, only making B.B. more upset. A few minutes of silence went by when a light came on inside Soltan's mind. "He's here!" he said as the pieces started coming together, fitting into their own special places. "Yeah, he's here in Chicago waiting on his opportunity. He doesn't know where we are, but he knows who we came for. He's going to watch the kid and wait for us to show up. Yeah, that's how I'd do it," Soltan said pacing again.

"Well, if that's the case then it should be easy to set a trap," said Jedi.

"No, I want him to come to me, if I know anything about Rico, he wants to take me out up close so he can look into my eyes. So no traps, I want him to feel in control of the situation. But we're going to need some more guys to pull this off," said Soltan. "I'm sure that won't be a problem. Will it, Jedi?"

"No problem at all my brother, we can talk to Frank about it, he's outside right now," said Jedi.

"Good," said Soltan as he began walking toward the door.

"So that's it?" asked B.B.

"Yeah, we'll move as normal, let's go," Soltan answered.

B.B. shrugged his shoulders and fell into step with him and they left the room. In the hallway Soltan turned around and said. "I'll meet you downstairs," and then walked in the opposite direction.

When Soltan made it the door he knocked lightly. He visualized Lauren's lithe body walking to the door as he listened to her feet cross the carpet. He could see her look into the peep hole, then a second later the door opened and he was looking into those radiant, lustful eyes. "Are you just going to stand there?" she asked.

But Soltan couldn't help himself, he was looking at a woman who wasn't just physically attractive, she was alluring. All she had on was a pair of boy shorts and a tank top, making her look absolutely delicious.

Soltan finally walked into the room, letting the door close behind him, but he was fighting the urges he was having at this moment. Now wasn't the time, but damn, he could use a release right now.

"You OK, baby?" she asked, seeing the wild look in his eyes, and she watched them as he scanned every inch of her body. She could tell he was turned on, and he knew she was ready to pounce on him herself.

Without another word she was kneeling at his feet and unbuckling his pants. She could feel his straining muscle thumping just below the surface. Soltan reached down, stopping her from completely freeing his penis just in time. "Not now, I just came to see if you were alright," he said, looking down into her beautiful face.

"I'll be alright once you let me take away your stress. I can see it in your eyes, you need a release, I can feel it, you're tense," she responded with some authority.

"My hunger can wait, right now there are more important matters at hand," he said, gently pulling her upright.

"But what about my hunger?" she asked in a pouty voice.

"Later, right now I need you to listen. Things have changed. While I'm gone don't leave this room and don't answer the phone or the door. Do you understand?"

Lauren looked at him now perplexed, "What's wrong?"

"Nothing I can't fix, but do you understand?" he asked again.

"Yes. I understand, so I'm just supposed to stay here by myself?"

"You will be safe here until I get back, trust me. Get some rest and relax, you have a long day ahead of you tomorrow," Soltan said as he finished buckling his belt and turned around to walk out the door. "Remember, don't answer the phone or the door."

Not knowing what else to do, Lauren got angry. She was angry because she was horny, and angry because there was nothing she could do about it right now. But, no matter, she walked to the door and turned the knob, setting the deadbolt, and swung the safety latch into place. She would follow his instructions for right now and get some answers later. She knew something was wrong by the look in his eyes, but he obviously didn't want to tell her what it was. So *what else is new? I might as well enjoy this luxury while it lasts*, she thought as she settled onto the king size bed.

Picking up the TV remote, she pointed it at the huge flat screen that was fitted into the wall and began channel surfing.

# Forty

**"A, you gotta be fucking** joking right? Are you serious? That motherfucka right there is bangin', son!" Jedi said as he looked at the Lamborghini Frank was leaning against.

"A two thousand eight Lamborghini Reventon? At six hundred fifty horsepower, it'll do zero to sixty in three seconds flat. It's the most powerful Lambo ever fuckin made my brother and it's all yours, said Frank.

"Are you fucking joking right now, yo, don't play with me son, this is me?" Jedi asked, running his hand across the shining paint.

"Yeah my brother, all yours, you deserve it, all these years we've known each other I couldn't ask for a better friend. Plus it's a great tax write off and business is doing well. You like it?"

Before Frank could brace himself, Jedi had walked over to him and gave him a giant bear hug. "Ease up man, I can't breath," said Frank.

Junior started laughing as he stood off to the side watching the two men.

When Jedi released him, Frank took a second to fix his clothes and then asked, "Ok, now that that is over, where's Soltan?"

"Here he comes now," Junior spoke up as he saw Soltan get off the elevator.

As he made it to the sidewalk, Soltan noticed the Lambo and said, "Nice car, Frank," as he made his way over to him to shake hands.

"Yeah, it will get you from A to B quite nicely," Frank answered, turning his head and looking back at the car.

"Alright gentlemen, now that we're all here let's handle this business. Jedi, what's the deal with our equipment?" asked Soltan.

"Don't worry, I'm sure Frank here is gonna have everything you need," said Tuffy.

"Soltan got some business he needs to handle and he's going to need a few toys and some transportation," said Jedi.

"Is that all? Soltan you know that if I got it, you got it. I was thinking that there was some business that needed some old fashioned attention, know what I'm saying? Shit, it's been a while, but I can oil these old bones and joints up and get with the best of 'em," said Frank.

"Well we just might have some of that after all my friend. It's just too early in the game to tell," said Soltan. "Don't worry then, you're family, so whatever the problem is we'll solve it together. Let's go to my shop and we can talk about it there with some degree of privacy," said Frank.

Everybody agreed and headed to their vehicles. Junior led the way to the truck, as Soltan and B.B. followed. Frank handed Jedi the keys to the Lambo and walked around to get in the passenger seat as Jedi settled in the driver's seat and turned the motor over.

*Triple Crown Publications presents . . .*

# Forty • one

**Arriving at Gold Coast Exotic Imports,** both vehicles came to a stop right in front of the showcase window. Inside were all manner of amazing cars: Ferrari, Porsche, Maserati, Jaguar, Rolls Royce and Benz were all on display. The building was a moderate two-story brick structure, giving you a view of the cars on the showroom floor through the huge picture windows. The building was connected to another structure that only showed two garage style roll-up doors with a line of much smaller windows that ran the length of the building all way to the end of the street.

A few seconds passed before one of the garage doors began to lift and Soltan watched as the low clearance Lambo crept under it as they had to wait for it to fully open to get inside. Once parked and out of the vehicles, Soltan looked around and admired the caliber of cars he saw and the amount of room the building furnished. "It looks like you doing good business Frank, top of the line as usual. Now I see why you and Jedi get along so well, you both have exotic cars fetishes."

"Come over here and check this out," said Frank as he led everyone over to a covered car under a lift rack.

Frank reached down, grabbing the edge of the car cover and pulled it off. "A 2009 Koenigsegg CCXR Edition," Jedi whispered as he approached the car and ran his hand over the midnight black paint job that was polished so well it looked wet.

"Got it just last week from Forza Collezione, hit me for two point five, but I figured it was worth it," said Frank.

"Are you fuckin kidding, of course it was worth it. This car is so exclusive they only made six. It runs on Bio-fuel and gets 1018 horsepower, it's probably the only one in North America. How did you pull it off?"

"I pulled a couple strings," answered Frank.

"When can I take it for a spin?" Jedi asked.

"We'll see, we'll see, right now let's get back to the business at hand." said Frank.

Soltan and B.B. exchanged a quick glance and then both simultaneously shook their heads in disbelief.

Junior said, "It's like this every time these two get together. They're just motor heads, they can't help themselves."

"Right, cause I damn sure don't give a shit about year, make, and model, I just need it to drive," added B.B.

"It's good that you don't like cars, Junior, because your job is to shoot people up when we need you to," said Frank. "I hope you get as hard looking at guns as I do looking at cars."

"And you know this, man," Junior fired back with his best Chris Tucker impersonation. They all enjoyed a quick laugh and then Frank led the way upstairs to his office.

Once inside the room it was obvious this was not just a warehouse for cars. There were crates marked U.S.

Government everywhere. Big crates, small crates, long and short, some stacked two and three high. "You said you need some toys, so what all you need?" asked Frank.

"This is all U.S. Government shit, Frank," said B.B. with a level of concern.

"Don't sweat it man, I'm connected, it's one of the perks of being an ex-SEAL," said Frank.

Soltan looked around silently for a moment before he said, "Ok, let's see what you got."

Frank walked over to a set of crates and removed the lid to show a chrome-polished Gatling gun. "This will definitely get you some action right, gentlemen," he said, lifting it out of the box with a grunt.

"That's fine if you're going to be in World War III, but fortunately we shouldn't be having that big a problem," said B.B.

"He's right, all we need is some good clean hardware and possibly some body armor. You got something like that around?" asked Soltan.

"Absolutely," said Frank, putting the gun down. "Come over here."

Frank led them over to what amounted to be a small display case showing a bunch of different makes, models, and calibers of handguns and silencers. "Is this what you are talking about?" asked Frank.

Soltan didn't answer verbally, but once he picked up a forty-five Socom HK that was fitted with a Trijicon night sight, the grin on his face said it all.

In the display case there was a variety of hardware, from more forty-fives to nine milli's. There was also a variety of small machine guns, a few Uzis and Macs as well as numerous MP-5s. There were also plenty of attachments as well, from laser aiming modules, to Knight's Armament suppressors. Stacked next to the display case was plenty of ammunition to go along. Federal hydro-shocks, regular copper heads, regular hollow points and the famously outlawed Black Rhinos.

"Don't be shy Soltan, what's mine is yours, take whatever you need," said Frank. Soltan gave a nod over to B.B. who began pulling out guns and silencers from the case.

"What about some body armor and holsters?" asked Soltan.

"No problem … Junior, bring that duffel bag there," Frank said, pointing at a bag across the room.

In the bag were four bullet-proof vests that had no slots for extra plates or Velcro straps. They looked like regular shirts, but at a closer look, you could see a scale-like surface. "These, my brother, are what we call Dragon skin. This is state of the art body armor that will stop a 7.62 bullet at twenty four hundred feet per second. The impact is a little greater, but the bullet ain't got a chance in hell getting through," he said with a smile.

"It's real thin Frank, you sure it will do what you say?" asked Soltan.

"I would put my life on it, baby."

"We might be," said B.B.

Soltan and B.B. gathered what they thought they needed for this mission and once they had everything they settled in to discuss the game plan. "Alright, so within the last twenty four hours I've lost two dear friends and a third is MIA. The first two seem to have been killed by an extermination crew. I believe I know who's responsible for it and if I'm right he's going to pay. I currently have business here with a young man by the name of Emilio Gonzalez. He works at the Federal Reserve Bank not too far from the hotel we're staying at."

Everyone was paying attention to Soltan as he spoke, nobody wanting to miss anything that might be important.

Soltan continued, "That's why we're here, but I'm afraid the crew that killed my friends is also either on its way to finish me and B.B. off, or is already here keeping an eye on our target waiting for us to show up. My guess is a trap will be set for us once we try to apprehend the target. So, I'm going to need a back up team to watch who's watching me. I don't know exactly what to expect, but I can tell you if I'm right about the extermination team, we're dealing with trained men. I don't want to intentionally put any of you in harm's way, so if any of you decides you want no part of this operation I understand."

"So basically what you're asking us is you need somebody to watch your back while you handle your business here in the Chi?" said Frank.

"Basically, yeah. But if I'm on someone's list, then just watching my back puts you in danger. If I can grab my target with no problem, then fine. But, things get ugly, then blood is going to run in the streets."

"Soltan, we're brothers and I'm with you no-matter what, whatever the situation is, I got your back," said Jedi.

"Same here," said Frank and Junior.

"Good, but were going to need a few more guys for this," said Soltan.

"That's no problem either, I got guys that live for drama, not saying that I want any to pop off. But if there's any type of mayhem going down they want in. I'll get with them and have them here tonight," said Frank.

"That's good, but I need guys who follow orders and have training," said Soltan.

"We all have training, so trust me, I got you." said Frank.

"Alright, you say tonight? Good, that gives me

enough time to get everything else lined up right. We'll go over exactly what to do later," said Soltan.

B.B. remained quiet the whole time, just sitting back and observing everyone and gauging their reactions and body language. He knew that he was in on anything and everything that Soltan was involved in. He was bound to Soltan, in this life and the next. But he had his doubts about the others' motives in this little get-together. But what made him happy was that Soltan didn't tell them that they were going to kidnap and kill the son of the man who ran largest and most dangerous drug cartel in the world. All because their employer wanted to start a war that would land him in power once everyone else was dead. It really didn't matter to him about the who's and why's though, he was told what to do and did it, trying to enjoy himself in the process.

# Forty • two

***Trump received the call almost*** an hour ago about the four homicides on Summer Ave. This was turning out to be a very busy week, he decided, as he pulled his squad car up to the curb in front of the house. When he first arrived at the corner, he couldn't believe his eyes. Crowds of people were gathered on both sides of the street all the way down to the convenience store. Apparently the homicide victim sitting in the car at the convenience store drew just as much attention as the victims in the house.

There was yellow crime scene tape everywhere, and he could see his department was out in full force. Some officers were still interviewing witnesses, while others were on crowd control duty. From the looks of things, there was no obvious way to tell if the victim down the street was connected to the victims at this location. But if he was lucky, they would be, at least that's what his gut was telling him.

According to the reports he'd heard, there was also a Narcotics Detective shot in connection with whatever happened here. The Narcotics Detective was not a good friend, but he'd seen him around the department on numerous occasions. They had also run across each other a few times while working the same cases. Drugs and violence seemed to go hand in hand, so he was familiar with the detective.

Even though Detective Clayton was a bit too flashy, he was a good cop. Everyone knew he used some unconventional tactics to get results, but who didn't? All he knew and needed to know was that, Detective Clayton's heart was on the right side of the law. He could forgive some of the ways justice had prevailed a long as the good guys scored more than the bad guys.

Walking up the steps to the porch, a uniformed officer turned and asked for I.D. before letting him go any further. After seventeen years he thought he knew everyone in the department. Fucking rookie.

Flipping his wallet open, revealing his badge, the uniform said, "Right this way sir," leading him inside.

The graphic images he saw inside made him blink a couple times. It seemed that what he was looking at, his frontal lobe didn't want to accept. "Has anyone touched or moved the bodies before I got here?" he asked, almost having to choke the words out. After all the years he'd been in homicide, seeing things like this never got easy.

What was left of a woman's head lay sideways, attached to her naked body. And from the looks of it, she was having some kind of sexual encounter with the man that was half on top of her, half lying to the side. The guy was naked from the waist down, his pants pooled at his feet. He lay at such an odd angle that it was hard to determine exactly what had happened. What was certain was this man was missing half his head also. Blood splatter, bone fragments and brain matter/tissue painted the walls and floor in a macabre tableau.

As Trump brain began processing the carnage, the uniform led him further inside to show him two more bodies. Seeing these other two victims lying in pools of their own blood made him think, *"This was a hit."*

Seeing the precision of the gunshots and lack of any signs of struggle, he knew this was no random set of homicides. These people had been killed intentionally. "This wasn't a drug deal gone bad, this was a massacre."

Around him, the house was being processed by crime scene technicians taking pictures, dusting for prints and taking measurements. The department's crime scene Forensic Serologist was also present, taking blood and DNA samples from the victims.

The uniform spoke again, "There's also some blood out back on the ground with plenty of shell casings. We believe that is where Detective Clayton was shot."

"When is the Medical Examiner due?" he asked.

"She was called when we discovered the first body down at the gas station, so she should be here soon. We had to get her out of bed sir," the uniform said to him, trying to explain why she wasn't on the scene yet. Monica isn't going to be happy about his little brouhaha, and that's probably why she was taking her sweet time getting here.

Making his way out back to look at the scene there, he tried to mentally add up the pieces. Two dead on the porch; both by gunshots to the head. Possibly an interrupted sex act, but the guy lying next to the woman didn't fit. He's wearing what looks to be tactical gear under a full length trench coat. The other two in the living room were also shot in a controlled fashion. While one was shot in the face like the others, the larger one was shot in the back. These people were clearly executed, but why?

Looking down in the grass, he could clearly see the

yellow teepee's that marked the shell casings and their locations. "Hey, let me hold your flashlight," he said to the uniform.

He took the flashlight, using the beam of light to guide his steps. There seemed to be at least twenty or more shells on the ground and what looked like a trail of blood, starting at the fence and then disappearing into the woods behind the house.

Handing the light back, he decided he wanted to see the rest of the house to get a better feel for what may have taken place. He navigated his way back through the living room around all the techies and into the bathroom hallway. Making a left, he entered the first of the two bedrooms of the small house to find it being searched and inventoried.

Scanning the area, he could see that there were no real belongings here. Everything in this room was either old-fashioned, outdated or secondhand. It didn't look to him that someone would actually be comfortable sleeping in, night in and night out. The bed was low quality, probably Salvation Army, the TV was obsolete, the carpet badly stained and matted. What didn't fit were the new boxes of tennis shoes and brand new clothing hanging in the closet. Flipping through some of the hangers, he noticed there were store tags still on most of the clothes. This signified they had never been worn. Moving a row of the clothes to the side in the closet, he noticed a hand-stitched portrait of some kind hanging on the wall behind them. Initially looking at it, he didn't know what to make of it. The picture showed an ashen face with dark circles around the eyes. It looked like a ring master from a circus, feathered top hat and all. But upon closer inspection he saw the skulls that adorned the brim, and that the painted face was to give the illusion of a human skull.

"Does anybody know what this is or what it could be?" he turned and asked anyone.

Everyone in the room shook there heads no, or replied in the negative. One of the techs said, "We're running it now sir, we should know within the next twenty minutes."

Looking back at the picture, he thought he saw something on the floor where the boxes lined the closet. Kneeling down, he flipped the lids on a few of them with an ink pen, careful not to touch anything, thereby leaving his prints. He flipped one box, whose lid was already half open and found a yellow satellite phone. "Has anyone inventoried this closet yet?" he asked. "Not yet sir," someone answered.

"Give me an evidence bag," he said to a nearby tech dusting the door handle for prints.

He took the bag, picked up the phone, careful to let the phone slide right inside, and then zipped the top shut. Standing up, he turned around to see everyone in the room doing their individual tasks. Everyone was concerned with their work for the moment, so he saw no reason to further disturb them. He walked out of the room with the phone in hand, deciding to take it to the lab personally.

Back in the living room he saw the medical examiner had arrived and was kneeling over the female body on the porch. He walked up asking, "Do you know the cause of death yet?"

Monica looked over her shoulder, eyed him, and then stood speaking in a groggy, irritated voice. "Hmm, let's just say for right now, mind you, that it wasn't natural causes."

He couldn't help but smile at this beautiful woman he didn't have a chance with. "Good observation, doc."

Her response was a little more agitated, "What the

hell happened here? I've got a young lady down the street missing half a head and face and then I come here to see not only do these two have the same problem, but it looks like this was a rape in progress. I won't be sure until my examination at the lab, but there's too much blood covering her down here..." She said, taking a pointer and signaling the area around the anus, "to be consensual."

"It looks forced, but what I don't understand is why he's got all this equipment on," she said, puzzled and angry.

"What are you talking about, what equipment?"

As he spoke, he began to focus in on exactly what she was referring to. He noticed the ear-piece now, and the transmitter clipped to the dead guy's belt. Then he noticed the armpit holsters and extra magazines stored in their place. "Where's the gun?" he thought. He didn't understand how he missed all this when he first saw the bodies. He noticed the trench coat but paid no attention to anything else.

*Damn, I'm slipping, I shouldn't have missed all this the first time. Maybe it was seeing all this death that made me overlook it. Fuck! I'd promised myself that when the day came when the deaths clouded my mind that I would retire.* He was thinking to himself.

"He's one of them, he's one of the killers." he said, talking out loud now.

He knelt down to get a better view of the receiver and noticed it was still on, possibly transmitting. Looking around, he noticed the ME's bag and reached inside for a pair of rubber gloves. Putting them on, he reached at the transmitter and pulled the wire out that connected the earpiece.

*Triple Crown Publications presents . . .*

# Forty • three

**Domingo ordered his crew** to make sure they left no evidence in the vans, so the three soldiers were busy wiping down the interiors with acetone and packing up all their equipment before setting the vehicles on fire. And as far as Antonio, he would be dealt with later for his carelessness. Killing one of his men and leaving him behind was surely an unforgivable act, no matter the circumstances. Not only was there evidence of their technology, but an actual member of their squad was left behind as absolute proof of their existence. But the more he thought about it, it would seem only proper to let Rico deal with him. That would definitely be a better course of action.

Standing in the hangar near their chartered jet, while it received the final preparations for flight, Domingo tapped the black videotape against his thigh. According to one, the female with the cop was clutching it before she died.

Climbing the stairs boarding the plane, he went directly to the TV, popping the tape into the VCR and pushing the rewind button. He waited only a few seconds until it stopped. Pushing the play button, Domingo waited some more to see what was actually on the tape. Once the image came into focus, it looked as if it was some kind of party. He saw who he knew to be B.B. and Sammy come into view as some half-naked females pranced around the room. The party quickly turned into an orgy as he continued to watch, with sex acts happening in every corner. The women in the video were performing with the men and each other as the camera turned, scanning all the couples in the room, then suddenly he saw an all too familiar face. Pressing rewind, Domingo couldn't believe his eyes.

*This has to be a mistake*, he thought in disbelief. He pressed play again and waited, heart racing as fear and excitement overcame his body. There she was again, it was her, no doubt about it, it was definitely her. She had been missing for two years now. Though no one was able to locate her exact whereabouts, it was believed she was in this area. And right here Domingo was looking at the confirmation. If only she knew how much trouble she had caused, how many people's lives were taken because of her disappearance, his own life almost being one of them. There was so much blame cast in the all the wrong directions that everyone had developed a bad taste in their mouth when it came to her.

She had become the modern day Helen of Troy, almost bring down their whole operation with the stunt she pulled. Using FARC to help smuggle her out of Colombia in one of their Narco-Subs damn near stopped all supply to their western customers. The General dealt death from Panama all the way up to Mexico City, everywhere that the sub stopped. If it was up to him she would pay for all the trouble she had caused, but the truth was that she wouldn't. The Devil himself was her protection, her savior. All the General wanted was his daughter back and it was Domingo's job to make sure she made if home safely. It was unfortunate, but he would do what was necessary - because his life depended of it.

Ejecting the tape now, he stuffed it in his pocket as he leaned out the doorway of the plane. "Finish what you're doing now, and load the plane. We're leaving in ten minutes!" he yelled to his men.

He didn't know whether to call Rico now or not, but he thought it was probably better for the General to see it for himself first.

Coming down the step of the plane, Domingo told the pilot to prepare a flight plan for Colombia and prepare for take off. Once he was back in Colombia he would get instructions from the General on what to do next.

# Forty • four

**Back at the hotel,** Soltan and B.B. finished unpacking the equipment they requisitioned from Frank. "I don't know what to say about all this outside help. You know I don't like working with strangers," B.B. said about their current situation.

"They are not strangers, B.B., they have been doing business with us for a while now, and you know we can trust Jedi."

"Yeah, Jedi, But what about his friends?"

"Don't worry, if Jedi says they cool, then I trust his judgment. I personally would like to have our guys here, but we'll see them on the other side. For now we concentrate on the task at hand, and get this job done, alright?"

"Yeah, I guess you're right, but I want to make the motherfuckers who are responsible for this shit pay. And I do mean pay dearly."

"I do too, brother, but if we think about what has already happened instead of what needs to be done then we're gonna slip. If we slip, we end up dead also, and we can't help no one if we're dead, feel me?" Soltan said, finished getting his gear together, and facing B.B.

"Yeah, I feel you," answered B.B.

"Good, I'll see you later tonight," said Soltan, picking up his bag and dragon-skin vest off the bed and heading for the door. "Relax B.B., everything is going to be alright," Soltan said before exiting the room.

"If you say, if you say so," B.B. mumbled to himself.

*Triple Crown Publications presents . . .*

# Forty • five

**Casi was holding a closed-door** meeting with his chief advisors about the future of Haiti's borders and what the investigation of his son's murder turned up. As his advisors talked about giving in to the Colombians to keep the peace, Jean Pierre was having more radical thoughts, thoughts of revenge and retribution. There was no doubt in his mind who was responsible for his son's death. He knew he would have to fight fire with fire in order to keep the respect of his countrymen. He had long heard the name of a man that was so feared in his country that when people spoke of him it was in a whisper. Supposedly this man was such a fierce and deadly hit man, people were afraid to even speak his name in public, for fear of becoming a target. He wasn't just a normal killer - reports say he didn't just kill, he took souls as well. In his country, taking one's soul guaranteed the victim would be eternally damned. For his actions against his family, Casi wanted General Gonzalez to pay for what he has done to his family. The gloves were coming off.

Casi got up from the table, knowing what he had to do. To him, the conversation taking place was like background noise compared to the humming in his ears. "Is everything alright Mr. President?" asked chief advisor Neville when he noticed Casi was on his feet.

"No, everything's not alright. My son has been murdered and I'm under consent pressure from this Colombian scum. I'm tired of it!"

The room went deathly silent as he spoke. "Is this what I get for trying to keep control of my country? This is not how it's going to be, not while I'm alive and President. I will not let any other country control us. All your talks are about giving up, I will never give up!" Casi said, slamming his fist on the table. "This meeting is over, Neville, we need to talk in my office now," he said, storming out the room.

~ ~ ~

Casi sat at his desk, looking intently into Neville's eyes. Neville was a short thin man who had an ever-growing bald spot at the top of his head. He wore plaid wool pants with a striped shirt and scuffed leather shoes that screamed neglect.

Casi had know this man for over twenty years and knew he was as loyal as they came. So he was confident that the conversation that they were having would never go outside the thin walls of his office. "Are you telling me this man will handle this situation with the utmost efficiency and discretion?" asked Casi.

"Yes sir, he will ask no more than he needs to know. His only concern is his fee, from what I'm told. And..." Neville hesitated a second, "if you would require some extra suffering, I'm informed he is our guy," said Neville.

"What to do you mean extra suffering, what can be worse than death?" asked Casi.

"Sir," Neville started in a hushed voice, "he practices

the arts of the Black Magic, the Voodoo."

Casi didn't break eye contact, but mentally he was somewhere else. He had always known about the rituals his countrymen were partaking in, but he had always turned a blind eye to it because it was not a subject he liked to discuss. He took a few moments to think about what Neville said then spoke, "Yes, yes, that will do nicely. Call this man and set it up, I want it done as soon as possible. Let me know of any progress."

Neville stood, and with nothing else to say, it was time to set the wheels in motion.

Back in his office Neville settled into his chair behind his desk and picked up the phone. Dialing the number, he waited for the voice mail to pick up. When it did he left a message, "Call me."

# Forty • six

**The next morning Monica,** the medical examiner, walked through the door to her office, sipping on a cup of Starbucks' finest latté, after getting only one hour's rest. She was thankful for the jolt the caffeine gave her. The night before had proven to test her body's endurance and mental resolve.

After doing her initial examination and filling out the preliminary reports of the carnage at the house on South Rivers, it was already five in the morning, so the thought of any sleep was strictly out of the question. The best she could do was go home, take a shower, change clothes and head back to the office. She was hoping the local Starbucks had something strong enough to wake her body up. *So far so good,* she thought, making her way into the examination room.

She sat her purse down and took another healthy gulp from the steaming cup. She reached for the phone receiver on her desk and dialed the police department. Finding out that Trump hadn't made it in yet, she left a message to call her when he arrived.

Monica was what some called a working stiff - her life was death and she took pride in her work. Being on the job for twenty years she had become immune to people's total disregard for human life. She had seen gunshot wounds, burn victims, poisoning, stabbings, any and every way a human could and would come up with to kill another one. The scope of her job was to decide what the actual cause of death was and how the person had died. It wasn't her usual to try and figure out the why's - it was her job to figure how. Performing autopsies was not a normal procedure for all those who died. It was a tool to determine specific means and causes of death in murder cases or cases that were suspected to have some form of foul play.

Her job was to help the homicide department obtain enough information and evidence to solve cases. But within the last couple days she found herself asking Why.

A few days ago she had received the mutilated body of a victim.

After performing her duties and logging her report, she thought she could just move to the next case, but to her surprise she couldn't let go of the image of the man with his internal organs on display. For some reason or other it haunted her. The image made her feel uncomfortable, trying with no success to pass it off as a lack of sleep.

She washed her hands, took another sip of her coffee, and began going through the mental checklist of the procedures she was going to perform. Already in her blue scrubs, she pulled on some booties, a disposable apron, two layers of latex gloves and finished off her ensemble with a mask and face shield.

Monica walked over to the first examination table and hit the switch on the overhead lamp that descended from the ceiling. The strong fluorescent light revealed the cadaver of the young woman from the night before. She had already been prepped and drained by her assistant who was interning from the nearby university, so all that was left for her to perform was the autopsy.

She reached out to an instrument tray off to the left of where she stood, taking off the blue napkin that covered the finely polished and sterile utensils. On the tray was her tape recorder, which she picked up and started her examination. "Monica Thomas, I.D. number, seven, six, two. The date is March eighteenth, time is 7:12 a.m. Autopsy examination of suspected murder victim," she said, speaking clearly into the recorder. "Dark skinned black female is identified as a Renae Tasha Harris. Date of birth, February 12, 1985, making her twenty four years old. Weight is one hundred and thirty pounds, with the height being sixty-eight inches, which is five feet six inches. Body development is muscular, with the body being cool and rigid at this time. Body temperature is cool, at room temperature which is sixty-five degrees Fahrenheit. The body nutrition level seems adequate. Bruising is noted on front of both thighs as well as chest and stomach area, likely due to livor mortis."

"Now starting full external exam, at the head: hair is shoulder length, permed, black; eyes are dark brown with pupils dilated at two centimeters; there are no signs of petechial hemorrhaging. The nose is broken, caused by force trauma indicated by a purple box-like bruise on the left side of the face. Both lips are split down the left side, also likely the result of the blunt force trauma. Upper set of teeth are natural with the left incisor and inner premolar teeth missing. Bottom set are natural with all teeth intact. Overall oral cavity shows signs of scarring with lacerations to left cheek and tongue. Besides the entry and exit wounds through the brain, no other lumps or deformities are present."

"The neck is symmetrical, with no lumps, deformities or signs of trauma. The chest region appears to be normal, nothing unusual noted. The abdominal region shows signs of swelling and no bulges are noted. The pelvic region shows signs of trauma, likely due to forced entry to the vagina. Bruising is noted on outer labia."

"Inspection of shoulders and arms are consistent with other injuries noted, showing force and body manipulation. Fingernails are short, clear, with minimal to no debris underneath. Thighs show brownish yellow bruising as noted earlier due to livor mortis. Lower legs show no sign of trauma, feet flat with bunions. Toe nails are short and healthy with no debris underneath. External exam is now complete. Move on to determine cause of death."

"Suspect cause of death, rupture of frontal lobe by projectile from a firearm. Wound appears to be a close contact wound, displaying burnt skin and tattooing around entrance,"

She paused as she pulled out a ruler and measured the size of the hole and distance from the right eyebrow. "Entry wound is 4 centimeters across and approximately eight centimeters above the right eyebrow. Suspected small or medium caliber, high velocity bullet, assumption of hollow point is still undetermined. Exit wound is approximately nine centimeters wide, located at the base of the skull Bullet trajectory appears to be a downward angle, specific degrees is undetermined."

She put the ruler back on the tray and continued her process.

~ ~ ~

As she droned on, she finished all three autopsies in the next few hours. The time had flown by to the extent that she forgot her body was tired. Once she began cleaning herself up, Trump walked in. "Hey Monica, I got your message."

She turned around from the sink while soaping her hands, a bit startled. Trump noticed her reaction, saying, "Your secretary let me in."

Monica turned the water off after rinsing, then grabbed a few paper towels from the dispenser. She made a mock gesture of looking at her watch, saying, "That was four hours ago, why didn't you just call?"

"I wanted to see what you found in person, plus I needed an excuse to get away anyway. The Captain has the department in the meat grinder because the Mayor had him for breakfast this morning. He wants this case cracked, yesterday."

Monica took off her apron, revealing her shapely frame, proving long hours at in the gym do a body good. She headed for her desk where she had set down her clipboard of notes and tape recorder. "Well, so far I have basically concluded these three were killed by gunshot wounds around eight to ten p.m. last night. There wasn't any specific pattern I could see other than they were all killed in the same house."

Trump stood in front of her as she talked, staring at her face and gazing into her eyes, trying to keep his mind off sex. He couldn't help noticing the contours of her body and the way her hair fell delicately over her shoulders, making her look amazing.

When she looked up from her notes she saw the look in his eyes and noticed that she had an all too familiar feeling of her own. Not knowing what else to do, she broke eye contact by sitting in her chair and turning toward her computer screen.

She tapped the spacebar, killing the screen saver. Trying to refocus on the subject at hand and not the past, she said, "But, what I did find was that the other body from the day before, the one cut open was not the first of its kind." As she punched keys, she could feel the heat of Trump's body at her back as he moved closer and bent down to look at the computer screen.

"What do you mean? Are you saying someone has done this before?" he asked, surprised.

"You got it. And you're going to love this," she continued as pictures of two similar victims popped up on the monitor. "They weren't done in this country. These two winners were found on a Colombian freighter docked in Port au Prince."

"Haiti?" Trump asked."

"The one and only."

"I don't understand, are you saying these two are related to the one I got the other day?" he asked, confusedly.

"I don't know, but they all have the same M.O. The same cuts, same wounds, same pattern. It's known as the Haitian Crucifixion."

"But you said these two were on a Colombian freighter, right? What the hell is going on? What the hell is a Colombian ship doing docked in Haiti?"

"I don't know, but it's your job to find out, Detective."

"Hmm, they look the same, but they couldn't be done by the same person, could they?"

"If it's not the same person, then we got two different Einsteins trying to recreate the same wheel, from the looks of it. I wouldn't know for sure unless I examine the other two, but from what you see here," pointing to the screen, "they are strangely similar."

"How the hell did you find those two?" Trump asked about the pictures on the screen.

"Well, during my examination, I started to think the act was too grotesque to be a first timer. You know what I mean? So I entered the wounds and the way the victim was cut open into the FBI's VICAP - Violent Criminal Apprehension Profile - just like they were coordinates and voila, the search engine shot back theses photos with a brief history. That's how I know what it's called. Apparently it's quite legendary in the Caribbean."

"Shit, this doesn't look good. The way I understand it is that the people who stayed in that house on Summer were Haitians." he said to her.

"Are you sure?"

"As sure as I can be right now. This is not good," was all Trump could say. It was bad enough he had bodies stacking up like building blocks, but now he had a possible Colombian and Haitian war going on in Charleston. This was just to much to take right now. Carved-up bodies, execution style murders, maybe it was time to retire after all, he thought. He questioned whether or not he wanted to continue in this line of work. Time was definitely taking its toll. Definitely.

# Forty • seven

**General Gonzalez was in his** office on the phone with the man in charge of one of his cocaine manufacturing plants. "How could you let this happen Pablo? It is your duty to make sure the raiders don't get anywhere close to my operation."

"Sir, they had a man on the inside this time, and it wasn't the usual fire bombing. The traitor placed a bomb inside the facility with a timer," said Pablo in his defense.

"Have you identified this... traitor?"

In the thick country of Calamar and Mira-Flores was where this particular problem had occurred. This was just one of the hundreds of Gonzalez's facilities throughout the country. While he was perched in Envigado, close to Medellin, Gonzalez ran his operation through people like Pablo - promising death if his demands weren't met. He tried to stay away from his facilities as he could, because of the threat of assassination. The revolutionary Armed Forces of Colombia - also known by their Spanish acronym FARC - had maintained a tight security net around him and his operations, but they too could be corrupted and turned against him. The rebels in his country would love nothing better than plant his head on a stake. Gonzalez felt he had fought too hard to gain control of the cocaine distribution system he had. Sending his product through the Caribbean was tough, so he began to use the untamed Pacific Coastline, all the way to the Gulf of Mexico. He maintained shipping for the constant demand for the product. Even though his operations produced tons of the white powder, any mishap was unacceptable to him. Because most of his manufacturing was in the middle of the fields to keep production high, it made them easy targets for the rebels. The rebels found that their locations gave them easy access to destroy factories and then easily blend back into the countryside and small villages. The factories were usually protected by heavily armed guards, but this did not deter the attacks.

Domingo stuck his head into the room, hearing Gonzalez's question. Seeing his face at the door, his brother waved him in.

"Yes sir, the man apprehended him after one of the women identified him as the one who placed an old looking box by the ether barrels."

Domingo stepped in and took a seat in the Victorian-style chair in front of his brother's desk. "We will take care of this traitor and any family he has will also be identified and taken care of," continued Pablo.

"No, no, that won't be necessary, send him to me, I will deal with him myself," said Gonzalez.

"Yes sir, but what of the family?"

"Do as you intended, and do not delay on the reconstruction of my facility. That is the second one in three months, Pablo. Maybe I should be a questioning your abilities to protect my interests. Do you need a replacement?"

"No sir, I will work most expeditiously and I shall not have any more bad news to report."

Pablo knew the implied threat given by Gonzalez. His replacement would be on the account of his untimely death. He now had to work harder to identify any more traitors before it was too late.

"Very well. I will be expecting the traitor within the hour," Gonzalez said before hanging up the phone.

"More bad news in the country, brother?"

"Another facility was destroyed, and Pablo says it was an inside job. A worker planted a bomb by the ether drums. It seems Pablo has become less effective in keeping production up than I originally thought."

With a wave of his hand he switched subjects. "Did all go well in America?" he said as he was reaching into his humidor and retrieving a fresh cigar.

"It seems Soltan has evaded us again," said Domingo.

"How so?"

"I think he's getting inside information from somewhere or he's one lucky son-of–a–bitch," said Domingo.

"I don't understand."

"When in America, we only got a few members of his crew. We could not obtain the whereabouts of him or B.B."

"That's because he's in Chicago. I believed we could catch him before he left, but no matter. Go to Chicago and help Rico with his mission. Report to me only when Soltan is dead," Gonzalez said aggressively.

"One more thing," said Domingo.

"What."

"I think I've located your daughter," Domingo said hesitantly.

"Where?"

"I believe she was at the target's location. I have a

video from a party that she attended."

"A video? Why is she connected with Soltan? If you have located my daughter then why haven't you brought her to me?" asked Gonzalez.

Domingo thought for moment - he didn't want to put his own neck on the chopping block, so he had to play this one smooth. "We are in the process of apprehending her now."

"Then you haven't located her, have you?"

"I will bring her to you as soon as we have her," Domingo stated carefully.

"Very well, I expect a progress report soon."

"Here's the video..." Domingo squeezed out, taking the tape out of his pocket and setting it on the desk.

Without another word Domingo stood and walked out the door with a sense of urgency.

Gonzalez turned in his chair, picked up the tape and put it in the VCR. Silently he looked at the TV as he watched all types of debauchery going on. When the tape finished he turned it off and thought about his daughter. She was so much like him - stubborn, arrogant, and conniving. He thought he was a good father to her. Giving her anything and everything she ever wanted. But her mother's independent gene always reared its ugly head. Like her mother, she would have to learn that independence from him was not an option. If you weren't with him, you were against him. It was that simple, daughter or not.

# Forty•eight

**Soltan and B.B. had been** watching their target for two days now and from what Soltan saw, this was going to be very easy. He was careful not to let the target know he was being tracked, but his gut told him that Rico was there tracking him and B.B. He and B.B. had split up a couple of times but had remained in contact using hand held radio receivers that came with ear pieces to remain inconspicuous. Jedi's men were shadowing their every move, but had yet to spot Rico. Soltan didn't expect Rico to be detected so easily anyway - he was always good at staying hidden until he was ready to strike. On the other hand, the boy was a predictable as the second hand on a clock. He showed up for work at seven in the morning, took his lunch break at eleven thirty, walking down to Rose Cafe, always sitting in the window seat while he ate. He always left work for the day at five on the dot and headed for home. At least that's what they thought, because as far as Soltan was concern, he was ready to pick the boy up.

~ ~ ~

Lauren had seen the guns and other equipment but still hadn't said anything about it. She was acting like being around the stuff was just as normal as having the TV in the room. Soltan was waiting on the questions from her, but they still didn't come, making him curious.

In the shower now, they bathed each other. As Soltan ran a soapy washcloth across her breast he made a point to tease the nipple. Lauren just held onto Soltan's shoulders as he continued to clean her body. When he picked up her left leg, he washed it all the down to the foot. Then he repeated the same routine for the other one. When he finished with that foot, he brought the cloth up to her pleasure spot, still holding her leg in the air. As he gently rubbed her private area, Lauren let out a soft moan, throwing her head back in the spray of water, wetting her hair and letting the water cascade the front of her body across her breasts to her core. Soltan took his time and was careful not to let her orgasm as he massaged her sweetness.

Soltan meticulously bathed this fine specimen of a woman knowing he was manipulating her and didn't care. His father had taught him how to turn his flings on and off, saying to him, *On the battlefield, you have no feelings, the only thing you have is your will to survive.* And to him this was a battle he was fighting. In his war he only wanted to do one thing - win.

After drying off, they both kept their towels wrapped around themselves at the waist. Soltan admired this woman as he watched her pad around the suite topless, showing she was comfortable with herself in front of him. He made up his mind early that morning they would be going after the boy tomorrow. Knowing Lauren was a major piece of the puzzle to get the boy, he felt now was the time to let her in on the plan. He sat down on the bed, pulling her by the hand so she sat down next to him. He noticed the glow she had and the smile on her face and realized that she had definitely fallen for him.

"You remember I told you I wanted you to meet someone?" he asked, measuring his words.

"Yeah," said Lauren as she gazed into his eyes.

"You're meeting him tomorrow, so we're going shopping today. There are some things you're going to need. The man I want you to meet is actually a friend of a friend. I need you to talk him into going somewhere with you," he said, watching for her expression to change as what he said sunk in. Not getting any kind of noticeable response, he tried again. "I want you to talk to him, gain his confidence and bring him to a certain spot and I'll take it from there."

At that moment recognition hit her eyes, and then she asked comically, "Are you asking me to help you kidnap someone?"

"Yes," he said stone-faced.

"Are you serious?" she said, her face now frowning.

"Yes," he repeated with the same expression. "Calm down."

Lauren's eyes went wide, then she closed them and shook her head as if she was trying to shake the thought loose. She snatched her hand back, then put both of them to her head while she shook it. When she opened her eyes she was different.

"What the fuck did you just say to me, nigga?" She said, standing up. "Calm down? Nigga, you want me to help you kidnap somebody, and you want me to calm down! What the fuck is wrong with you," she said, dropping her eyes to floor, "What the fuck is wrong with me? I'm so stupid! I knew deep down something wasn't right, I knew it!"

She was pacing the room now as Soltan watched carefully. She said, "Ok nigga, entertain me, what did this person do, he owe you money?"

"No."

"Fuck your wife?"

"No."

"Steal something from you?"

"No."

"Humor me then, what the fuck you kidnapping him for then?" Lauren asked, clearly angry.

"I can't explain it to you, but it is going to happen with or without you," he stated flatly.

"So what the fuck is this, why you asking me this shit? Is that why you been seducing me and fucking this pussy so good, to make me do your dirty work? Is that what the truck and condo is for? Oh my god," she said as she stepped in the middle of the floor, putting her hands to her mouth. "You planned this whole thing didn't you? You've been planning this shit the whole time," she said with tears in her eyes. *What have I gotten myself into?* She wondered to herself.

She stumbled backward a bit, then decided to sit down on the chaise lounge across the room. Soltan waited, and watched as she began to shake as she bawled, then she stopped suddenly and wiped her face dry with her hands. When she looked up at him she was serious again, no fear in her eyes. "So what is your plan if I refuse?" she asked, looking straight at him.

Soltan returned the stare, saying nothing. She was nearly yelling now. "Oh my god, you'll kill me won't you? That's the benefit of bringing me here, no one knows I'm here, do they?" she said, half talking to him and half to herself.

Soltan was very impressed as this woman put the pieces of the puzzle together right in front of him. He saw a hint of fear for a moment and just as quickly as it appeared, the hardness took hold of her again as she spoke. "Nigga, you better say something over there, what the fuck is wrong with you?"

*Finally,* he thought. He had to give her credit - she possessed exactly what it took to do this type of job.

It took an hour for him to run things down to her, but he made sure she understood everything she needed to know. He left out the fact he was at war with a Colombian cartel and that they were probably waiting on him to make his move on the boy. But when he had finished, he was almost sure if and when she cooperated he was going to have to kill her. He didn't like it, but she was too volatile, she had given him a chill or two while she went through her emotional roller coaster. He had lied to her when he told her she wasn't in any danger from him or anyone else. But the look she gave let him know she knew the truth.

"Can we go shopping now?" he asked as if nothing happened.

She said nothing, but got up from the lounge and removed her towel to get dressed. Soltan looked at her, almost mad with himself that he had to get rid of such a beautiful woman.

~ ~ ~

*I can't believe this shit! I let this motherfucker trick me. Who the fuck did he think he was. And which Colombians are they?* She decided that she would play ball for now. She didn't give a fuck about what he wanted her to do, if he would have just asked, she might have done it anyway. But now she felt like her life depended on it. That look in his eyes told her everything she didn't want to know. So for right now, he's got his cake, but if she could help it in any way, he damn sure wasn't gonna eat another piece.

Right now they were by themselves in the boutique, but his right hand man was outside the door. He had said something to him on the cab drive over, but she could not make out what was said. Soltan sat on the little bench inside the dressing room as she dressed and undressed, trying on different clothes. He had her trying on pantsuits in different colors. But what she had on now was a skirt with a blouse, something she felt comfortable in. The skirt was with a sky blue blouse underneath. As she dressed in front of him she could see the lust in his eyes, which upset her more. "How's this one?" she asked of the outfit.

"I think that's the one, now all we have to do is find some shoes and I think we got a winner," he said.

*Yeah, we got a winner all right. I'm going to hold onto you for a while, I believe you have what it takes to be something real special. Yeah, you are going to do just fine. Just to make sure, I want to see how you do with the boy, then I'll make my final decision. No matter what, you belong to me, Lauren, me and only me.* Or so he thought.

# Forty•nine

**Trump had just gotten off** the phone with one of the techs who processed the house on Summer Ave. After receiving some info about the crime scene over the phone, he mentioned some of the details he had gotten from the M.E. The tech listened to him without interruption, letting Trump say what he wanted, and when he finished the tech did the equivalent of punching him in the gut. Because what he'd just heard had taken all the air out of him.

"You're not going to believe this," Trump said to Monica as he put the phone in its cradle.

By sitting still for so long, Monica was now feeling the effects of sleep deprivation as she came down hard from her caffeine high. "Try me," she said.

"There was a picture in the closet of one of the rooms in that house on Summer. Nobody knew what it was or represented while we were on location. It has now been identified as Baron Samedi," he said now, confused and disgusted.

"So what are you saying? Who's Baron Samedi?"

"Well according to the tech, he's the all-knowing Voodoo Haitian voodoo *Loa* of the dead."

"Voodoo? So what you're saying is... what?"

"Apparently, Haiti and Colombia are at war over who's going to control the drug trafficking in the Caribbean. So if my hunch is correct, the victim of what is called the Haitian Crucifixion and these executions are connected and their war has spilled over into our city."

"This is not good," Monica said, shaking her head.

Then Trump had an idea. If he could have someone in the area of Summer Ave identify the composite sketch of the suspect of the murder on Rivers, it was possible he might catch a break and identify his suspect. It was a long shot, but it could help him try to put another piece of the puzzle together.

# Fifty

**Soltan and Lauren had agreed** on some nice navy blue Giuseppe heels to go with the outfit and were now sitting down in Benihanas, waiting on their meal. Soltan and B.B. talked as if Lauren wasn't there, which was cool with her because she didn't want to talk to them anyway. All she could think about was how she was going to get out of this mess. She couldn't believe how stupid she was for getting herself mixed up in something like kidnapping.

This was the main reason she left her father's house, because of his machinations. Her father was very dear to her, but he was always scheming and hurting people and he had no problem whatsoever letting her know his exploits. His lifestyle wasn't the type of life she wanted to lead - she wanted a normal life. She wanted to go to college and work like the girls her age did on TV. Her father hated for her to even think of doing something so low-born. He provided a tutor for her schooling since she was little, as well as a nanny. As she got older she began to feel like she was missing out on life. Everything was being given to her on a silver platter. She was waited on hand and foot, she never got the chance to experience the only reason for living: LOVE.

What kind of life was that? Her father would not only disapprove of any of her male friends, (as if she had many), but the ones who were brave enough to try and get close would mysteriously disappear. Not to mention the fact that she liked black men. She knew if her father found out her secret he would surely kill her. Once she left her father she began to experience life. She had only recently started to enjoy her freedom and lo and behold, just when she thought she found someone she thought she could love, she realizes he is so similar to the very man she was running away from.

They finished their meal with Soltan and B.B. talking amongst themselves, then headed back to the hotel. Once there, they went to their rooms, but instead of Soltan just seeing her inside and leaving like before, he stayed with her.

To her surprise, she was not afraid in the least around him, but she found it hard not to display her anger toward him. He walked to the bathroom and seconds later she could hear him peeing in the toilet. She walked over to the bed, picked up the remote from the night stand and turned on the TV. As she was flicking channels, he came out the bathroom and sat down next to her. "Let it out, tell me why you are upset with me. It will make you feel better to get it out."

*Great, now he wants some pussy, so he gonna act like everything's normal*, she thought. "Are you serious? You can't be fuckin' serious, you've been using me, using my body this whole time and you want to know why I'm upset with you?" she asked, turning to face him, staring into his eyes.

"No, I know why you're upset, what I'm asking is for

*Triple Crown Publications presents . . .*

you to let it out."

"Ok, you want me to help you kidnap someone, so you can do Lord knows what to him, for whatever he's done to you and you don't think I should be angry? Not to mention, I think that I know too much at this point and am no longer here on my free will."

Soltan just stared at her, almost amused by the way she thought. If nothing else, she was smart. When he didn't answer she added, "Well, am I right?"

"No."

"Right, just like I figured. So what surprises you got for me? Am I going to end up on a milk carton somewhere too?" she asked, really not wanting to know the answer.

Soltan didn't know for sure the answer to that question himself so he just played it safe, "No."

"Right, I don't fuckin' believe you."

"Well, if you don't believe me, why aren't you fighting me? Why aren't you trying to leave or escape?" he said. "If you think your life's on the line, why aren't you fighting for it?"

"I don't know," she stated honestly, lowering her head as she spoke.

When she looked back up at him she said, "I'm not afraid of death, but I don't think you want to hurt me. Am I right?" she asked, hoping for the right answer.

Soltan's eyes softened when he spoke. It was slight and you had to really pay attention to see it, but he could see that she noticed. "I'm not going to hurt you Lauren. I don't want to hurt you, I never did."

He knew he had made a mistake when he spoke but he couldn't help it now. She had melted at least a little of the ice surrounding his heart. "Then why are you asking me to do this?" she asked honestly.

Soltan looked at her and made a decision. It was now

or never. If he was going to love someone or have someone truly love him, he knew it would be Lauren, so I was time to give it a shot.

He reached over her, grabbing the remote and pointing it at the TV, turning it off. He shifted his posture toward her, commanding her undivided attention. "Lauren, what I ask of you is a small task compared to what I'm doing for my people. I come from a place where poverty rules and violence is a common language. I have taken up the cross to do my part to help my people, even though I am but one man. I believe I can make a difference. I want more for my people because they have nothing and no one will give them anything without a price. So everything I accomplish, I do so for my countrymen, not for me. I come from a very strict military home run by precision. My father was a General and my mother a homemaker. I grew up in my father's military and learned discipline and honor. Because my people are a proud people we are outcasts to the world. We are so frowned upon that when we want to come to America for refuge or even opportunity to seek prosperity we are jailed for long lengths of time and sent back. The world doesn't like us because we won't let them sink their claws into our politics, our resources or our brains. I am from a people who will not be manipulated. So what I do has a greater meaning. It's not just for me, what I ask of you, it's for my country," he paused to see if she wanted to ask a question.

"So what are you saying, you're a one man crusade to help a whole country and actually think you can make a difference?" she asked.

"Yes, and yes. I have plenty of resources at my disposal and I have been making a difference. As we speak, my country's economy has skyrocketed, there is new construction going on creating thousands of jobs and my country's political system is now beginning talks with other countries such as the U.S. and Canada to open up new trade. We are exporting record amounts of sugarcane, coffee, and cocoa, giving a boost to our economy. People in my country have hope now, and renewed sense of meaning."

"But aren't you a drug dealer? How the hell does that help your people?"

"Look at America, the epitome of the decadent west. How do you think they became so powerful? They built their country with drugs, arms trading, warfare, and on the backs of slaves. They dealt with countries like Peru, Colombia and Bolivia to import their cocaine and heroin to produce revenue for their country. So are drugs bad when they help a nation grow?" he asked.

"Drugs destroy countries, they destroy people and they destroy families. Yes they're bad, drugs are the devil's candy," she said, getting angry again.

She knew all too well what drugs can accomplish, how they can destroy good people. "Then so be it. If that's what it takes for my people to get what they deserve, then I believe it's worth it in the long run. This is a war, and in war you have casualties, I'm willing to make certain sacrifices for my people."

"You keep talking about your people, who the hell are you talking about?"

"I'm from a country called Haiti, a small country on the other side of the Dominican Republic. Do you know the place?"

"Yeah, I think I'm familiar," she answered sarcastically.

"Then you should know my people struggle to survive in that triangle of no-man's land. We've used the drug trafficking trade to generate capital, but it has created a war between us and the Colombians."

Lauren looked at him - it all made sense now. She hadn't noticed it before, but now it was obvious. She could see it in his features now, he was telling the truth of who he was. "Then how did you get the name Derrick. That's not a Haitian name."

"My name is Soltan, Derrick is the name I use in America. Soltan Marsay, I'm the son of General Francois Marsay of the Haitian army."

As he spoke his father's name goose bumps formed on Lauren's skin. His father was the defining factor of why she left home. She had heard that name being talked about by her father. Hearing what her father wanted done to General Marsay was the final straw. The hatred she heard in her father's voice made staying in his house, even one more night, unthinkable. Even though she didn't know the man, the anger and hatred she heard coming from her father was something she couldn't believe a human could have for another. She realized her father was a monster, and that made her decision to leave easy.

But right now she hoped Soltan didn't see the goose bumps or the recognition of his father's name on her face or in her eyes. But at the same time, she knew that this was a man she admired, a man with a good heart, willing to sacrifice himself for another. A man she could see herself with, someone she could love. She decided that she would help him in his struggle and be committed to him.

But her fear now was of how much to tell him about herself. She didn't like the fact he was involved in such activities, but his reasons and cause seemed noble to her. Plus, any enemy of her father was a friend of hers, and maybe with a little luck she hoped to change his tactics to more conventional methods.

Watching her reaction, Soltan thought he saw a flicker of recognition flow across her face. "You know my father?"

"I have read about him," she lied, hoping he bought it, "He was a good General."

"My father was a tyrant," he said, not catching the lie. "He had no compassion or tolerance for anything but order and discipline," he retorted with a little too much emotion.

She noticed that he had not yet gotten over something when he displayed all that emotion. "Are you alright, what's wrong?" she asked soothingly.

He stared off into the center of the room, reliving the day his father died and his mother disappeared. "On May 31, 2007, my father was murdered and my mother disappeared. I came home that night and found what was left of my father's body lying in the middle of the living room floor. His head was severed and laying on his chest. His arms and legs were missing and were never located. My mother was never found either - she is also believed dead. It was believed that a band of rogue militia from our lands tortured and crucified my father because of his tyranny. But I don't believe that. Even though my father was a hard man, the people loved him. I think it was made to look like his own people did it. I'll know the truth someday."

When he finished talking, he thought to himself that this woman had definitely found his heart and took hold of it. He didn't know why he'd just told her the truth about his father, he'd never told anyone else before.

Seeing Soltan break down in front of her melted her heart. So she moved from her defensive spot on the bed and scooted over to him, grabbing hold. She embraced him against her body, arms wrapping around him as she kissed his head and rubbed his back. "I'm sorry baby, I'm so sorry," she whispered, trying her best to comfort him.

The Cartels Daughter

Soltan welcomed the warmth and the comfort she gave, and he knew this was something he'd been needing for a long time. And it felt good, like she really meant it. But no tears fell for his parents because he knew they would be avenged properly.

Sitting back up, he grabbed Lauren's hands with his and looked into her eyes as she gazed back at him. "Lauren?"

"Yes."

"You can never leave me now," he said, ice returning to his voice.

"I won't my love, I won't," she answered, putting her hand on his face and pulling him toward her, kissing him on the lips.

It was clear to her now, they were bound together by fate, but could she ever tell him the truth of who she was? Would he still accept her, or would he kill her? It wasn't her fault what her father had done, she had no control over that. If Soltan found out, she wondered, would he understand?

# Fifty • one

**Soltan was up and about,** getting everything together for the snatch and grab. It was two hours until dawn, a time when most people would still be in bed, dreaming away. This was the time he liked to operate, it was quiet and peaceful, which gave him time to think. He had already called Jedi and let him know to muster the troops. Frank arranged for a plain white van to be parked in the underground garage a block away, for them to use. Soltan had also been to B.B.'s room, finding him up and alert as usual, getting his equipment ready.

Once he went over the plan one final time with B.B. he went back to his room to wake Lauren. But when he walked through the door, he was surprised to find she was already in the shower. He thought about the fact he had actually exposed himself to her, even though he left out some key facts. The most important one being that he enjoyed killing. One thing he noticed, was when he was with her he didn't get that boiling sensation within, the urge to kill. Maybe it was because they had plenty of satisfying sex - they were definitely compatible in that area. She knew how to please him as their bodies merged, satiating his urges. They didn't have any kind of sexual contact last night, not because she wouldn't let him, rather because he didn't want to. He needed to be alert and ready for action because today was going to be very interesting. He knew Rico was close and when Rico thought the time was right, he was going to make his move. That was the one thing he could trust in that Colombian.

Finished with her shower, Lauren turned off the spray, but stood still trying to gather her thoughts. *What am I thinking? Am I really going to go through with this? Hold up, hold up. Stop flipping back and forth. It's time for me to stop running from my feelings. I love him and that's all I need to know. I think he loves me, but that doesn't matter anymore. I'm in love for the first time in my life and it feels good. I ain't letting it go for nothing. My mind is made up and I'm not going to change it. Even if what we're about to do is wrong, I'm all in.*

Lauren came out of the bathroom, having not bothered to cover herself, and she took a seat on the chaise lounge by the window. She met Soltan's eyes, but said nothing as she sat across the room naked, spreading her legs wide, exposing herself to him as she dried off.

Soltan felt an almost uncontrollable urge within to satisfy his hunger for her, but fought it the best he could.

She never took her eyes off him, and after she finished drying herself she smiled gleefully at him.

It took them an hour and a half to get ready. Soltan went over what he wanted her to do, showing her a picture of Emilio Gonzalez. He explained in great detail how he wanted her to handle the situation and then dressed her. In the process of dressing her, he wired her for sound with a two-way transmission system. It came with an earpiece that fit snugly into her ear that could not be seen without some effort.

When they were done they went to B.B.'s room and she watched as Soltan and B.B. suited up as if they were going into battle. By the time they were finished the sun was just peeking over the horizon, shedding its first rays of light on the city.

Lauren turned at a knock on the door, then watched as Soltan went to open it.

When the door opened she saw three Latino guys walk into the room. Her heart missed a beat until she realized they weren't Colombian. They were probably Puerto Rican, she guessed, because of the arched eyebrows. She hoped nobody had seen her surprise. She eyed the three men, the first being short and stocky with a bald head. The other two with him had an air about themselves as being purely dangerous. To her, the bald headed one carried himself like a ladies' man instead of hired muscle; good-smelling cologne, nice clothes, well-groomed. But she could tell at a closer look this man possessed a promise of extreme violence underneath his inviting exterior. She'd seen plenty of men like him working for her father.

"Everything good to go, Jedi?" asked Soltan as they walked in.

"Yeah, we good to go on my end. My guys are dug in pretty good, been there for about eighteen hours already. They haven't seen any kind of activity so far, but the day is young," answered Jedi.

"Come get your radios," Soltan said as he turned, letting them follow him to the bed.

When Jedi saw Lauren he immediately asked, "And who is this gift to mankind?"

"She's help," Soltan answered, not even turning around. But Jedi could tell by the tone in his voice that there was more to it than that. So he left the subject alone.

The guys couldn't help themselves, so they just stared at her, not saying anything, eyeballing her. She attracted the men's attention like moths to a flame.

Lauren was stunningly beautiful, the way her hair was done; pulled back in a tight bun, exposing her long slender neck. The skirt she wore fit her body, accenting the contours of her hips and ass. And with her long shapely legs housed in all white thigh-high stockings with tiny sky blue bows running up the seam in the back, and the strappy six-inch heels put the icing on a very nice cake.

While everyone was checking their equipment and weapons, Jedi walked over to Soltan.

"I need to talk to you privately for a minute."

Soltan looked at Jedi, seeing that he had something serious on his mind.

"Alright, give everyone a minute to finish up, then we'll talk," said Soltan.

When the group was ready to go, Soltan announced, "Everybody knows what to do and what we're dealing with, so all I'll say is thank you all for your help and be careful." Then to B.B., "Take her with you downstairs, me and Jedi will catch up."

B.B. nodded, then Lauren walked over to Soltan, grabbed his face with both hands and kissed him on the lips. Then she turned on her heel and walked out the door with B.B. right behind her.

When Jedi and Soltan were alone, Jedi spoke first.

"What the fuck was that?"

"Help," was all Soltan said as he tried to hide his emotion.

"Well, can we trust 'Help?' asked Jedi, seeing through the front.

"Yes. Now what's up, you said you wanted to talk," Soltan said, trying to change the subject.

"Yeah, listen. Remember the job you did in the Dominican Republic?"

"Yeah," Soltan said, now curious.

"Well, remember that I told you there was a leak somewhere?"

Soltan nodded.

"Well, I found it. This guy Rico was the one that gave the information to the appropriate people. They just reacted too slowly to his tip, so that's why you were able to finish the job. I just found out last night. After you told us who you thought we were dealing with, I made some calls. My source says that he's also the one who killed your family." Jedi waited on a reaction.

"What!" Soltan asked, as surprised as he'd ever been.

"My source says he's the one the contract on your mother and father went to. He was supposed to make it look like your own people did it. Whoever wanted them dead wanted them out the way for a reason. The hit came from within the government. That's what my source says. I know this is not a real good time to tell you this, but if it's really Rico out there then you have all the more reason to catch this muthafucka and give him your regards, feel me?"

Soltan stared at his friend as rage and hatred made his body temperature rise and his heart pump faster.

"Are you sure? Can your source be trusted? I need this information to be accurate, I never believed my father and mother were killed by our own people. So if what you say is true, our priority for this mission has changed. Rico is now my priority, so we use the boy as bait now, he's not to be harmed," he said to Jedi.

"Are you OK?" asked Jedi.

"Yeah, I'm cool. Thank you brother," Soltan said

extending his hand, then pulling Jedi in for a hug.

"You ready to go get this muthafucka?" asked Jedi, stepping back from him.

"If you only knew. Let people know to keep their eyes open and be careful man, this ain't a game."

"You be careful, I don't need your emotions having you make a mistake out there. I got your back as always brother, feel me?"

Making their way the catch up with the others, Soltan was deep in thought. If what Jedi said is true, and someone inside his country's government had his family killed, then his whole agenda has now changed. Now he would dedicate his time to questioning members of his government. So when this was over, his next priority was to go home. It was time he went back, and he knew the first person he needed to see. The only person he thought that could give him the kind of information he was looking for was the one and only Region.

# Fifty • two

**B.B. parked the van almost** two blocks from the entrance of the bank. Soltan checked the receiver on Lauren before she exited out the door, making sure they could communicate.

She walked confidently in the heels, hips swaying, careful not to make direct eye contact with anyone. The sidewalks were packed with men and women of today's business world, so she blended right in.

When Lauren walked into the bank, she looked up at the large clock and read seven-eighteen a.m. She walked to the front lobby desk with a purpose, getting into character.

"Welcome to the Federal Reserve Bank of Chicago, how may I help you this morning?" the receptionist said as soon as she approached the black marble desk.

"Ok gentlemen, we're in. keep your heads up and be ready, anything can happen," Soltan spoke into his radio.

Lauren could hear Soltan through her earpiece as well, and that brief moment, his voice in her ear, calmed her and motivated her at the same time. She didn't want to let him down. Then nothing but silence filled the air when he stopped talking, making her feel alone just as fast.

"Yes, my name is Daphne Davila, I'm a member of the Colombian Consulate. I'm here on official business," she said, handing over an International Diplomatic I.D.

She took a quick scan of the area and noticed an armed guard stationed right beside the desk. Another was posted by the elevator off to the right, leading down the hallway. Both the guard by the elevator and the one by the desk were intently watching her.

The receptionist scanned the I.D. while Lauren glanced at the guard.

Satisfied with the identification, the receptionist spoke, "So what can we do for you today, Ms. Davila?"

"I'm here on official business to see Mr. Emilio Gonzalez, he's not expecting me."

"One moment please."

Lauren watched as she picked up the telephone and dialed an extension.

"Yes, this is reception, I have a woman here from the Colombian Consulate requesting to see Mr. Gonzalez. Yes sir, she's here on official business. Yes sir," she said, ending the call.

"He'll be down in just a minute," she said to Lauren.

Satisfied, Lauren stepped to the side of the desk where a couple of expertly-crafted Italian leather chairs were and sat down crossing her legs, allowing the security guard to see just enough to make him avert his eyes.

Ten minutes later Emilio walked out the elevator toward the reception desk.

Lauren recognized him from the photo Soltan had shown her. His facial features were the same but up close she noticed he had an almost boyish body, short and slim with his large head looking out of proportion to his body. After a few words at the desk, he looked her way, nodded to the receptionist and approached her. Lauren was standing by the time he reached her and she could see he paid her looks no attention. He had a worried or even scared look on his face, but as he got closer there was something else. Something about him she couldn't put a finger on, but whatever it was, it was familiar.

"How are you today, Mr. Gonzalez?" she asked, extending her hand. "My name is Daphne Davila and I work for your father." She dropped the bomb immediately.

Emilio did not take her hand, but in response he said, "What is this about, Ms. Davila, is this some kind of joke? My father is dead," he said, all high-strung and uppity.

"Mr. Gonzalez, I have been sent here by your father to get you to safety, he believes you to be in danger," she said, ignoring his comments.

She figured he was too arrogant for her to be subtle, so she wanted to scare his ass into compliance.

"Danger?" he retorted, forgetting his father was supposed to be dead. "Who the hell are you?"

"My name is Daphne Dav..."

"No, no, who do you work for? Let me see some I.D." He fired off the question and demand, not letting her finish her sentence.

Lauren reached inside her briefcase, pulling her phony I.D. out and handing it over.

He took the I.D., examining the billfold closely, then looked up at her, asking, "If there is danger, why are you here alone?" He passed the I.D. back to her.

*Bingo! You believe me don't you, little man,* she thought.

"Your father wanted to get you to safety as discretely

as possible. There are men outside waiting for us in a white van, you must come with me immediately." She stated, putting urgency in her voice.

Emilio looked skeptical. She could see the cogs turning in his head as his eyes shifted and his face hardened. He looked over to the receptionist's desk, then stepped closer to her, saying, "If you are who you say, then you should know the procedure for something like this."

"Yes sir, Mr. Gonzalez, I'm aware of such a procedure," she stated confidently.

"Ok," he said, pausing for a second. "What is the meaning of life?" he asked.

Lauren couldn't believe her ears, she couldn't believe what her heart and mind were telling her. He couldn't be. His name was Gonzalez though, and that question. What the fuck was going on?

Lauren watched him brace himself for the answer. She knew if she said the wrong thing then he would immediately alert security, and she would have to do her best to get back outside to the van or be approached as an impostor. She knew that if she was caught, she would be brought up on charges and carted off to jail.

Without warning her earpiece came to life with Soltan giving her the answer. But she already knew the answer, it was drilled into her head from the time she could remember.

"Mr. Gonzalez, the meaning of life is blood, sweat and tears, sir. Now hurry, we don't have much time. You need to come with me immediately."

Recognition crawled across his face and fear flooded his eyes. He asked one final question, "Where is my mother?"

"She is being alerted as we speak, and you will be reunited with her at the safe house." She ad-libbed off the top of her head, not expecting the question.

Before she could finish her sentence, Emilio was already moving.

"Let's go," was all he said as she turned to lead him out the front door.

Once they were street side, Lauren noticed the van was directly in front of them. She led Emilio to the side door, helping him step up and in, and then closing the door behind.

The van drove off before the door was shut. Immediately sitting inside, Emilio could see he had made a mistake. He had been fooled, and probably would end up paying for it with his life.

Soltan had his gun pointed at Emilio as soon as the little man was inside, but Emilio hadn't seen it until he sat down. Too scared to say anything, Emilio looked at Lauren and wondered to himself why he believed her, and how she knew the password.

"Emilio, if you do as I ask you will not be harmed, but if you attempt to escape I will kill you. Are we clear?" asked Soltan.

Emilio looked into Soltan's eyes and knew what he said to be the truth and nodded slightly in understanding.

"Good, now turn around and put your hands behind your back."

When Emilio turned in his seat, putting his hand behind him, Soltan pulled a large zip-tie from his pocket. Grabbing both of Emilio's hands, he looped the tie around his wrists and tightened the restraints. Turning Emilio back around, Soltan put a piece of duct tape over his mouth, and a black bag over his head, repeating the procedure with the zip-tie around his neck, just loosely enough for him to breathe.

# Fifty • three

**_Rico saw the white van_** park down the street. He couldn't see in the van because the windows were tinted black, but he knew Soltan was in there. Rico had seen his men spread out and watch, knowing Soltan was going to make a move now. He'd seen the clumsy counter-surveillance team Soltan had in place, watching him, but it didn't bother him. As long as he'd known Soltan and his tactics he knew he had a place to take the boy before he made his demands, or killed him. So being patient would definitely pay off in this case. He figured he'd follow Soltan to his destination, then wait for him to settle in and give him the surprise of his life.

~ ~ ~

Finishing with Emilio, Soltan looked over at Lauren for the first time since she got back into the van. He noticed the look in her eyes, and he couldn't understand or believe what he was seeing. The look she was giving him was so feral and distracting he had to break eye contact just to concentrate on what he was doing. Picking up his radio he spoke to the team.

"Package received, and being delivered. Is everyone clear?"

Soltan listened as everyone checked in. He waited to hear from someone letting him know Rico had shown himself and was moving, but to his surprise, no one reported anything unusual.

Looking back over at Lauren, he noticed her condition hadn't changed.

"Are you alright?" he asked her.

She cracked a smile before licking her lips as if she had something tasty on them.

"Soltan, he's here," said B.B.

"Where?" Soltan asked, snapping out of the trance Lauren had him in.

"Two vehicles back, he's behind the shadow."

Soltan picked up his radio, "Jedi, our shadow has grown a tail, you copy?"

"Yeah, we see it. It's happening just like you planned. We showed him sloppy surveillance and drew him out, keeping our real team invisible. What do you want us to do? You want us to clip the tail?" asked Jedi.

"No, don't make a move unless they do. Let them follow, then find out where they set up. Then we'll make our move," Soltan spoke into the radio.

"B.B., you know what to do," Soltan said to the front of the van.

"We'll be there in two minutes, let Frank know to be ready," B.B. said over his shoulder.

~ ~ ~

Rico and his driver watched the van trying to figure out why they had stopped. It wasn't an ideal area for an ambush, so that option was out. He didn't even think Soltan had seen him, so it couldn't be a set-up. Then out of nowhere, the shadow vehicle pulled up to the driver's door of the van. Rico didn't understand what was going on, but he knew this wasn't the place where they were taking the boy because no one go out of the van.

~ ~ ~

In exactly two minutes they were parked in front of the city's old water treatment plant. The place had been empty for the last eight years. The city water works signs were still in place, but the windows were boarded up and the doors chained.

Inside the van, Soltan pulled the carpet off the floor, revealing a hatch. He pulled the hatch open, showing they were stopped directly over a manhole cover.

B.B. parked the van just right, using a pre-drawn mark to line up the two holes. He then jumped in the back with everyone else, waiting on the signal.

"We're good, green light, green light," Soltan said into his radio.

Seconds later, the shadow vehicle pulled up alongside the van, with Junior hopping out. Then the driver's door opened and Junior climbed behind the wheel of the van. The shadow vehicle's main purpose was to shield the van, preventing anyone from seeing what happened next. "All set," said Junior.

Soltan gave a slight nod, looked at B.B. and Lauren, then said, "Open, sesame," into the radio.

At the signal, the manhole cover popped up and moved to the side, showing a ladder inside.

"Muevete, papa," one of Jedi's men said from inside the hole.

B.B. moved first, climbing down the ladder halfway and then stopping. Soltan grabbed Emilio, moving him toward the hole, saying, "There's a hole in the floor and then a ladder. Use your feet to find the steps, and someone is going to help you all the way down. Do you understand?"

Emilio gave a nod and a grunt as Soltan postured him

to descend into the hole. B.B. helped secure his footing, then guided him down into the tunnel. Once he had Emilio inside, Soltan turned to Lauren saying, "Let's go, I'm coming down right behind you."

She still had that look in her eye, but said nothing as she climbed down into the hole and down the ladder.

Soltan turned to Junior and said, "You know what to do," and then followed Lauren, letting the hatch down inside the van and replacing the manhole cover.

At the bottom of the ladder Soltan turned around to find Lauren face to face with him. The others must have already started walking down the tunnel. Without warning, she grabbed his head with one hand and began to kiss him deeply, while her other hand worked to unbuckle his belt.

Soltan felt the passion in her kiss immediately, causing his own to ignite.

With total disregard to their surroundings, Soltan allowed her to pull his pants down, freeing him. He reached down, pulled her skirt up and her panties to the side, and guided himself inside her. She was so wet and hot inside that all he was concerned about at this point was what she was offering.

Pleasure.

Lauren lifted her left leg, placing it around Soltan's waist as he moved in and out of her. Soltan's strokes were fast and strong as he rushed toward a climax. His right hand found her leg, gripping her thigh and pulling her toward him as if he were trying to merge their bodies.

The air around them was electric, and laced with an animalistic instinct of need and survival. Soltan gave two more hard thrusts that brought a low guttural growl from him and a soft whimper from her. He stopped, looked directly into her eyes while she did the same.

Then pulled himself free and grabbed her by the shoulders, spinning her around.

With Lauren facing the wall now, he reinserted himself in from behind with one hard upward thrust. He was so forceful that she had to throw her hands against the wall to brace herself.

Soltan continued with the deep thrusting as he grabbed her around the throat with his right arm, putting her into a choke hold. Using his left hand he reached around the front of her, finding her clit, and using his index finger he began driving her wild. She didn't protest any of his actions - her only response was to lean into him and move her body in rhythm to his thrusts.

Ten minutes later they both exploded in orgasm, with Soltan pushing himself in her as far as he could go as his body jerked in release.

Soltan could feel Lauren squeezing him as her vagina pulsated around his penis. They were both breathing heavily as he pulled himself free and began pulling his pants up, getting himself together.

Lauren turned around, smoothing her skirt down with her hands and trying to dust off some of the dirt and dust. She never took her eyes off of Soltan, and when he caught her stare he stepped closer to her and kissed her deeply. The kiss took away what little breath she had left. He stepped back, grabbed her hand and said, "Let's go."

They followed the tunnel to the old abandoned control warehouse just two blocks south of the decoy van's destination. The tunnel was part of a grid underneath the city's water treatment plant used for quick repair purposes. Jedi received the plans from one of Frank's contacts and devised the plan accordingly. The tunnel was warm and humid, with cobwebs hanging from the walls and light fixtures. The ground was concrete like the rest, but was covered with layers of dirt, gravel and dust, giving the tunnel the smell of an old rail car made of wood and steel. The tunnel provided the inconspicuous route Soltan wanted, knowing no one had been inside it for years. When they came out of the underground passageway into the warehouse, Frank was there with a group of men. Frank helped pull Emilio up the ladder, sitting him on a chair in the middle of the structure.

B.B., Lauren and Soltan followed.

"Sit right here and don't move papa, comprende?" Frank said, then turned to Soltan. "You ready for some action, my brother?" Then he looked over at Lauren who was standing beside him.

Frank noticed the flushed look in Lauren's cheeks, but couldn't decide if the reason was what he thought it could be, or if she was just excited. Making his mind up, he smiled, then focused back on Soltan.

"Well, well, somebody's already shot their gun."

Soltan gave a slight grin, but didn't attempt to look at Lauren, not wanting to confirm any suspicions.

B.B. stared, not really caring, but knowing something had happened, because Lauren and Soltan had fallen behind in the tunnel. It didn't concern him at all that much because she would be dead soon. Soltan was just playing with his food, so it didn't matter what he did with her at this point.

Soltan looked around, seeing Frank had brought a few guys with him. He thought, *good thinking*.

"How many are at the decoy site?" Soltan asked.

"There's five inside, two in the back and three out front. I also got one on the roof across the street with a 308 sniper rifle on a tripod, ready to give out new breathing holes."

"Are they good?"

"Some of the best Uncle Sam has ever employed," Frank said arrogantly.

"I hope so, because if I know Rico, he brought the best trained men with him too," Soltan said, matter-of-factly.

Frank got on his radio and began telling his men it was show time. The bait had been cast, now it was time to see if they could get a bite.

~ ~ ~

Rico watched as the van drove into the underground parking area of a building that was still under construction.

"Slow down, let's see where the van parks," he said to his driver.

"All posts be advised, once the van parks, surround it and capture Soltan, but proceed with caution," Rico said to his men who were riding in two other cars ahead of him, running alternating tails on the van.

# Fifty•four

**When Frank turned the corner** he could see the van was parked in the location they had planned. The Coalition's men were spread out in the underground garage of the building, waiting on the action. They were professionals at digging in any environment, so you would be hard pressed to find them if you weren't looking for them. "This is Falcon one, a car with three occupants just passed me going inside," one of the three men at the front entrance alerted.

A few seconds later one of the men at the back entrance signaled, "This is Bravo three, I have a vehicle carrying two coming in the rear."

Frank stayed where he was, at the newsstand across the street, as he watched the second vehicle pull around back. When the car disappeared out of sight Frank went on the move. He jogged across the street and around back, spotting the car just before it disappeared again into the parking area.

"Zeus, do you have a visual?" asked Frank.

"Yeah, I got three bad little piggies closing fast," the

sniper on the roof responded.

"Good, wait for my signal."

"Roger that."

"Jedi, what's your location?" Frank asked.

"I'm in the northeast corner, looking at three future cold cases."

"Ok, good. Wait for my signal."

"Roger that."

Frank pulled his weapon out and went back to his secure location, hoping that Soltan was right. If Rico was as smart as he said he was, then this whole fiasco should go off without a hitch.

~ ~ ~

Rico watched the first car go inside the building through the front and decided it would be better for him to bring up the rear. He used this as an opportunity to see if anyone else was behind the building also. The building was still under construction, with walls missing, plastic tarps hanging over exposed iron beams, and half-filled insulation panels. This made anyone able to see through most of the building, and that in and of itself disturbed Rico. He didn't understand why Soltan would kidnap the boy and then bring him to an open area that anyone who wanted to look could see what he was doing. That didn't make sense to him, so he decided to hang back and see what was really going on.

~ ~ ~

Junior sat in the driver's seat, listening intently to the transmissions as everyone alerted each other to the activity going on around him. He kept shifting his eyes from the side mirror on his left back to the one on the right. While his head moved from side to side, his hands stayed gripping the gun resting in his lap. Using all his senses, trying to anticipate what would happen next, he was amping himself up and mentally preparing for the battle. Suddenly, out of the corner of his eye he saw movement. Snapping his head to the left, he watched the mirror and saw two armed men approaching.

~ ~ ~

Zeus saw three men approaching the van at such a fast pace he didn't have time to warn Junior. Instead, he did the next best thing - he took aim and began to fire.

# Fifty • five

**Domingo had talked to Rico** as soon as he arrived in Chicago last night. They talked about what he'd seen on the tape before they met up with each other. Once he'd heard what was on the tape, Rico devised another part of his plan, which was to get rid of his brother's main distraction once and for all. Domingo didn't care one way or another about it, so he agreed.

Right now he was sitting back watching. He'd seen the van stop and then drive off again, but he was curious as to why they had stopped. He was still pondering that as he sat back and watched his men join Rico's as they converged on the van.

~ ~ ~

Soltan was pacing back and forth, not really paying attention to his surroundings. He was too busy trapped in his own thoughts. Something about this whole ordeal wasn't right, he felt it in his gut.

He walked over to where Emilio was seated and stood in front of him. Three of the men were posted inside the warehouse with him, one at each doorway, front and back, with the other one standing right next to the manhole he'd had used to get there.

Lauren was tucked off in a nearby control booth where she couldn't be seen. She didn't like what Soltan had planned, but trusted him to know what he was doing. So she remained still and quiet.

Soltan wanted to take a closer look at Emilio, so he removed the hood covering his face. Once he began removing it, his hand brushed against Emilio's skin. At that moment he had a vision. It showed him being shot as he stood talking to Rico.

He went down clutching at his chest as Rico laughed in triumph. Snatching his hand away from Emilio, Soltan looked away, startled.

He scanned the room, looking at faces, his only thought being, *this is it.* Tossing the hood on the ground, he turned to the man. "It's time, go to your positions. No one makes a move until I give the signal. Do you understand?"

"Don't worry Soltan, you're in good hands."

Then they all went to their positions, leaving Soltan alone with the boy in the center of the room.

*Triple Crown Publications presents . . .*

# Fifty • six

***The first bullet made the guy*** closest to the door's head explode. Not thinking about his own safety, Junior stepped out, firing his gun, hitting another as he himself took a bullet in the leg. With so much adrenaline coursing through his veins, Junior didn't even flinch. He kept firing at his target as bullets flew by him, hitting the van, putting holes in the sheet metal and shattering glass. He turned around, looking for another target as he popped a full clip into his gun. As he looked for an escape he realized he was surrounded. Dropping down behind the wheel of the van gave him the necessary shield he needed for the moment. "Shit, these motherfuckers is like roaches."

He could hear footsteps coming toward him slowly. He wanted to get the radio and find out where the help was, when all of the sudden gunfire erupted again. But this time he was welcoming that scary sound, these were his guys, and they were shooting their guns with purpose. Taking a look under the van he could see the Coalition was driving the enemy back. "Yeah! That's what the fuck I'm talking about!" he shouted. Then, when he tried to stand up and join the party he finally realized had been shot.

Looking at his wound, he thought to himself, *Fuck it,* and stood up anyway, despite the pain.

Leaning over the hood of the van, Junior squeezed off multiple rounds, taking careful aim. Rico's men were well trained, and even though two of them lay dead at his feet they weren't all that easily killed. They had to have on some kind of body armor. He was sure he had seen a few of them get hit. So now he was aiming at parts that couldn't be protected: arms, legs, neck.

Taking careful aim, he began to see promise. Instead of them backing up, Rico's men were dropping. He yelled out, "They have on armor, shoot the soft spots!"

As Rico's men were being driven back to cower behind whatever would give them cover, Frank took advantage of the fact that he was behind them. It took Rico's men too long to realize they were in a cross fire as Frank's men picked them off one by one.

When the firefight began to slow, Frank ducked out of the fire. He was waiting to take a survey of the situation and check with his men to find out the casualties. He hoped Soltan's plan worked because it if didn't, lives were being put up for grabs for no reason.

~ ~ ~

Domingo sat still, the wheels inside his head turning fast. Pieces of this puzzle didn't fit the way they were supposed to. He listened to the gunfire and knew his men had run into something unexpected, because it would be impossible for Soltan by himself to put up that much of a fight. He fought the urge he had to get out and join the battle. He hadn't seen Rico, or anyone for that matter, come out of the structure.

He looked up at the building across the street and

saw muzzle flashes, and then a shimmer of light, some kind of reflection out the corner of his eye. *Sniper.*

Reaching down into the seat, Domingo grabbed his binoculars and focused on the area where he'd seen the reflection. Scanning the area, he located the source, a man on his belly using a sniper rifle, taking shots at Domingo's men from the rooftop. Fury filled his veins with red hot lava.

Jumping out of his vehicle, Domingo trotted across the street and behind the building. As he made his way up to the roof, he could hear the silenced fire of the rifle get closer and closer. He moved as quiet as a cat, making no sound as he stalked his prey. He could clearly see the sniper facing away from him, training his scope on another one target. Pulling out his weapon, Domingo took aim and put two bullets in the back of the sniper's head from about forty yards away. Being an expert marksman made the shot unfair to the victim – but no less fair than the sniper was being to Domingo's men.

Walking over to the body, Domingo kicked the lifeless mass to the side and picked up the rifle. It pissed him off that there were blood and brain fragments all over it. One of the bullets went straight through, spraying the immediate area with tissue and gore. Now using the sight, Domingo searched the building across the street to see who would be next. As he scanned the garage area, he saw a few of his men down, probably dead, but he also saw the enemy. Taking aim, he leveled the crosshairs at the man's head who was firing his weapon as he leaned across the hood of a van.

Domingo exhaled like he was taught, then squeezed the trigger. The man's head exploded like a water balloon. Domingo swung the rifle into another direction, looking for another target, found one and repeated the process.

~ ~ ~

Backing out of the alley, Rico told his driver to speed it up. "Are you sure Soltan's not in the van?" asked Rico, using his radio and talking to one of his men in the garage.

"Sir there was only one person in the van, no one else. I'm standing right here now," came the voice through the speaker.

To his driver he said, "Go back to the place where the van stopped."

"Yes sir."

~ ~ ~

"Rico's leaving, I think he's figured it out. Let's go. I can hear sirens coming, we need to get ghost yo!" Frank said to Jedi over the radio.

"Everybody out! Get back to the spot!" Jedi yelled back.

Without hesitation, Frank got on the radio, "We got what we came for, everybody out, get out. Regroup at the rendezvous point. I repeat, get out, we're done here!"

~ ~ ~

Domingo heard the radio come to life with someone giving the command to get out. He realized immediately what his gut had been trying to tell him - it was a setup. This whole circus was staged. But what did they want? What had they come for? There was nothing here in the building ...

Unless it was a person. Yeah, that was it. Soltan knew they were being followed, didn't he? Soltan played his hand just right. He let Rico come straight to him, and Rico should have known better.

Domingo dropped the rifle and took off at a full sprint across the roof. He needed to make it back down to the alley to see if what he thought was right. He had never

seen Soltan come, but he was sure he was here somewhere. He gave Soltan a lot of credit - he had set a very
effective trap.

Domingo figured he had either slipped in while the
firefight was in full swing, or was already there, ready
and waiting on Rico. It would be too easy for him to just
kill Rico. Knowing Soltan, he liked to see his victims suffer, so he would probably take him somewhere to inter-
rogate him for information.

As he made his way around the building into the
alley, he recognized one of the guys he'd seen shooting
at his men while on the roof top.

He crouched back against the brick wall of the building, cursing himself for leaving the rifle. But it really did-
n't matter, he could still make the shot with his forty caliber. He heard the man as he moved, out of the rear of
the building and down the alley. But he couldn't figure
out where he was going. When he thought his target was
close enough he spun around the corner with his gun
sighted down on him.

"Drop the gun!"

Frank jerked to a stop when he saw Domingo standing there with him in his sights. "Whoa, take it easy
friend. What seems to be the problem?" asked Frank, trying to buy time. Domingo could sense Frank was about
to make a move.

"Don't," was all he said.

"Easy, easy, friend. We can work this out," Frank said,
standing completely still.

"I said drop the gun. I won't say it again!" Domingo
continued after seeing his reaction.

~ ~ ~

Jedi heard the order to get back to the rendezvous
point, but in the position he was in he thought it was
better to do a back sweep of the area. The nearing sirens

put an end to most of the drama as both sides made their escapes. Coming through the garage, Jedi made his way to the van Junior was driving and stopped in his tracks when he saw him laying across the hood. Half of his head was missing as it rested atop a pool of blood. Jedi crossed himself, said a tiny prayer for his comrade and kept moving. He walked past several dead men that weren't members of the Coalition. Coming around the back of the building toward the alley, he heard voices. As he got closer he realized it was Frank, along with one stranger. It could be Rico, he thought. Getting closer still, coming up behind Frank he noticed they were having a standoff, with Frank being confronted at gunpoint. When he got close enough, he saw movement behind the man holding the gun.

~ ~ ~

At that moment, Frank saw B.B. coming up behind Domingo and decided to take a gamble. If he wanted to shoot him, he would have done it by now, Frank thought about his assailant.

B.B. motioned for Frank to drop his gun, then moved a little to the side for a clear shot. Domingo spoke. "Now, where is -"

BOOM! Domingo went down face forward after being shot in the back. He hit the ground with a loud thud, his gun flying out of his hand on impact.

Reaching down to retrieve the gun, Frank put the gun in his waistband and picked up Domingo's. Jedi came up from behind, getting everyone's attention as they both pointed guns at him.

"Whoa, take it easy," Jedi said, both hands in the air.

"You're the one sneaking up on people. I almost shot your ass," said Frank.

"I love you too baby. Good shot B.B. - you saved me from having to rescue his old ass, again," said Jedi.

"Let's get the fuck out of here," said B.B., not responding to Jedi.

"Yeah, let's go," Frank said exchanging a look with B.B. that said everything.

# Fifty • seven

**Rico had his driver park** in the same spot he'd seen the van parked in. He looked around but couldn't figure out why the van had stopped here. He got out of the car and stepped up on the sidewalk and looked up and down the street.

"What do you think?" Rico asked his driver.

"I don't know. There's nothing here, the street is empty. And the buildings are old and abandoned."

"Soltan didn't stop here for nothing. Unless he knew we were tailing him."

"He couldn't have known - I stayed well behind their shadow vehicle. If he knew he was being followed he would have made the adjustment. His shadow vehicle would have gave him a signal."

"Yeah, but what if he planned for it. What if he was expecting me the whole time, waiting on me to attack? Maybe he stopped to see if I would ambush the van here. It's a good place to try a reverse ambush," he said, looking at the buildings with boarded up and shattered windows. "There's only two ways to go this street. No side streets or alleys, so it would be easy to box us in and use the high ground. But it didn't happen that way, the van parked another five blocks away," he said doing a three-sixty, looking up and down the street. "Where the hell did you go, scum?"

Sirens in the distance got his attention. Then his radio crackled to life, "Sir, Soltan's men are retreating, and they're leaving the building."

"Have you spotted Soltan yet?" asked Rico.

"No sir, no sign of Soltan. What is your command, sir?" asked the soldier.

"Get back to the rendezvous point." said Rico.

"What about the wounded and dead sir? We took a few casualties."

"Leave them, let the locals deal with the problem."

Walking back to the car with his radio in hand, Rico stepped off the curb, grabbing the car door handle. Putting one leg in and sitting down, he reached out with his right hand to close the door as he pulled his right leg inside the car. Looking down, Rico saw the street's water drain. The metal grate was fitted into the curb to allow water to drain directly into the sewer. Then he looked up and read the faded sign on the building in front of him. *Chicago Water Works.*

"Move the car forward," demanded Rico.

"What?"

"Move the fucking car!"

Without any more questions, the driver eased the car forward ten feet, and then Rico got out and looked at the manhole that was right beneath them.

"Get me a tire iron," Rico said, never looking back at his driver.

A minute later his driver was handing him the l-shaped bar. Rico put the flat end into one of the holes in the manhole cover and removed the fifty pound lid.

Looking down into the hole, he saw that the light bulbs were on.

"Soltan, you are smarter then I thought."

He looked back up at his driver and said, "Regroup the men at the rendezvous and wait for me."

"Sir?"

"I'll handle Soltan and meet you there later."

"But sir -"

"Leave!"

Without another word, the driver walked back to the car. Rico was climbing down into the hole as the car pulled off.

~ ~ ~

Domingo's right arm twitched as he regained consciousness. He struggled to open his eyes. He was feeling pain all through his body. Moving his head, his vision blurred, and it did little to help him figure out where he was. As if somebody was around to help anyway. Using his ears, he thought he heard sirens in the distance, but he wasn't sure because of the constant ringing inside his head.

~ ~ ~

Walking through the tunnel, Rico used the fresh footprints to guide him to Soltan. More than one person had tracked up the dust and dirt so he knew he was on the right trail. The footsteps stopped at a ladder that led to another manhole cover up above. Stepping up the ladder, Rico paused to listen for voices. Hearing none, he eased the cover up and to the side - only to see Soltan not fifty feet away, standing over his nephew Emilio in the center of the room.

*Soltan, I've got to give you some credit, your smarter than I thought you were. But not smarter than me,* Rico thought, easing toward Soltan and pointing his gun at his chest.

Aloud he said, "Drop the knife and step away from the boy."

Soltan looked at Rico as he approached, showing no emotion.

"Took you long enough, I've been waiting for an hour," Soltan said, now grinning as he dropped the knife.

"Now drop your gun," said Rico, "slowly."

Soltan grabbed the butt of his gun and eased it out of its holster, then made a show of holding it in the air by his thumb and forefinger.

"Drop it," repeated Rico.

Soltan kneeled down on one knee and placed the gun lightly in the concrete.

"Kick it to me."

"Is there anything else I can do for you since you are making all theses demands?" asked Soltan.

"In due time, I'm in no rush. Do you know how long I've waited to spill your blood, Soltan? I've dreamt of this moment, to look in your eyes and see fear in them. The same fear I saw in your father's eyes as I cut him into pieces."

Soltan raged on the inside at Rico's words, but tried to keep his composure and voice level.

"I long to see the pain in your eyes when I'm cutting you into pieces."

As Rico looked closer at Soltan, he realized that Soltan was not in shock to see him.

"You're not surprised to see me, are you?"

"Not too surprised, Truth is, I was hoping that you were smart enough to catch me. I gave you all the clues I thought you would need."

"Is that right?" Rico said, circling Soltan. "So you want to die, is what you're telling me."

"Absolutely not. But you do, and that's why you're

*Triple Crown Publications presents . . .*

here. You tracked me down so I could kill you," Soltan stated calmly.

"I like you Soltan. Even though you're scum, a Haitian dog, you still have arrogance 'til the end. You're here, about to die and still have the courage to act like you have the upper hand," said Rico.

"I do."

Standing directly in front of Soltan now, Rico laughed a deep, throaty laugh. "Is that right?" His gun was pointed at Soltan's chest.

Something caught Rico's attention from the corner of his eye, a red beam, but it was too late.

"Agh!" cried Rico as a bullet tore through his hand, making him drop the gun.

Once the shot was fired and the gun dropped, everyone came out of their hiding places as Soltan picked up Rico's gun. Soltan smiled.

~ ~ ~

"Bring another chair over here," said Soltan.

When Soltan walked over to the control booth Lauren looked surprised to see him, but stood and hugged him tight anyway.

"Is it over? Are you OK?"

Soltan kissed her on the forehead and then peeled her away from him, because he still had business to take care of.

Lauren's only concern was Soltan, so she never took the time out to look at the man he held captive. In the center of the room B.B., who had just arrived, sat Rico next to Emilio. Soltan walked over to him with fire in his eyes, but B.B. stopped him before he got too close.

"Slow down Soltan, we got him. We got him. Let's find out what's going on first, get him to talk," said B.B.

"Je suis venu," Soltan said.

Startled, B.B. looked into Soltan's eyes, at the same

time noticing his body was turning cold.

"What?" asked B.B.

"Je suis venu. I am here to claim a most precious prize. Get out of my way servant, or you will be next," were the words that came from Soltan's mouth, hollow and echoing through the room.

"Soltan, what the fuck is going on?" asked B.B.

"Soltan is no more. He has served his purpose," the voice croaked as Soltan's right arm moved in a sweeping motion, sending B.B. flying across the room.

The impact of his landing knocked the breath out of him, but in between gasps he managed the words, "Baron Samedi!"

"You speak the name in fear? After all the protection I have given you, why? Have I not given you your heart's desires? You pray to me and send me many souls, but when I come to you, you are afraid?"

Samedi's voice traveled through the room as if it was a blizzard engulfing all life force.

"The curse is real," B.B. said to himself, kneeling as if in prayer.

"I am no curse, servant, I'm inevitable. I ask you again, why are you afraid?"

"Baron, I don't fear you. But you have possessed the body of the man who has been a loyal servant to you as well, the man who taught me your ways. Why are you here?" B.B. asked humbly.

"I am here because Soltan has been given too much power, so it's his time to come to the other side. He has been a loyal servant and has done my bidding well. So I have come to claim him personally."

Everyone in the room looked stunned as they eyed each other, wondering if this was really happening.

As soon as Soltan started talking weird, everyone froze except B.B. and Lauren. "Soltan!" Lauren called out.

Samedi/Soltan turned to look at her, admiring the bond that she had with Soltan. He could feel it in Soltan's body, he could feel everything. Walking over to her, her wondered how she was able to break his spell, as he reached out to caress her face. But when he made contact he knew immediately of her power.

"Ahhh, love. You care for this man deeply, I can feel it. But do you think your love is strong enough to stop his hatred?"

Samedi felt that this woman possesses the only thing that could break death's hold. And the feelings she had were so strong for the man whose body he possessed that he felt that there could be a chance she could save him. The path he was on, he was being consumed into the dark side. On the verge of pure evil, with no redemption.

"Leave us alone!" came Soltan's voice.

Feeling Lauren's love for him gave Soltan enough power to regain some control of himself. Still blinded by rage and anger, he drew his blade and took small tentative steps toward Rico.

Before he could make it to Rico, gunfire erupted from B.B.'s gun, and Soltan's body jerked with the impact of each slug.

"No! No! Stop it! Stop it! You are killing him!" Lauren screamed out.

With the impact of each bullet the Samedi spell weakened, allowing Jedi, Frank and the rest of the men in the room move again.

"No matter what you do, he can't stop the killing, it's his way. The more souls he sends to me the more the thirst has to be fed. It is an imminent demise, and his time is now!" Samedi said before fading.

Soltan fell on his back, hitting the ground hard.

Lauren was already running toward him but unable to get to him before he landed. Sliding to a stop next to him, she grabbed his head.

"No, this can't be it. Baby wake up, wake up," she pleaded, tears rolling down her cheeks.

She took a second to look at his body, noticing that there was no blood. Confused, she slid her hand under his shirt and felt the vest.

"Thank God, baby, open your eyes. Dammit, Soltan breathe!"

But he just lay there, not moving nor breathing. Lauren didn't know what else to do, so she leaned down and kissed him on the lips. "Baby, I love you, you hear me, I love you, so wake up!"

Soltan's eyes shot open, and the image he saw brought a smile to his face as he took a deep breath.

"You look like you could use a hug," he said to Lauren.

She smiled at him, then kissed him again with tears of joy flowing freely.

"Help me up," he said to her.

When he was on his feet he took a look around and noticed that Jedi and his men had B.B. at gunpoint.

"Don't you have a better target to point your guns at?" Soltan asked everyone.

Jedi and company turned around amazed to see Soltan on his feet.

"What the fuck is going on?" asked Jedi.

"Well, let's start with you and your guys letting my brother up, and giving him his gun back," Soltan said.

Reluctantly, Jedi told his men to put their weapons up and give B.B. his pistol back.

"How do you feel?" asked B.B.

"A little weird, but I'll make it. I won't say anything about how my ribs feel, Jedi might get angry at you again," joked Soltan.

"Alright, do you always change your voice and freak niggas out like that, or is this a special occasion?" said Jedi.

Soltan and B.B. exchanged a look and then Soltan spoke.

"Short version, you just met Baron Samedi, the all-knowing Haitian voodoo *loa* of the dead. He stands at all the crossroads where the souls of the departed pass on their way to *Guinee*. He guides the dead safely. And yeah, sometimes I get these ... spells ... and I can't control myself. And sometimes that is the voice people say they hear."

"Are you fuckin' serious?" asked Frank. "What I just saw is some poltergeist shit. I don't want to be here anymore. This shit only happens in Hollywood, shit, I'm out."

"Chill," said Jedi, walking over to him and putting a hand on his partner's shoulder.

Frank looked pale and afraid.

"So what was all that about? Why did he possess you, and why did you shoot him?" Jedi asked, looking over to B.B.

"I don't know why that happened, except a lot of weird shit has been happening to me lately, and I thought I was going to die. But that begs the question, why did you shoot me?" asked Soltan, looking over at B.B.

"I took a gamble. I figured that if I could make you believe I was killing you that the voice would leave. I knew you were wearing your vest, and Frank said he'd bet his life on it. So, I bet your's - and mine." Answered B.B. "I figured that you were going to die anyway, so it could only help, not hurt." He continued.

"That's some crazy-ass logic," Frank squeaked out.

"But I told you, you could bet your life on the vest, true. But you muthafucka's is crazy for real. But as usual, my word is good." He said, smiling as he folded his arms.

Lauren and Soltan stood there, looking at Frank, both happy he knew what he was talking about when it came to his equipment.

"Ok, enough of the Tales From The Crypt shit, let's get back to business," Soltan said, mind back on track.

"Yeah let's, I ain't got all day." Rico said from the center of the room.

Hearing Rico clearly for the first time sent Lauren into shock as she twirled around. She finally *really* looked at Rico.

"Uncle?"

"You got to be fucking joking!"

For the first time Lauren had walked over to see the man sitting in the chair next to the boy they had kidnapped from the bank. His hands were bound behind his back, blood pooling from them because of the hole in his hand.

"Uncle, what are you doing here?" She turned to Soltan. "What is he doing here?"

Soltan walked over and looked at her, then at him, Rico was smiling from ear to ear.

# Fifty•eight

**"Yeah, Soltan, what am I** doing here?" Rico asked.

"Is this really your uncle, Lauren?" Soltan asked.

"Yes, now tell me, what is he doing here?"

"Don't worry Soltan, I'll help you out," Rico said.

Everybody in the room was shocked. Some moved closer to the conversation while others stayed where they were. But everyone wanted to hear what was going to be said.

"Your boyfriend, Soltan here, is going to kill me, isn't that right loverboy?"

"What?" Lauren shouted.

"Yeah, that's why I'm here. I'm next on his list. And all I was trying to do was protect your brother."

"My brother?" She said, but when she heard the words come out of his mouth she knew they were true. Somewhere deep inside her, she knew his words to be the truth, as she looked at Emilio. But still, she had to ask.

"What the fuck do you mean, my brother?"

"Yes my lovely niece, the man sitting next to me is

your brother. His mother fled the country years ago trying to get away from your father, the same way you did. So your father sent me here to protect him from your murderous boyfriend, who in case you didn't know, is an assassin for hire. The contract on your brother's life just happened to fall into your boyfriend's hands - how ironic. By the way, did you know that he also likes to cut people up while they're still breathing?" Rico said, smiling at Soltan.

Lauren looked over at him, searching his eyes and seeing the truth.

"Yes, my lovely niece, your boyfriend is a monster." Rico continued.

"Shut up! Tell her how you chopped my father up and killed my mother! Tell her that," Soltan said, slapping Rico across the face with his gun, unable to remember when he had drawn it.

Rico raised his head, laughing at Soltan as blood poured from his nose and mouth.

"I did enjoy killing your father, listening to his cries of pain as I severed each limb, but I didn't kill your mother. She was too good in bed."

Before he knew what he was doing, Soltan was hammering away at Rico's face and head. Blood was flying every time he made contact. No one dared step over to try and stop him. Getting involved with the rage they were witnessing wouldn't be wise – especially after the weird shit with the Baron's voice.

Minutes later Soltan was out of breath. He took two steps back and looked at the damage he caused; Rico's eyes were swelling shut, his mouth was bleeding as well as the side of his head - which had a six-inch gash, leaking blood heavily.

Covered in blood and missing a couple of teeth now, Rico gained his bearings and spat blood at Soltan.

"Is that all you got?" taunted Rico.

Soltan took a step forward to hit Rico again, but Lauren stepped in between them.

"Soltan, stop," said Lauren, her hands on his chest.

"That's right my dear niece, save your uncle from this monster. I see he has the same weakness for you as your father."

"What? What are you talking about?" she asked, now facing Rico.

"You're bad for business, sweetie. When you left, so many people paid the price for helping your pretty ass get to America. We found out you were in Charleston, so your father wanted us to bring you home. But I had a better idea - since you cost so many people and families their lives, I find it only fitting for you to repay the debt. With yours!"

Lauren stepped back, stunned at her uncle's words, unbelieving.

"What?"

"He should have killed you a long time ago, like he killed your mother."

"What?" Lauren said, wide-eyed, taking another shock to the system. "You're lying!"

"Am I?" said Rico.

Lauren reached back and slapped Rico hard across the face, "I'd kill you myself if I could you bastard!"

"I wish the same for you, my dearest. But unfortunately, I think your boyfriend isn't going to let me live through this, so I won't be able to kill you like I originally hoped," said Rico.

Lauren stepped to the side and began crying as the truth of his words set in. It was true, her mother did die under suspicious circumstances, but she never would have blamed her father for it. Turning back toward him, she leaned in and spit in his face, "I hope you burn in hell!" she said, and then she backed up and stood next to Soltan.

"Well, I guess that means she's done with me. What about you Soltan? Are you ready to kill me now?"

Soltan was having trouble controlling himself, but he knew that for what he wanted to do he needed to be alone. Turning to Lauren, he said, "Do you trust me?"

Looking at him with tears rolling down her face, she answered.

"Yes."

"Do you love me?" he asked her.

"Yes."

"Then leave me now, go back to the hotel and wait for me." Soltan said to her.

"No, I want to stay with you." She begged him.

"Go, go now," Soltan said, and then turning to Jedi and Frank, who were watching everything silently, he said, "Thank you my brothers. I'll take it from here."

Now he turned to B.B. "Take her back to the hotel, I'll see you later."

B.B. walked over to Lauren, ready to usher her along as Jedi and Frank gathered their men and began to file out of the building.

"What about the boy?" asked B.B.

"Take him with you. No harm will come to him before me," Soltan said.

B.B. didn't question it, he just walked over to Emilio and cut him loose. He'd been quiet the whole time, no doubt listening and watching everything in awe. So when B.B. went to cut his bonds, he flinched and started shaking.

Lauren saw Emilio's reaction and walked over to him, "It's OK. No one's going to hurt you, I promise. Let's get you out of here, brother."

Lauren's voice soothed Emilio, and he got up and

stood next to her, trusting the words she spoke. Without thinking, he reached out and hugged her tight, holding on for dear life. When he released her, he glanced back at Soltan and said, "Thank you."

Before she walked out of the warehouse, Lauren kissed Soltan on the lips, and whispered in his ear, "Make him suffer."

Soltan looked at her and grinned a wide toothy grin. "Don't worry."

When they were finally alone Soltan stood in front of Rico, whose face looked like a smashed pumpkin, and pulled out his blade.

"Well, it's just you and me now. Your demise is imminent, but let's see how much pain you can really take.

# Fifty • nine

**By the time Soltan had made** it back to the hotel, the building was quiet and empty. Of course, it being four in the morning probably had a lot to do with the silence. Taking the elevator to his floor, he felt an overwhelming sense of accomplishment. It was finally over. He had made sure that Rico endured as much suffering as possible before he allowed him to die. Not really caring about what would be next, he was finally able to exorcise one of his demons.

At the door to his suite, Soltan wondered how Lauren was going to accept her uncle's fate. Was she inside crying, or would she be ready to turn him in for murder? Either way, Soltan didn't care, what was done was done. Now it was time to move on. If the Baron came to claim him for good, so be it.

Knocking lightly on the door, Soltan heard footsteps coming in his direction from the other side, immediately. He could see the peephole go black, and then the doors locks were released.

When the door opened Soltan was looking at a fully

dressed Lauren with no signs of tears or suffering, look-ing right back at him.

"Are you OK?" she asked.

"Yeah, I'm fine. How are you holding up?"

"I'm good," She answered, still standing in the door-way.

They stood their looking at each other for a few sec-onds, gauging reactions and taking a mental inventory of each other. Finally, Soltan broke down and said, "I'm tired."

Hearing this, Lauren stepped into him, wrapping her arms around him and giving him a hug. Letting himself go, Soltan accepted the embrace, wrapping his arms around her as well. "It's over," said Soltan as he laid his head against hers, whispering in her ear.

Lauren pulled Soltan into the room, letting the door close behind him. Pulling away from his embrace, she stepped behind him and locked the door.

"Where's your brother?" asked Soltan.

"When I finally got him to calm down and listen to me, he agreed to stay the night in one of the available rooms here until we could talk more later."

"Is he going to be someone I'm going to have to worry about? I mean, I know he's your brother, but you don't know each other. So I guess I'm asking if he's going to call the police or something?" Soltan asked wearily.

"No, he's not going to do anything like that. He's just as confused and scared about all this as I am, but he's willing to listen to gain a complete understanding first. I'll admit, he's not used to things like this happening, but he's a soldier. He's got our father's blood in him, and he's going to be fine. Like the rest of us, he just wants to get away from his past and move on." Lauren said, looking Soltan in the eyes.

"Your father... did you know who I was, I mean when I told you who my father was? Did you know then that your family, your uncle was the one who killed my family?" Soltan asked, not really prepared for the answer.

"No."

"But you knew something didn't you? You knew that somehow your family and mine were connected in some way."

"I knew I heard your father's name in my house before. And that was the reason I escaped Colombia for the United States, Soltan. I didn't know at the time who you or your father were, but I heard so much anger and hatred in my father's voice towards your family that I just couldn't take it any more. I know who my father is and what he's done to people and I'm not proud of it. I hate him for it. I hate him for all the wrong he's done to everyone, not just your family. Do you believe me?" she asked as her palms began to sweat, as he stood inches from her with her back to the door.

Soltan looked at Lauren, seeing that she really cared about him. Not just lust, but real, true, love.

"So now what. I do know that I love you, Soltan, and I want to make this work – Baron Samedi and all." She said honestly.

"Are you serious? I manipulated you, used you for my own evil purposes, and you want to be with me?" he asked, confused.

"Yes."

"I think you're crazy."

"I'm not crazy Soltan, I'm in love. Something that I have never experienced before with a man. I love you, no matter who or what you are. I'm not going to judge you, I'm here for you. So don't push me away. Do you love me?"

Soltan stood still while he continued to weigh his

answer in his head. He was looking at a woman whose uncle is now dead because of him and she knew it. Yet, she still professed to love him, after all his manipulation and conniving ways. Two days ago, he was ready to kill and discard her when he finished with her. She was nothing but a tool, something to be disposed of when he was finished with this assignment. But he couldn't believe the words that came out of his mouth.

"Yes. I do love you. But that doesn't mean anything, because it'll never work between us."

Lauren looked at him, furious now. He admitted his love for her, but was doing his best to find an excuse for them not to be together.

"Have you ever been in love before, Soltan?"

"No." Soltan hesitated.

"Then why are you fighting it? I know you're scared. I'm scared too, but I know what I want and I want to be with you. I know who you are, I felt you the first time we met. I felt you Soltan, but I also seen that you have love for me as well, don't deny yourself. We are one, and nothing is going to change that."

"So what is it you're really saying to me? That you accept everything about me at all cost? That you are willing to risk your life with me and for me. Is that what you're saying? 'Cause there is a lot of shit to deal with back in Charleston, if we ever make it back there."

"I love you. And if that's what it takes, then yes, Soltan. My life is yours to do with how you see fit. Whether we ever see Charleston again or not. And personally, I say we stay the fuck out of that town."

Soltan waited a few seconds as he continued gazing at her, then he held out his arms, beckoning her to come to him. She came to him in a rush as they once again were tangled in each other's arms. This time they both stood in the middle of the room, squeezing each other

*Triple Crown Publications presents . . .*

tightly, and crying together.

Soltan said, "We need to go back to Charleston for a minute, but then I have some business to take care of in Haiti. I still don't know who betrayed my father." He paused. "I think you probably have some unfinished business with your father too."

Lauren looked up but didn't say anything. She didn't have to – Soltan recognized the look in her eyes. The same look that had been in his eyes for most of his life. *Revenge.*

They've already gone through Hell to get here together - what could the future possibly throw at them that they couldn't handle?

~ ~ ~

Outside the hotel, an unmarked police car sat. Detective Trump sat inside with three FBI agents. A female agent, sitting in the driver's seat, looked toward Trump and said, "Okay, we have the building surrounded, and our agents await my signal. Are you ready?"

Trump drew his pistol and nodded. "Let's do it."

The FBI agent lifted her radio handset and gave the signal.

# ♛ Triple Crown Publications

## Order Form
P.O. Box 247378   Columbus, OH 43224

| Name | |
|------|--|
| Address | |
| City | |
| State | Zipcode |

| QTY | TITLES | PRICE |
|-----|--------|-------|
| | A Down Chick | $15.00 |
| | A Hood Legend | $15.00 |
| | A Hustler's Son | $15.00 |
| | A Hustler's Wife | $15.00 |
| | A Project Chick | $15.00 |
| | Always a Queen | $15.00 |
| | Amongst Thieves | $15.00 |
| | Baby Girl | $15.00 |
| | Baby Girl Pt. 2 | $15.00 |
| | Betrayed | $15.00 |
| | Black | $15.00 |
| | Black and Ugly | $15.00 |
| | Blinded | $15.00 |
| | Cash Money | $15.00 |
| | Chances | $15.00 |
| | China Doll | $15.00 |

**Shipping & Handling**
1 - 3 Books        $5.00
4 - 9 Books        $9.00
$1.95 for each add'l book

Total $_____

Forms of accepted payment: Postage Stamps, Personal or Institutional Checks &
Money Orders.  All mail in orders take 5-7 business days to be delivered.